CIU

Celebrating
30 Years of Publishing
in India

CIU

CRIMINALS IN UNIFORM

SANJAY SINGH AND RAKESH TRIVEDI

TRANSLATED BY SNEHA BAWARI MAKHARIA

HarperCollins *Publishers* India

First published in India by HarperCollins *Publishers* 2023
HarperCollins *Publishers* India, Cyber City, Building 10-A, Gurugram, Haryana-122002, India
www.harpercollins.co.in

2 4 6 8 10 9 7 5 3 1

First published in Marathi by Mehta Publishing, Pune, 2022
Hindi edition published by R.K. Publication, Mumbai, 2022
This English edition translated from Hindi by Sneha Bawari Makharia

P-ISBN: 978-93-5629-658-9
E-ISBN: 978-93-5629-659-6

Typeset in 11/14.5 Sabon LT Std at
Manipal Technologies Limited, Manipal

Printed and bound at
Repro India Ltd.

HarperCollins *Publishers* , Macken House, 39/40 Mayor Street Upper, Dublin 1, D01 C9W8, Ireland

To the art of writing,
where names are changed but not the story

Contents

Preface

After the phenomenal success of *Scam 1992: The Harshad Mehta Story*, which first aired on SonyLIV in 2020, its producer and director titled the second season *Scam 2003: The Curious Case of Abdul Karim Telgi*, based on our book *Telgi: A Reporter's Diary*. This has been a matter of great pride and inspiration. So, here's the latest and most sensational book in your hands.

The two of us have over two decades of experience in the field of crime and investigative journalism and have unearthed numerous scams and conspiracies in the past. Often, in crime reporting, it becomes difficult to present a cohesive picture of an ongoing case by piecing together breakthroughs in a sequential manner. Even more challenging is to present behind-the-scenes stories in a matter of minutes. In such a scenario, there is great responsibility on a journalist's shoulder to report an incident, or the events unfolding around him or her, impartially. This is a task a journalist can do more justice to by donning the hat of an author. For journalists who cover day-to-day developments of an incident or a scam, direct eyewitness accounts and experiences serve as the research, guide and control room.

In fact, consider this. If journalism is called history written in haste, then a book written by a journalist can be considered the first draft of history written at leisure.

News has a short shelf life and a small canvas. Apart from the limitation of words and time, it is fragmented and divided into so many bits and pieces that it is difficult to ascertain a beginning and an end. However, the possibilities are endless when it comes to a book. A book can give you the complete picture through a sequential narrative. A story told in the author's distinct style, in a simple and easy-to-understand way, without leaving out crucial details, is possible in the case of a book.

If a news item is considered foreplay, then the book that follows is the actual deal. It was with this in mind that we conceived and executed the idea of this book. With our overall experience in investigative journalism, and because we witnessed the events first-hand, we feel that the dangerous and sensational incidents described in this book are a story worth telling. Never before in the world of media has a story as startling as this come to light. We don't think it's very likely in the future either.

Many governments and prosecuting and investigative agencies have been mentioned in this book. It is definitely not our intention to malign or defame any of them in any way. We believe that, keeping in mind the way these agencies have rendered their duty to the country, they do not need any certificate of honour. Their stature is such that their image cannot be tarnished by any form of fictional writing. Thousands of dutiful personnel sacrifice their lives for the country and the proud history of these agencies cannot be sullied because of the misdeeds of a few. Yet, year after year, the news about a few employees from these agencies being caught in illegal activities and corruption cases always comes forward; books, films and web series are made, too. This book, too, is the story of a few black sheep who tainted the name and reputation of their respective agencies. As a result, there is anger and displeasure in these agencies and public–political leadership, and we also share the same sentiment. Hopefully, this book will serve as a strong lesson for all the still-hidden black sheep and deter them from defaming their organizations.

Enjoy the book. We hope you have a good time reading it.

Sanjay–Trivedi

1
Breaking news

BREAKING NEWS: Conspiracy to bomb Asia's and India's richest man, Kuber

News anchors across channels hollered this news. 'An abandoned car was found outside Mr Kuber's residence. It was stuffed with explosives. A bomb squad, the Crime Branch and the Anti-Terrorism Squad (ATS) are present at the crime scene and investigation is on ...'

Utter chaos ensued inside and outside the newsroom. Panicked individuals ran back and forth between desks as if the country itself was under threat. Screams and shouts, interspersed with expletives, added to the bedlam. The scene was similar across all news channels in the country as they relayed the breaking news of the hour.

Images and videos of siren-blaring police vehicles, Kuber's photographs at his residence—Kuberia—stock footage of him, and the explosives-bearing vehicle being examined by a bomb squad dominated all TV screens.

About an hour ago, Aman Choudhury had driven into Kuberia in his impressive white Range Rover. Tall, with short white hair and a muscular build, Aman had barely crossed the gates of Kuberia when a file of security officers saluted him. The security personnel had already been informed of this suited and booted man's arrival; the gates had been opened in anticipation.

Kuberia was a symbol of opulent grandeur enjoyed only by three people: Kuber, his socialite wife, Meeta, and their young son, Dhruv. Located in the poshest area of south Mumbai, adjacent to Peddar Road, it was an uber-luxurious multi-storeyed building that stood facing the sea majestically. It was home to India's richest man, and crores and crores of rupees had been spent on it. From innumerable servants to multi-level parking, gardens, an in-house tennis court, swimming pool, movie theatre, auditorium and banquet hall, Kuberia had it all. The interest surrounding this magnificent residence was so intense that the news of any threat to it continued to maintain the top spot across headlines.

Having retired early from the R&AW (the Research and Analysis Wing), Aman had not only been the head of security of the Kuber family for decades, but also their most trusted person. While Aman enjoyed Mr and Mrs Kuber's unbridled trust, Dhruv was another matter. His strange and adventurous ideas were often risky and put Aman in a tight spot. Currently, under Aman's command were hundreds of trained and armed commandoes responsible for the security of the Kubers.

Kuber was a gracious host. On account of the numerous soirées and business meetings he hosted, Aman's duty hours often extended till late into the night, which was why he usually reported to work in the afternoon. Today was no different. As usual, Aman reached Kuberia in the afternoon and headed straight to the temple to pay obeisance to Ma Amba, after which he took in the specifics on the security front from his juniors. Post this, as per routine, a route parade followed wherein the security guards patrolled the roads within a two-kilometre radius of Kuberia. The roads were sanitized from a security point of view, with the objective of spotting suspicious persons or activity and addressing threats.

The upmarket area around Kuberia, Peddar Road in south Bombay, was the abode of the very wealthy. On an average, each family there owned at least two cars. There were families where each member had his or her own car, with some having a separate vehicle designated just for their pets. Cars priced in crores were often parked directly under the blue sky on this road and, for security reasons, the number plates and other information pertaining to the owners of these luxury vehicles were always with Aman's security team.

Today, too, the patrol had commenced at the scheduled time. The buildings flanking both sides of the road, their balconies, the security guards manning the gates—Aman minutely scrutinized it all. His eyes scanned the cars parked on either side of the road as he slowly drove past the BMWs, Mercedes, Audis, Porsches, Jaguars and the Scorpio. Something clicked in his mind. He quickly reversed his car and gazed at the Scorpio. The registration number looked familiar. It belonged to one of the cars in the Kuberia fleet, but that vehicle was not a Scorpio. Unknowingly, his hand inched towards the Ma Amba locket around his neck. He quickly got his cell phone out and dialled a number. The call was disconnected. Aman dialled again.

The Gamdevi Police were the first to reach the scene, with other agencies following. Mumbai Police's CIU (Crime Investigation Unit) trailed in just behind the local unit. Then came a bomb squad, followed by the ATS and the IB (Intelligence Bureau). Even the officer of the CPF (Central Police Force) who had granted Kuberia Z+ category security descended on the scene. In short, people who had no reason to be there also arrived to partake a slice of the action. An uncalled-for ambulance and fire brigade joined the melee, too.

Curious residents began to gather on their balconies to get a view of the happenings below. Some even started recording on their phones, unaware that just one phone call had led to an enormous gathering of invited and uninvited authorities outside Kuberia. The hullabaloo made Inspector Andhle's head spin for a second. His three decades of experience in the police force came to his rescue. As in-charge of the local police station, he knew that the media would follow soon. He was aware that his role in the case would be limited to registering the case, which would most likely be passed on to the CIU, ATS or another agency for investigation. His role would slip to that of a host, whose only job would be to ensure a seamless supply of tea, snacks and mineral water for the officers, along with managing traffic at the scene.

The bomb squad that had arrived minutes ago thoroughly recced the Scorpio and then proceeded to open it. What they found inside was troubling. A Jay Bharti pink jersey and a bag bearing the Jay Bharti logo were in the boot. Jay Bharti was a PCL (premier cricket league) team from Jaipur owned by Kuber. During the premier league matches, a host of parties had been organized for the players at Kuberia. But the tournament had not begun—it was one and a half months away—so why the jersey and bag? And then the squad found false number plates, gelatin sticks sans a detonator and a letter that read:

Dear Bhaiya and Bhabhi,

This is just a trailer. We have made arrangements for the entire family. Stay safe.

The moment the letter was retrieved, a contest ensued among the agencies present, with each wanting to be the first to photograph it.

Readers should know that gelatin is an explosive substance, but without a detonator, it cannot be used as a bomb. It is commonly used in industries as an explosive substance, but there have been incidents where terrorists have used gelatin to make bombs.

It was not difficult to imagine that Kuber was the intended target. The richest man of Asia, with wealth greater than the GDP of many countries, had been accosted. Be it Bollywood stars or world leaders, everyone wanted to be in Kuber's good books. This was probably why Maharashtra's home minister, Sardeshpande, did not waste any time in breaking the news on social media.

Having uploaded the video, Home Minister Sunil Sardeshpande was ready for this meeting. The participants comprised the top brass: the home secretary, the commissioner of the Mumbai Police, the DGP (director general of police) of Maharashtra, the ATS chief and the IB's regional director. Because the target was Kuber, an exception to official protocol was granted. Kuberia's security head, Aman Choudhury, had been allowed at the meeting and was seated at the back.

The home minister justified Aman's presence in the government meeting on the grounds that he would be a useful source of information pertaining to the security and movement-tracing arrangements at Kuberia. Upon not receiving an encouraging response to this justification, the home minister continued, 'It is decided. The local police station will not be investigating this case. It's too high profile for them. Now, you decide the next course of action. We will not be recording the minutes of this meeting.'

The meeting progressed with the IB director, Om Pachnekar, saying the bureau had not received any intelligence regarding this. No phone chatter or tapping had picked up any mention of this incident, and no terrorist organization had come forward to claim responsibility so far.

The next half hour saw the ATS chief, Vishwajeet, and the Mumbai Police commissioner, Mahavir Tomar, at loggerheads with each other. The ATS presented the argument that since the case was related to terrorism, they should handle the case. Commissioner Tomar believed that in 2013, when Kuber had received a threat from the Indian Mujahideen, they had handled the case. According to Tomar, for the sake of continuity and because they had prior experience, the case should be handed over to the Mumbai Police.

Pachnekar suggested that the ATS take over the case, but Commissioner Tomar counterargued that the police had more manpower and resources in Mumbai compared to the ATS, and that they also had highly skilled technocrat officers capable of handling such cases. He also suggested that Yatin Sathe take the lead in this case. This irked Pachnekar, making him stand up in defiance and declare that the bureau would take no responsibility if something went wrong. Even ATS chief Vishwajeet was not in favour of API (assistant police inspector) Sathe leading the investigation.

The final card was dealt when Commissioner Tomar said, 'I vouch for API Yatin Sathe. I will personally monitor him. I am also acquainted with the Kuber family, which makes it easier to communicate with them on an unofficial level. Mr Kuber does not open up immediately to new people.'

With such a senior police officer taking guarantee for API Sathe, the pleas of the others lost steam. The ball was now in Aman Choudhury's court. His 'no objection' would determine which agency would investigate.

Now, Aman had been closely watching this tennis match of words. When he understood that he would be the deciding authority, he did not say anything. Instead, he shrugged. A broad smile spread across the commissioner's face. Only a formal announcement by the home minister remained.

The case was handed to the Mumbai Police. The home minister tried to console the slighted ATS by throwing a bone; they could conduct a parallel investigation just for academic record, but the main investigation would be carried out by the Mumbai Police's CIU. The home minister then summoned his assistant and instructed him to record a new video announcing the same.

The moment he heard the media call out his name, API Yatin Sathe understood that the CIU had been handed the case for investigation. Since he was the head of the unit, he knew that he would be the chief investigating officer.

Just then, he received a call from the commissioner. 'With great difficulty, the CIU has been handed this case. I have given my personal guarantee. Our future depends on it.'

'Yes, sir. Everything is proceeding as per plan.'

'What's the progress?'

'Sir, the chassis and engine numbers were wiped off. Not possible to locate the car's owner. I am looking into everything else.'

'Just ensure that the ATS does not meddle,' the commissioner said and disconnected the call.

The local police had put up a barricade at some distance; the increasing number of media persons was required to report from behind it. The police were on high alert, and Sathe knew that this was to impress Kuber. Every news portal and channel showed sincerity in reporting, faithfully devoting themselves to broadcasting every detail they could get. After all, Kuber held either a minority share in most of the media houses, or they relied on the advertising revenue they received from the Kuber group. This was the perfect opportunity to show solidarity and to use it to their advantage.

The rumblings of the episode at Kuberia were felt in the corporate world and the share market, too. Celebrities from the world of Bollywood and cricket took to social media to offer their two bits on the incident. The heads of states of various countries did not lag behind and expressed concern through tweets and phone calls.

Needless to say, the security at Kuberia and that of the Kuber family was doubled.

API Sathe spotted Sanjay Trivedi of Crime First Channel in the media gathering. Sathe had a bad history with Sanjay, which was why he walked past without acknowledging him. Resting against the suspect Scorpio with a cigarette in his hand, the CIU head casually took in the drama surrounding the car. He was aware that a journalist like Trivedi would not desist from raking up his past.

Sathe's eyes focused on his seniors, on the concern etched on their faces. He knew that even though they were his seniors, they could not handle a case like this. A huge responsibility rested on his shoulders. After all, he had been the investigating officer of the Mumbai Police's five high-profile cases in the last few months. Used to hauling in eighteen-hour shifts, Sathe was often unable to go home and usually got some shut-eye at the office or a nearby hotel. This lack of sleep had given him dark circles. He had a mask on his face and his shiny half pate glistened under the sun. To add to this, the age of fifty sure did not make for an attractive appearance on TV.

The Crime Branch, a special unit of the Mumbai Police, was set up to solely handle criminal cases. It had twelve units across the megacity, but the most important one was the CIU. Twenty years ago, when the CIU was established, Sathe had been a sub-inspector under the command of Dilip Verma, the unit's erstwhile head. Today, he was its head. Normally, only an inspector rank officer was given such a premium posting, but Sathe had been given charge despite being an assistant inspector.

Sathe, before speaking to the media, decided to give the car a once-over as the investigating officer. He was heading towards the Scorpio when Inspector Andhle from the Gamdevi police station congratulated him. Sathe kept walking without as much as a nod.

'What is the central government's perspective on this case?' ATS chief Vishwajeet asked his senior and the IB's regional director, Om Pachnekar. The two of them were walking down a corridor in the home minister's office block.

Pachnekar, a former Mumbai Police commissioner, offered a response that was not very reassuring. 'I spoke for a minute with the union home minister. He said he was busy and wanted to see how the state would handle the matter.'

Vishwajeet laughed and quipped derisively, 'Forthcoming elections in five states. Is he busy with that?'

'He is an unconventional and unpredictable politician. I am going to recommend that the NIA (National Investigation Agency) be given the case.'

'What will the NIA do now? The case is not as straightforward as it seems.'

The regional director lowered his voice to a whisper. 'Yes, but this case concerns Kuber. We have to show our earnestness and, in any case, our batchmate heads the NIA.'

'Yes, but he was snubbed the last time.'

'What I can't comprehend is Commissioner Tomar's enthusiasm to take up this case. Generally, under such circumstances, the commissioner is happy to hand over the case to the ATS, the NIA or the CBI (Central Bureau of Investigation) because they are already overloaded with maintaining law and order. What's more difficult to digest is that he insisted for Yatin Sathe to handle the case. Why would a senior IPS officer vouch for an API whose reputation has already been tarnished?'

'Something is amiss. Why else would he agree to walk the tightrope?'

'He is not averse to taking risks; he has always been daring. But I agree, there is something fishy, which is why Commissioner Tomar does not want anybody else to handle the case.'

'What about Sathe?'

'I will talk to Sanjay Trivedi about him,' said the ATS chief before getting into his car.

Seething with anger, Sathe plonked himself into a chair. He had been on his feet for ten straight hours and, as a result, had cramps. He took off his shoes, pushed them under the chair and sighed with relief. Having not had a morsel to eat in the past seven hours, he called out to a constable to get him a sandwich. Already plagued by an acidity problem, Sathe was feeling hungrier thanks to his anger.

With his hunger addressed, Sathe returned to his tumultuous thoughts, the focal point of which was Sanjay Trivedi. When Sathe had gone to speak to the media, rather than focussing on the case at hand, Trivedi had chosen to dig up his past. He had cast doubts on his capability, something he had done seventeen years ago as well. Today was no different.

'Bloody idiot! He could not manage his own affairs and is out keeping a tab on others. Investigative journalist, my ass!' Sathe said to himself.

His thoughts were interrupted when the sandwich was placed before him. He had just taken a bite when he heard shoes clacking. Sathe recognized this sound too well; a police officer had just saluted. He turned around and saw the ATS team led by DIG (deputy inspector general) Mandeep Palande. A Maharashtrian, Palande was from the Bihar IPS cadre, presently with the ATS on deputation.

Palande had been given the moniker Singham (lion) for his daredevilry in innumerable cases in Bihar. He was fearless, just, easily accessible and prompt in doling out justice. He did not spare anyone who did wrong; for him a criminal was simply that, a criminal, social standing notwithstanding. Palande, however, was not averse to vanity and wore tight uniforms or muscle-fit T-shirts that showed off his biceps, and he always tucked his tummy in on camera. Sathe had seen a lot of Palande's videos on YouTube and knew that behind his success lay his politician father in-law's blessed hand.

As per protocol, Sathe stood up, but without his shoes, and a sandwich in one hand and a plate in the other. He was not in a position to salute. Sathe expected that Palande would let this slip, but he did not. He waited for Sathe to salute him the way his seniors, the ACP and DCP, had done. The other policemen standing close by watched this spectacle with amusement.

It is common knowledge that discipline and hierarchy are the very ethos of the police force. Especially in Palande's cadre, a senior officer was treated like a demigod, with genuflecting juniors always eager to serve. Since Sathe did not follow the norm, Palande was uncomfortable. He knew his juniors from the ATS and the Mumbai Police, not to mention the media, were watching. His reputation was on the line.

On the other hand, this was not an abnormal situation for Sathe. He had become a celebrated officer who enjoyed the support of the commissioner. This made him slack in his duty of saluting his seniors. The Mumbai Police did not condone this behaviour, but they knew Sathe was sheltered by the commissioner and thus kept mum.

Thankfully, the silence was broken by the media persons. Palande waved at the press and ordered his junior, Nitya Shetty, 'I will be back in a bit. Take down the details.'

DIG Palande had just started walking towards the media when Sathe's words fell on his ears. 'Please, this is our case to solve, not the ATS's.'

One insult heaped upon another, Palande thought. He considered making a U-turn and setting Sathe right, but then he thought better of it and moved on. He did not want to give off the wrong signal. Palande was also worried that the unpredictable Sathe might embarrass him again. He decided it was best to let it go for now.

Palande approached the media and informed them that he had just arrived at the scene and would talk to them once he had more information.

Meanwhile, Sathe had been munching on his sandwich and observing Palande. He saw Palande approach Trivedi and whisper into his ears. The fact that Palande's junior, Nitya, was standing in front of him added insult to his already injured ego.

Palande returned and asked Sathe, 'Where is the Scorpio?'

Sathe, his mouth stuffed with the sandwich, took a few seconds to respond. Palande's gaze had not wavered. Sathe turned around, noted that the car was no longer there and replied, 'The car is not here.'

'We can also see that the car is not here. *Aatta Scorpio kuthe aahe* (Where is the Scorpio)?' This time the question came from Nitya.

Sathe answered, '*Malaa naay maahit* (I don't know).'

Nitya was allergic to Sathe's face and voice.

His anger evident, Palande took out his cell phone and called his boss, ATS chief Vishwajeet, and said, 'Sir, they are not cooperating. I think we need to raise and bring this issue on record with the proper authorities.'

Though Palande was speaking on the phone, his intention was to let his words reach both the media and Sathe. A sagacious Sathe realized there was no point in confronting Palande, Nitya and the media together.

Finished with his sandwich, and with his shoes back on his feet, he stood up and said, 'If you are so capable, then you know the protocol. We cannot leave the Scorpio here for the media and people's entertainment. The forensic team needs to look at it.'

Sathe was looking at Nitya, but his intent was to put DIG Palande in his place.

'*Aatta kuthe aahe*?' Nitya asked again.

Sathe responded by looking at Palande. 'In the premises of the Yellow Gate police station. That place is isolated. Here at Gamdevi it would have been difficult to collect forensic evidence ... sir.'

Sathe's one-second pause before calling Palande 'sir' went unnoticed because DIG Palande had already started walking off with Inspector Nitya in tow.

Seeing them retreat, Sathe spoke in a loud and confident voice, 'You won't find anything. The number plate is fake, the car's papers are missing and the chassis and engine numbers have been wiped clean, so we cannot trace the owner of the car.'

Sathe then called his junior, Sub-Inspector Fakhruddin Haji.

It will help the reader to know that a chassis number is a unique number allotted to a car. It can help trace the owner. Often, small-time criminals change the number plate, but they do not tamper with the chassis number. This makes it easier for the police to find the owner. But if both the engine number and the chassis number have been erased, you can be sure that it is the work of a seasoned criminal or terrorist, who is well aware of the fact that this will make the investigation difficult for the cops.

ATS officers Palande and Nitya knew this. Under normal circumstances, the ATS would have walked away from the case since it had been handed over to the CIU and they had been sent only as record keepers. But Sathe had soured their mood by not behaving appropriately. Instead of turning their car towards their office, the ATS officers headed to the Yellow Gate police station.

There are over ninety police stations in Mumbai, but the Yellow Gate police station is different. Any crime that is committed in the Arabian Sea, on the western coast of India, is registered there. It is located in the port area of Mumbai, giving it seclusion and making it easy to control the media from barging in. This was why the Scorpio had been taken there.

A police officer in plain clothes approached the ATS vehicle and saluted DIG Palande and Nitya as they disembarked.

Nitya said, 'Sir, this is Fakhruddin Haji of the CIU. He is with Sathe.'

Haji escorted them towards the Scorpio and said, 'Sathe Sir called. He told me to come here and offer my full cooperation.'

'*Nazar rakhne ke liye bheja hai tere ko, gandu. Mere ko malum nahin kya? Janta nahin kya main usko*? (He has sent you to keep an eye on us, asshole. Don't I know him?)' Inspector Nitya quipped back and called out to his team that proceeded to open the bonnet of the Scorpio and began a technical examination.

'Useless Sathe is trying to project a good image. He was with me in the CIU. He would follow his boss around like a loyal dog. I have done eighty-five encounters; he is not half the man I am. Sathe has not one solo encounter to his name. He would attach himself to the team and take credit for the encounter. Even the job of catching the criminals and beating them up was left to me and the boss. If a dog is present at the encounter scene, will we call the dog an encounter specialist? Seventeen years ago, because of his so-called smartness, he defiled the image of the Crime Branch. Officers who weren't even involved suffered because of Sathe,' Nitya said.

This tirade was the ATS's well-thought-out strategy to unnerve Haji. They knew that Sathe would send his man to keep an eye on them. The idea was to distract Haji while the rest of the team examined the Scorpio uninterrupted. Any evidence found was to be collected stealthily.

Nitya continued to speak. 'He is behaving as if all the other police officers are incompetent. Don't we know how he landed those high-profile cases?'

Sathe updated Commissioner Tomar on the phone—the ATS team was scanning the explosives-bearing Scorpio, but there was no clue whatsoever that would lead them to the owner.

The investigation seemed to have reached a dead end.

Sathe's friends in the media had requested a video byte, which he now began recording on his phone. 'I was Mumbai Police's first technocrat officer. The nature of crime has changed and technical know-how has become the key to solving cases. I have been outside the police force and honed this skill for seventeen years. My cases have been handed over to me based on merit. Whether it was the case of a news channel faking TRPs or the car modification fraud, I solved them diligently and filed the chargesheets on time. But this case is the most crucial one of my life, and we at the CIU are putting all our strength into investigating it. The chassis and engine numbers of the Scorpio have been erased and as of now we have no clue about its owner.'

'The most important skill is discerning that one clue that even the smartest of criminals leave behind, just like this criminal has done,' DIG Palande said and smiled, gazing at something.

The Scorpio was examined thoroughly. Nothing was found inside. Sub-Inspector Haji, who had been a mute spectator, now stood with a grin plastered on his face. Just when they were closing the car by rolling up the windows, Palande spotted something written in fine print at the bottom of the glass. He took a photograph with his mobile phone.

He handed a piece of paper to Nitya and instructed, 'The car was bought on loan. These are the details of the finance company, bearing the date of purchase. The print is so fine that the criminal would not have noticed it, thus failing to erase it unlike the chassis and engine numbers. We can trace the owner with this.'

Nitya took the piece of paper and dialled a number. A few minutes later the ATS had information: the name, address and contact number of the car owner.

'We will show your investigating officer what investigation is,' DIG Palande said contemptuously to Sub-Inspector Haji and called his boss, the ATS chief.

Sathe's video byte was playing on a loop across news channels. It was the headline of the hour. Almost all the anchors asked the same questions: Who parked this car? What's the point of planting explosives outside the house of India's richest man? Who wants to harm Kuber? Do the perpetrators intend to harm the economy of the country by harming Kuber? Are terrorist organizations supported by Pakistan responsible for this act? Is this a result of some corporate war?

API Sathe had just started to upload the media byte when the second phone in his pocket began to vibrate. There were two missed calls, one from the commissioner and another from Haji. He returned the commissioner's call first.

'Sorry, sir, I was actually—'

Before Sathe could complete his sentence, the commissioner shouted at the other end, '*Chutiye, phone kyun nahin uthata*? (Asshole, why don't you answer your phone?)'

'Sorry, sir.'

Commissioner Tomar was still angry. 'The home minister called. He informed me that the ATS has found the owner of the car.'

Sathe was shaken. The phone was about to drop from his hand. 'What ...'

'You said that there was no clue. How did they find it then? Motherfucker, didn't you check? Want to send us to jail or what?' The commissioner was thundering.

'Sir, from my end—'

'*Apni taraf se ghanta* (From your end, my ass)! I went out of my way to land you this case. The ATS was allowed to investigate purely out of academic interest. Now, because of your mistake, it has been granted permission to conduct a parallel investigation. Go and cooperate.'

'Yes, sir.'

'Listen, you better clean up your mess, or you will rot in jail for the rest of your life.'

'Yes, sir. Jai Hind, sir.' Sathe disconnected the call and wiped the sweat off his forehead. It was a cold evening, yet he was sweating.

Sathe wondered if the biggest case of his life was turning into a trap that would ensnare him before he knew it. His face lost all colour and, after much procrastination, he got his mobile phone out of his pocket and dialled. Before the person at the other end could speak, Sathe said, 'Boss, please do something. I am in deep shit. If we don't do something fast, if we don't stop the ATS, it's going to be a big, big mess. We will all be screwed.'

2

What you are seeking is seeking you

A month ago in New Delhi, on the twenty-first day of the twenty-first year of the twenty-first century, a crowd had gathered to celebrate. In the biting January cold, the people had come to celebrate the birthday of Rajesh Dogra, aka Daring Dogra.

Dogra was the country's NSA (national security advisor). He was the country's third most powerful man, even more than the cabinet ministers. After the prime minister and the Union home minister, it was mostly Dogra who called the shots. He was the prime minister's eyes and ears, a position he had earned purely based on merit.

Now, Rajesh Dogra was called Daring Dogra for a reason. From being an undercover spy in Pakistan to his exploits in a cross-border operation, he had proved his mettle over and over again, making him a living legend in the Indian police circle and the spy establishment. He had his own fan following and his protégés—IPS officers—were present in every state.

During his seven years as the NSA, Dogra had used his clout to get his group's IPS officers the choicest of postings at the central and state levels. Because of this, the officers he had obliged gathered every year to celebrate his big day.

Inside, it was hot, courtesy of the free-flowing alcohol and heat radiators. All the officers were busy lobbying and networking. The corner occupied by the Maharashtra cadre seemed the glummest though. Even copious amounts of Old Monk had failed to lift their spirits. The reason for this was that one and a half years ago the government had changed in Maharashtra and the tri-party Maharashtra Regional Alliance had come to power. The new government had wasted no time in reassigning all of Dogra's officers to non-important side postings. The honeymoon period had ended for all the officers who had been given plum postings by Dogra during the reign of the JBS (Jan Bhakt Sangh). The only consolation for them was that the JBS was in power at the Centre and Dogra was JBS's man.

'Did you know that a retired army officer launched Old Monk in 1954? He was also presented with the Padma Shri for the same,' said Dogra when he reached the Maharashtra corner with a glass in hand. Dogra, whose love for Old Monk was well known, looked impressive in his well-cut blue suit. His romantic personality only added to his charm.

'Sir, if it were up to you, you would make Old Monk the national drink of the nation, especially once the sun sets during the winter months,' Om Pachnekar joked.

'Sir, you drink in happiness, we ...' said Naren Arya, leaving his sentence unfinished on purpose. Arya had been the joint police commissioner of Mumbai and the ATS chief in Maharashtra once, but the new government sidelined him because he was close to the former ruling party.

'Arya, your time will come. Rohtagi was also the joint commissioner of Mumbai and the state government sidelined him, but we absorbed him into the NIA, na?'

IG (inspector general) Rohtagi joined the discussion. 'Yes, sir. Actually, the new commissioner, Tomar, has managed to drag his lackey, API Sathe, in. Now he is milking it in the name of the Crime Branch.'

The post of the commissioner of the Mumbai Police was one of the most sensitive ones in the country. It was also the only post that was not occupied by an IPS officer of Dogra's choice.

Dogra had been trying to get Mahavir Tomar over to his side for a while now. But since the time he had been appointed commissioner, Tomar's loyalty had been with the state government and not the Centre. Dogra knew that Tomar had chutzpah and was opportunistic. It was not going to be easy to win him over without offering something lucrative in return.

An alternate communication route needed to be established so that Dogra could be apprised of the ongoings at the commissioner's office on a regular basis. This was why he had ensured the presence of a capable officer like Arya there. Arya was not happy about this; he was rotting in the side posting, aware that his capabilities were being wasted.

'Arya, we will do something for you as well. You are my only eyes and ears in Maharashtra. One soldier should remain on the field so that we don't give the impression that we have all run off,' Dogra said.

Naren Arya, however, perceived himself more as a watchman than a soldier. Before he could say anything, Dogra had walked off to the door where Aman Choudhury waited with a bouquet in his hand and Dhruv Kuber by his side. Ma Amba's locket glistened around Aman's neck. Dhruv took the bouquet from

Aman and handed it to Dogra, wishing him a happy birthday. They exchanged a few pleasantries and Dogra politely inquired after the well-being of the Kuber couple before asking about the progress on the helipad.

Arya was observing Aman and Dogra. He knew that unless he did something exceptional to prove his loyalty, Dogra would not get him out of Maharashtra.

At the ATS bureau in Mumbai, Inspector Nitya entered DIG Palande's cabin without knocking and began to speak immediately. 'Sir, this is interesting. The Scorpio found outside Kuberia is officially owned by a man named Mario Fernandez. We picked him up for questioning and he told us that the car had not been in his possession for three years, that it was with one Hasmukh Jain.'

'Why?' asked Palande.

'Hasmukh owns a business of spare auto parts. Mario had sent his Scorpio to Hasmukh for repairs, but the bill that Hasmukh raised had triggered a fight between the two. Since Mario did not clear his dues, Hasmukh did not return the car.'

'Then let's pick up Hasmukh for questioning.'

'That will be premature at this stage. However, what's intriguing is that Hasmukh had reported the Scorpio missing a week ago at the Vikhroli police station. There was some technical snag with the car, because of which Hasmukh had left the vehicle parked on the highway. When he returned the next day to pick it up, it was missing.'

Palande tried to put two and two together. 'This means that the terrorists stole the car. They changed the number plate and kept the car for a week before leaving it outside Kuberia, filled with gelatin. What did the Vikhroli police station do with the lodged complaint?'

'Sir, they did what is generally done in these cases. The car was Hasmukh's and not Kuber's such that an all-out search would be conducted. Vikhroli police station merely did the paperwork, but they did one good thing. They scanned the CCTV footage of the toll plaza and found that the Scorpio had been taken to Thane.'

'If we have CCTV footage from the toll plaza showing the car, then the driver must be visible, too?'

'No, sir. In Covid times, masks are compulsory. The driver's face was covered. His head was also covered.'

'Did they check the return footage?'

'No, sir, they thought that the thief had run away from Mumbai with the car. They did not expect him to return. And they definitely did not expect to find the car parked outside Kuberia.'

Annoyed by the police's oversight, DIG Palande ordered in a thunderous voice, 'Immediately call for CCTV footage of the entire city's toll plazas. Check the footage for when the Scorpio re-entered Mumbai.'

Back at the CIU office, the alert received from the cyber cell shocked API Sathe. A quick scan of the social media sites told him that the news had gone viral.

Jaish-ul-Hind had posted a message—'Terror at Kuberia'—on its Telegram page. It said that the terrorists who had planted the Scorpio outside Kuberia had reached the safe house. The message also stated that this was just a trailer. A demand for money was made, which if declined by Kuber would mean an attack on his son's car. The message said that he (Kuber) knew what needed to be done. It ended with: 'Wire the money demanded and stay happy with your "fat kid".'

All at once, the headlines changed. Jaish-ul-Hind was trending. Not much was known about this terrorist organization or its leader. Without investigating much, and as per an established and tried-out method, it had been assumed that Pakistan's ISI (Inter-Services Intelligence) was supporting this terrorist outfit. It was inferred that this organization, like others of its kind, targeted young and vulnerable Indian Muslims and brainwashed them to become terrorists.

Wasn't the ATS enough that now this terrorist fiasco has begun as well, Sathe thought, running his hand over his half-bald head.

Meanwhile, the state's home minister, Sardeshpande, called Commissioner Tomar and informed him that since Jaish-ul-Hind had claimed responsibility, the role of the Mumbai Police would become limited. The investigation would no longer remain under the sole purview of Mumbai. It was now a pan-India case, so it would be better to hand over the investigation to the NIA, Sardeshpande suggested.

At Tihar Jail in NCR, a special team of the Delhi Police, along with the jail officers, conducted a thorough search of sub-jail number 8. It was just a while ago that they had managed to trace the IP address of the mobile through which the message had been posted by the Jaish-ul-Hind on Telegram. The terror outfit had used the Tor proxy software to post without being tracked. Once uploaded on Telegram, the message had been broadcast to various social media groups. After this, the account through which the message was posted was shut down.

The Delhi Police sent this top-secret report to the Mumbai Police and the NIA.

Commissioner Mahavir Tomar updated Sardeshpande. Referring to the information obtained by the Delhi Police, he said that the handset used to post the message had been recovered from the barrack of Indian Mujahideen operative Tehsin Akhtar in Tihar Jail.

Akhtar, Tomar said, had no connection with the Jaish-ul-Hind. In fact, it was likely that the Jaish-ul-Hind was not real, that it was merely a virtual group. No government agency had any information about its members. The person who had posted the message was probably taking advantage of the situation and claiming responsibility for something he had not done only to enhance his terrorist profile.

Sardeshpande, convinced with Tomar's update, asked, 'What are we going to tell the media now, after creating such a hue and cry about the Jaish-ul-Hind?'

The Mumbai Police, meanwhile, shared a letter with the media, in which the Jaish-ul-Hind claimed that it had nothing to do with the explosives found outside Kuberia. The Mumbai Police took this latest letter at face value and, considering it to be authentic, closed the Jaish-ul-Hind chapter. In short, they were back to square one in the investigation.

Yatin Sathe heaved a sigh of relief. It had been a close shave. The case was not going to be transferred to the NIA. However, one question still remained. Some organization had planted the Scorpio outside Kuberia. If not the Jaish-ul-Hind, then who?

In the meantime, the ATS's Nagpur unit reached the factory from where the gelatin had been purchased. The company checked the serial number and affirmed that the said stock had indeed been purchased from there. How it had reached the terrorists was something the ATS got no answer for.

Incidentally, it's not difficult to procure gelatin sticks since it is used industrially. A licence is generally required, but it is not difficult to obtain through fraudulent means, which was why this angle of investigation, too, seemed to be heading nowhere.

At the ATS bureau, officers diligently sifted through piles of CCTV footage obtained from various toll plazas.

To put things into perspective, Thane lies adjacent to Mumbai, just like Noida and Gurugram in terms of Delhi and Hyderabad in terms of Secunderabad. A single toll plaza separates Mumbai from Thane. And since Mumbai is surrounded by the sea on three sides, to exit the city by road you have to cross one of the three toll plazas. This meant that if the stolen car was taken out of Mumbai and had re-entered, it had to cross one of the three.

'Sifting through all the CCTV footage is going to be a monumental task even if we have all hands on deck. One week, three toll plazas, forty lanes, thousands of cars and multiple cameras in multiple locations—it's a mammoth amount of footage to go through,' Nitya said sounding helpless.

Hoping to find another solution, DIG Palande asked, 'Hasmukh?'

'From his social media profile, it seems like he is a simple middle-class man. Likes music and swimming, and lives in Thane with his family. Has an auto spare parts business.'

'Any clue from the missing car complaint he lodged?'

'Hasmukh mentioned in the report that he was on his way to work when the car's steering began to give trouble. He parked the Scorpio on the side of the road and took a cab to get to work. The next day, when he returned, he couldn't find the car. He went to the local police station and filed a complaint. When he saw on the news that a similar car had been found outside Kuberia, he contacted the police.'

'I don't understand one thing; actually, there are so many questions in my head. I need Hasmukh to answer those,' Palande said and extended a notepad towards Nitya.

It had a list of questions, which Nitya skimmed through:

1. If Hasmukh owns an auto spare parts business, he must know several mechanics. Why didn't he call one of them to look at the car?
2. Assuming he returned home via the same route a few hours later, why didn't he see if the car was still there or not?
3. Did he return to the spot the next day with a mechanic? How many mechanics did he contact?
4. Does the location mentioned in his statement match with that of his phone?
5. Just by seeing the footage of a similar car on the news, how did he discern that it was his Scorpio, that too when the number plate had been changed? If he managed to recognize the car based on some identification mark or sticker, then he should tell us so that we can also easily spot the car returning to Mumbai in the CCTV footage.

Three hours later, DIG Palande and Inspector Nitya returned to the ATS office from Thane after grilling Hasmukh. ATS chief Vishwajeet was waiting for them. It was unusual to find him in his cabin so late in the night. But before they could give him an update, Vishwajeet gave them an earful. Commissioner Mahavir Tomar had called him and the ATS chief was simply executing a 'forward as received'.

The ATS's questioning had left Hasmukh shaken. He had been unable to answer quite a few questions to their satisfaction. Early that morning, Hasmukh had had to leave for the Vikhroli police station where he had filed the missing car report. After being questioned there, Hasmukh had made his way to the CIU office in south Bombay, where he had been made to wait for hours before his statement was recorded. He had been unable to go to work. To top it all, the moment he reached home the ATS had descended upon him like a pack of wolves. He had been questioned like a terrorist in his own house, with the ATS threatening to haul his sorry ass to their office for another round of questioning. As far as he knew, the CIU had been investigating the case and the same had been reiterated in the media. What had been the meaning of this additional investigation?

Hasmukh looked at his face in the mirror and felt that he had aged ten years in a day. The moment the ATS left, he had called Yatin Sathe in desperation and wept. A few minutes later, Commissioner Tomar had phoned the ATS chief.

Tomar was known for his Haryanvi swag and the ATS chief was aware that the commissioner's closeness with the current ruling party had fetched him this cream position. The chief had also heard whispers in the police circles that Tomar had paid a staggering hundred crores for the post and was now on the road to recovering this money. It was no secret that officers offered bribes for the coveted commissioner's post, but this time the amount had been record-breaking.

ATS chief Vishwajeet was in a conundrum. Commissioner Tomar was his senior; he was not someone Vishwajeet could confront alone and directly. Also, Vishwajeet did not want to ruin his chances of becoming the next commissioner of Mumbai or the state's DGP. He was not a player in this fight and did not want to take sides. He was also aware that the commissioner had direct links with the Kuber family. After weighing all the pros and cons, Vishwajeet had chosen his words carefully before reprimanding his juniors.

Tomar had made it clear that while he had no problem with the ATS running a parallel investigation, threatening and frightening Hasmukh could ruin the entire case. He had also warned Vishwajeet that if Hasmukh decided to open his mouth in front of the media, the Mumbai Police would lay the entire blame on the ATS and not take any responsibility. Vishwajeet would then have to deal with the government and the media on his own.

After thirty years in service, Vishwajeet understood what the commissioner had subtly communicated. He berated Palande and Nitya for their treatment of the complainant and witness, Hasmukh. He warned Nitya that he was not to use this case as an opportunity to get back at Sathe for a tiff that had occurred seventeen years ago.

It did not take long for Palande and Nitya to understand the situation. They guessed correctly that Hasmukh had called Sathe the moment they had left. Sathe had then called his 'caretaker', Commissioner Tomar, who had phoned Vishwajeet.

They knew Vishwajeet played it safe and had big aspirations for the future. So, even though his officers had done a good job, they were being admonished. Palande and Nitya also knew that Hasmukh's statement had its loose ends, but after being admonished by the chief, their suspicion had turned to belief. They knew there was something worth pursuing and they also realized that there would be no straight answers. But they had an ace up their sleeves.

Naren Arya carefully read every question in the list handed to him.

1. What was the logic behind erasing the chassis and engine numbers of the Scorpio? What could the terrorists gain by hiding the identity of the car's owner? If the owner was traced, how would that affect the terrorists?
2. Usually, criminals steal a car forty-eight hours prior to committing the crime. Why did the terrorists risk stealing and keeping the car for a week?
3. Why did they take the car out of Mumbai after stealing it? Everyone knew that the entry and exit points are under CCTV surveillance. Why didn't they hide the car within the city itself? And why did they risk bringing the car back to Mumbai?
4. Was the terrorist safe house in Thane?
5. CPF jawans are stationed outside Kuberia along with private security. The terrorists would not have parked the car directly in front of the residence. They would have recced the neighbouring areas. Did they conduct multiple recces?
6. They would have made numerous trips between Thane and Mumbai, and they might have crossed hundreds of CCTVs in doing so. Hadn't any cameras noted this activity?
7. Terrorist organizations and the underworld are not the same. The underworld is known for extortion, but which radicalized terrorist outfit extorts tax money?
8. The threat letter was written in broken English. The tone of the letter was regional Gujarati: 'Bhaiya-Bhabhi'. Which terrorist organizations use this kind of language?
9. After the Kuberia episode, no chatter had been picked up on social media sites, there had been no phone interceptions, nothing from the informers' network. Why? Was this the

work of a local group that physically met to decide what they would do next?
10. Was something else brewing under this guise of terrorism?

Arya handed the paper back to the officers and looked at them. The state government had appointed him as the additional director general (DG) of the State Security Corporation, but to him, this post felt like a watchman's. He had once been the ATS chief; he had had a glorious career. In comparison, this felt like a slight. Arya had kept up contact with his old team. The same team members, Palande and Nitya, were now sitting in front of him after the tough exchange with Vishwajeet the night before. The officers knew that Arya was well connected with the lobby in Delhi and the NIA. He also enjoyed favour with the former chief minister of the state and the current leader of opposition, Jitendra Nagpure.

Palande and Nitya had paid Arya a courtesy visit to seek some unofficial guidance about this case. But, most importantly, they wanted the information to reach the people who needed to be privy to this information. They wanted to ensure that any attempt by the ATS and the Mumbai Police to sweep the case under the carpet failed.

It was through casual banter that the two officers relayed what they wanted to, and Arya understood. He, too, could see that there was more to this case, something that could be turned into an opportunity. He also knew that the central leadership was busy with the upcoming state elections and would not pay much attention. He remembered the party at Dogra's residence and decided to settle some scores with the police officers in power. Also, he had not met Nagpure in a long time. Luckily, he was in Mumbai because the state assembly session was on.

Jitendra Nagpure thundered his way into the Maharashtra Legislative Assembly that morning. He surprised the state home minister, Sardeshpande, by highlighting sequentially aspects of the investigation that had not been noticed, or were deliberately omitted.

Arya smiled in his office as he watched the live telecast of Nagpure's speech. Nagpure had demanded that the NIA investigate the case.

A CBI inquiry was not possible because, like many other states, Maharashtra had withdrawn general consent. This meant that the CBI was duty-bound to seek the state government's permission before conducting any investigation in Maharashtra. And this permission would be difficult to obtain because the CBI had been accused of being partial and providing political benefits to the ruling party at the Centre.

While the state government could say no to the CBI, this did not hold true for the NIA. Nagpure had raised this demand after much deliberation. He also knew that the state government would not allow the NIA to enter without protesting, since the allegations against them were similar to those levied against the CBI. His only motive was to prepare the base for the long battle that would ensue.

The ruling party rejected Nagpure's demand, but the home minister, who had been snubbed in the house, summoned Commissioner Mahavir Tomar to his office.

As soon as the commissioner entered, the home minister lashed out, leaving him at a loss for words. It took the commissioner a while to convince Sardeshpande that the investigation was heading in the right direction and that the case would be solved soon.

It was clear to the commissioner that Nagpure had been tipped off by a police officer who had not only leaked sensitive information, but also explained to him how to circumvent the investigation, point by point. He suspected the ATS and wondered if the phone call yesterday had been too much. Having successfully implemented three of the four tenets of Chanakya's sutras,[1] he had to focus on damage control and establishing a communication link for the future. He weighed a few options in his mind and then called Dilip Verma, the erstwhile head of the CIU.

Meanwhile, the news about the former chief minister of Maharashtra questioning the credibility of API Yatin Sathe, and thereby the integrity of the investigation, spread like wildfire.

Sathe found himself in a Catch-22 situation. If he gave direct answers, he would become a part of the political rhetoric. If he kept silent, it would be misconstrued as an admission of guilt. After a few years of working with a political party, Sathe had realized that politics was not his cup of tea. He braced himself for the expletives the commissioner was bound to throw at him. He also prepared for the volley of questions the media was waiting to bombard him with. But the biggest danger he could sense was the ATS, which had lost no time in tracing the owner of the explosives-bearing vehicle.

Despite his age and years of experience, Sathe had not understood that when you are standing at a crossroads, when no direction seems safe, you should focus on cutting your losses and leaving. He had failed to put this bit of advice into action years ago, as a result of which he had spent seventeen

1 Chanakya, also called Kautilya, was a statesman and philosopher during the reign of Chandragupta Maurya. He said there are four ways of getting someone to do a task: saam, daam, dand, bhed. 'Saam' means to advice and ask, 'daam' means to offer and buy, 'dand' means to punish and 'bhed' means to exploit secrets.

years outside the police action. Today, again, he was caught in a similar bind.

Sathe stepped out and faced the cameras that were thrust at his face. The questions from the media burst forward, all pertaining to the Kuberia case. Sanjay Trivedi was present, too, but he stood a little apart as he had spotted Sanchini in the crowd. Trivedi had a history with Sanchini and wanted to avoid her at all costs. Just then, Trivedi's mobile phone beeped with a message. The message was a question that Trivedi asked Sathe almost immediately.

The API, who was leaving after having answered the last question, did not hear Trivedi clearly at first. When the question was repeated, Sathe understood who had really asked the question, using Trivedi as a medium.

'Sathe Sir, the ATS has found the owner of the Scorpio, Hasmukh Jain. Do you know him? I repeat, did you know Hasmukh Jain before this investigation began?'

Sathe paused before answering. 'No,' he said finally and left.

Two hours later, the signal in front of Mumbai's historical GPO building turned green. While other cars scampered ahead, one SUV obstinately stood in the middle lane with its parking lights on. A flustered man approached the car from the other side of the road and got in.

'The matter of the Scorpio is gaining steam. The problem is escalating. We are in deep shit. I have managed to come here with great difficulty, only because we have been friends for years,' he said as he sat down.

The driver of the SUV placed his hand on Hasmukh's shoulder, as if reassuring him, and said, 'We will be in deep shit if someone gets to know. We cannot let anyone find out that we know each other from before. The fight against terrorism is big business. Any game that you play in the name of national security, Pakistan, ISI or Islamic militancy, will be accepted by these blind nationalists, no questions asked. Because of this, we will stay in the safe zone.'

With this, Yatin Sathe, who was in the driver's seat, raced ahead.

3

Shit happens

Roughly a year ago

Four people took off in a helicopter from the Mahalakshmi Racecourse helipad: Sathe, Hasmukh, a bookie named Mahesh Bhor and Sathe's girlfriend, Nina Dias. They were headed towards Daman. Even though they had reached the helipad earlier, Kuber's helicopter was given priority and allowed to leave before theirs. This wasn't surprising given his status and wealth.

Mumbai looked different if you saw it from a helicopter and not an aircraft. With its skyscrapers, Nariman Point and BKC, the city looked like India's Manhattan. Dharavi, the world's biggest slum; and Marine Drive, one of the world's most beautiful seafronts; looked nothing like what you see when you are at eye level.

Of course, the different perspective was because a helicopter flies much lower in the sky, allowing you to recognize a lot of landmarks if you are familiar with the city.

The moment their helicopter took off, the four of them found themselves over Kuberia. Mesmerized, Hasmukh said, 'Kuber's building looks more majestic from the top, isn't it? I had only seen it from the ground before this.'

'You know, if Kuber needs to go somewhere, he comes to the helipad of the racecourse first and then takes the helicopter to an airport or his factory,' Sathe said.

'It takes him thirty minutes to get to the Mahalakshmi helipad. Don't these trips translate into losses for him?' Hasmukh asked.

'He earns about five lakh rupees per minute, which means five crores in thirty minutes. In one year, that amounts to five hundred and fifty crores,' Nina Dias said. She was very sharp when it came to money matters, which Sathe appreciated.

'If you go by Hollywood movies, the rich have a helipad on their roof itself. Kuber should also do the same. In two years, he will save about eleven hundred crores,' said Hasmukh.

'I will ask Kuber to appoint Hasmukh as his financial adviser,' quipped Mahesh Bhor. He had been silent all this while. This statement from him made the others laugh. 'But won't he know this bit about the helipad already?'

'He has been trying to get permission to construct a helipad on his terrace, but it has been denied so far. I think he will get it soon though,' said Sathe and looked down. He closed his eyes and his thoughts began to drift.

Present day

API Sathe was rudely jolted out of his power nap. He had just fallen asleep after completing a twenty-hour shift. Sub-Inspector

Haji did not speak. He simply turned on the television. Old highlights of a Sachin Tendulkar match were playing on Star Sports. Haji quickly changed the channel to the news. Amidst big banners of breaking news, Sanjay Trivedi was reporting live—the NIA had supposedly jumped into the case lock, stock, and barrel and begun a parallel investigation.

Sathe was shocked. *Who all were going to take a bite out of his pie?* First, it was the ATS, and now the NIA! 'The NIA, so suddenly? Why and how? The state government did not give the NIA permission. Commissioner Sir had told me that the state government did not want to involve the NIA,' he said to no one in particular. His half-asleep mind had barely conjured these questions when Trivedi offered answers from the television.

'A raid was conducted in a terrorist's cell at the Tihar Jail. Although he has not been directly linked to the Kuberia case, the Delhi Police sent a copy of their report to the NIA. Subsequently, the NIA began a primary investigation. Even though the Opposition's demand for the NIA to handle the case was denied by the state government, there is another provision of law which allows the NIA to conduct a parallel investigation without seeking the state government's permission. In the Kuberia case, in addition to the existing provisions of the Indian Penal Code, Section Four of the Explosive Substances Act is also applicable. According to that, the expression "explosive substance" shall be deemed to include any materials for making any explosive substance; also any apparatus, machine, implement or material used, or intended to be used, or adapted for causing, or aiding in causing, any explosion in or with any explosive substance. Wherever this act applies, the NIA can investigate without seeking anyone's permission.'

The anchor was not well versed in the nitty-gritty pertaining to the laws. Unable to think of a question immediately, she asked Sanjay Trivedi: 'Tell us, how will this impact the case and the politics of the state?'

Trivedi was quick to respond. 'Please note that three agencies are working on the case now: Mumbai's CIU, the Maharashtra unit of the ATS and the Centre's NIA. Besides this, the car with the explosives was reported stolen at the Vikhroli police station a few days ago. This is going to become a race more than an investigation. Each agency will want to prove that it is better. Of course, the good thing is that if one agency oversees a crucial detail, the other two will catch it.'

Trivedi wasn't done. He continued. 'And as far as politics is concerned, only yesterday the opposition leader and former chief minister, Jitendra Nagpure, disclosed some crucial information. He also requested an NIA inquiry, a plea that was rejected by the state government. But now there is no stopping the NIA. It will be interesting to see who solves this case first.'

A worried Sathe muted the television and went to the washroom to splash some cold water on his face. He didn't know what else to do. He was already under immense pressure and had a lot to tackle. And now he was in a race with the NIA and the ATS. He had lied to the media about not knowing Hasmukh and was prepared to be chided by his political bosses and the commissioner for it.

He got to work. First, he wrote a letter and handed it to Sub-Inspector Haji. He had to get hold of the CCTV footage of the Scorpio prior to the Kuberia incident. He ordered Haji to take into custody all CCTV footage, which was stored in the office of a housing society in Thane. Just then, he received a call from the commissioner's office, which he promptly answered.

2004

Yatin Sathe was a sub-inspector back then.

A bus had been blown up in Mumbai's eastern suburbs, causing substantial loss of life and property. The city had seen a bomb blast after ten years, after the serial blasts of 1993.

The IB had identified five people. They had been picked up for interrogation from different parts of the state by the Maharashtra police. Among the suspects was an engineer from Parbhani, Nawaz Salim, and a doctor, Arif Fatim.

Various units of the Mumbai Police tried to get them to divulge information, but despite being subjected to torture, the suspects refused to speak. Policemen with years of experience surrendered. They even suggested that though the names of the suspects matched those of the accused, it was probable that the wrong men had been taken into custody. It seemed impossible to extricate any information.

That was when Sub-Inspector Sathe had been summoned, as the last resort. He was young and dashing, a firebrand and the most tech-savvy officer of the police force. He showed no sympathy towards the suspects.

Entering the cabin of his senior officer, Dilip Verma, Sub-Inspector Sathe saluted sharply.

Present day

Sathe was headed to the commissioner's office. Dilip Verma was already there when he arrived.

Verma was Sathe's mentor and had got him entry into the Crime Branch. Verma was the only officer who held a record of carrying out over a hundred encounters, and he had given Sathe an opportunity to be a part of his team. A few years ago, after resigning as a police officer, Verma had contested the Vidhan Sabha elections on the ruling Shakti Samaj Party ticket but lost. He was on good terms with Commissioner Tomar and also had contacts in the current ruling party of the state. His presence in the commissioner's office signified that he had been called in for a special and specific task.

Sathe sat on Verma's left. The chair to his right was already occupied by a black leather bag. Commissioner Tomar came straight to the point. 'I think we started off with the ATS on the wrong foot, on a confrontational note. Verma has worked with the ATS chief earlier and can help us. We will have to pretend that we are cooperating with the ATS and the NIA, but we know what needs to be done.'

Sathe nodded in agreement.

Before the discussion could proceed, the commissioner glanced at the news channel on his TV and increased the volume. On the screen, Jitendra Nagpure was addressing the legislative assembly. 'The day Hasmukh's car was stolen, he was seen in the Crawford Market area, which is where the Mumbai Police Commissionerate is located. Incidentally, the CIU office is located inside the Commissionerate. Hasmukh came to meet someone there. But who? Let me remind you that Hasmukh and Yatin Sathe live in Thane and are old friends. I have proof that the two have been in touch. Mobile records are also available. Hasmukh is an important link in this case and should be given police protection.'

Both Commissioner Tomar and Verma looked at Sathe, whose face had lost all colour. The three of them agreed that a senior police officer was tipping off the opposition leader. Was it an ATS officer or somebody else? Sathe was right in suspecting that it could be Naren Arya. After all, Arya had friends in the ATS and was directly connected to Nagpure.

The commissioner warned Sathe. 'You have created this mess, and you will clean it.'

'If you don't have the balls, why bite off more than you can chew?' said Verma.

The moment Sathe stepped out of the commissioner's office, he saw missed calls from Hasmukh. The fact that Hasmukh had used his own phone to call Sathe on his official phone, despite being specifically told not to, meant that it was a serious matter. Sathe decided to use the 'secret' phone in his cabin to call Hasmukh.

The CIU office, where Sathe's cabin was, was located at a distance of roughly a hundred metres from the commissioner's office, which was packed with media persons. Sathe had expected this. He knew the media would want him to react to Nagpure's disclosure. Not being able to resist the camera was Sathe's weakness. He recalled how Sachin Tendulkar handled attacking bowlers and thought of dealing with the media the same way.

The moment he stepped out of the commissioner's office, the press descended upon him. On being questioned about knowing Hasmukh, Sathe said, 'Well, I guess just because we live in Thane, it has been assumed that we are acquainted. I have not met Hasmukh of late. Even when Hasmukh's car was stolen, I did not meet him.'

'The opposition leader said that Hasmukh came here the day his car was stolen. Did he come to meet you?' This question came from Sanjay Trivedi.

'He said that Hasmukh had come to Crawford Market. He never said that Hasmukh came to the Commissionerate. I have also read his statement; he didn't say that Hasmukh came to

Crawford Market to meet Yatin Sathe. It would be better if you check your facts before making assumptions. Speak only if you have evidence.'

In trying to hit a boundary like Sachin Tendulkar, Sathe had made a mistake. He had engaged in a one-on-one with the media. This was akin to wrestling with a pig in the mud, forgetting that the pig actually enjoys it.

Sanjay Trivedi shot back with another question. 'Are you denying that Hasmukh visited the CIU office in the last couple of days? Will your call records and CCTV footage from the CIU office confirm this?'

Sathe knew this was a tricky question. His lie had already been exposed once. Anything he said now would be noted and used against him as evidence in court proceedings or an inquiry at a later date. Even Sachin Tendulkar 'well-left' balls at times. Sathe decided to do the same.

Leaving the throng behind, he headed to his office saying, 'What is the evidence ... what is the evidence?'

All through the media interaction, Sathe's phone had been vibrating in his pocket with calls from Hasmukh. When Sathe got to his cabin, he called Hasmukh back but got no answer.

Bloody hell! Nothing is going right today, thought Sathe.

Hasmukh's mobile phone continued to vibrate under his towel on the sunbed. He swam whenever he was under stress. It was the ultimate stress buster for him; it was what he needed this day. A simple problem had metamorphosed into a big one. The CIU hadn't rattled him much because he knew Sathe would keep it under control, but the ATS had left him shaken. He had been questioned like a terrorist. And now the NIA was also investigating!

Sathe had told him to confess to the crime, to take the blame for parking the Scorpio outside Kuberia, and that he would help him get bail. His family, however, had flatly refused to let him do anything like that. Hasmukh's wife made her dislike of Sathe quite apparent; she considered him to be an enemy. And her hate was justified. Sathe was pressurizing Hasmukh to confess to something he had not done.

Sathe and Hasmukh were old friends. Now, Hasmukh knew that friends did not abandon each other when things got rough, so he decided to stand by Sathe. Hasmukh allayed his fears and told himself that if the matter went out of hand, he would do one of two things: he would go underground for some time or he would expose the entire truth. The problem with the first option was that his family would not agree.

It was with these thoughts, wondering if he should discuss them with Sathe, that he dived into the water.

2004

At the Crime Branch's Andheri office, Nawaz thought he would drown. Water splashed and spilt around him, and it continued to enter his mouth. He could not breathe because his nose and mouth were filled with water. The harder he tried to breathe, the more water seeped in. He could feel his lungs becoming heavy.

Two constables held Nawaz's head firmly. They intermittently removed the cloth covering his face, poured a jug of water over it and then covered his head again with the cloth. A young officer back then, Sathe instructed the constables in this procedure. He had seen this form of torture in English movies. The internet helped him keep a tab on the practices of police forces across the world and their tried-and-tested methods. Sathe had heard that suspects of the 9/11 terrorist attack in the USA had been tortured using this method. He had also heard that the Americans did this in the presence of doctors. But that was not the case here.

This technique, often called water torture or water boarding, involves water being poured over a cloth covering the face of an immobilized captive. The captive is made to lie on his back and his hands and legs are tied in a way that ensures that the neck and head are elevated.

The moment water enters the captive's nose and mouth, the body expels air as a reflex action. The captive then tries to breathe, but that only causes more water to enter the lungs. Now, because the neck and head are elevated, the lungs don't immediately fill up with water. The whole time, the cloth is kept on the face, so that no water is expelled. After some time, the captive is allowed to recover through coughing and vomiting. If the captive faints, he is revived. And the torture begins all over again. It's a very cruel technique where the captive feels like he is drowning.

Water torture is not condoned across the world, but a lot of police officers and agencies use this technique furtively. Done the wrong way—if excess water is poured, if there is no medical help on standby and if it's done by people who are not experts—it can even cause the captive's death.

This is often why water torture is the last resort. In Nawaz's case, all other techniques to extricate information had failed. Yatin Sathe had been given the golden opportunity to prove himself, that too after many stalwarts had given up. But even Sathe, who used conventional ways of torture and then water boarding, failed to get anything out of Nawaz. He remembered the big promises he had made to his seniors. He could see his aspirations of becoming a supercop slipping through his fingers, which was why he decided to increase the duration and amount of water used.

Just then, his phone vibrated.

Present day

At the CIU office, Sathe woke up to his phone vibrating. *Did Nawaz's appearance in his dream portend a bad omen?*

It was 3 a.m. The alarm had set off the phone. Sathe had managed three hours of sleep. There was no one else around except him. He adjusted one hard disk and two number plates in his bag. Then, from the CCTV monitoring room, he brought out similar-looking items and stuffed these too into the bag.

Five minutes later, his SUV was headed out of the Commissionerate and towards his house. There were barely one or two other cars on the road at that hour. All Sathe wanted was to go home, sleep for a few hours, have a bath, eat a home-cooked breakfast and wear fresh clothes before returning to the office. The next forty-eight hours were going to be critical in the Kuberia case.

Normally, the route to Thane from the Commissionerate traversed through Sion, but Sathe took a left turn and chose to take the long way home—via BKC, the Bandra Kurla Complex. This road was usually deserted at night, but because of the pandemic, not even a single soul could be seen. The bridge over the Mithi River, which flowed out of Sanjay Gandhi National Park and passed through BKC and towards Mahim Creek before emptying into the Arabian Sea, was deserted, except Sub-Inspector Fakhruddin Haji.

DIG Palande always reported for work on time, at 10 a.m. But today he was half an hour late. The moment he stepped into the ATS office parking lot, he saw Dilip Verma exiting the office. Palande stormed into the office of ATS chief Vishwajeet, demanding an explanation.

Ignoring protocol, Palande asked his boss why he had met Verma. Especially when Verma's role in this entire fiasco seemed to be suspicious. The ATS chief explained that Verma and he were old acquaintances, that he had known Verma since he was the DCP of Mumbai and famous as an encounter specialist.

DIG Palande, however, reminded the ATS chief of Verma's wrongdoings, saying that meeting him would send out the wrong signal. Now, the ATS chief also knew that Verma had come to see him with a motive and a message. But sharing that detail with Palande didn't seem wise. He concocted a story to pacify Palande and sent him on his way.

Outside the ATS chief's office, Nitya Shetty could hear loud voices. But he was not going to step in between two sparring IPS officers. Verma had been his boss. In fact, Nitya was called Verma's second-in-command at one point. Verma had been like a teacher to him, teaching him everything there was to know about an encounter. Together, they made a good team and even became famous with both the national and international media talking about them.

But then Nitya was jailed in the disproportionate assets case and Verma served time for an encounter. The remaining team had to face the consequences of Sathe's imprudence in the Nawaz case, as a result of which the entire team fell apart like a broken string of pearls. Verma, in fact, had tried to sideline Nitya on account of his fondness for Sathe. Nitya believed that it was Verma who had got him implicated in the disproportionate assets case seventeen years ago. This was why when he saw Verma entering the ATS office, he decided to eavesdrop from the next room. Placing his head against the wall, he heard everything—right from what Verma and the ATS chief spoke about to what DIG Palande and the ATS chief discussed after Verma left.

Nitya noticed one more thing. When Verma entered the office, he was carrying a black leather bag that seemed heavy. But when he left, the bag seemed flat. In fact, when Verma placed the bag on the seat, it flopped over, indicating that it was empty.

A little distance away from Aniket Housing Society, where Sathe lived, Hasmukh paced up and down frantically. Sathe had instructed him to never be seen near the society. But Hasmukh seemed to have no option. This day had begun on an even worse note. He had not even finished breakfast when the NIA had barged into his house. This after he had already been interrogated by the Vikhroli police, the CIU and the ATS.

Being questioned again, by the NIA this time, was not new for Hasmukh. He parroted what Sathe had taught him. But then he was asked questions that Sathe had not prepared him for. The NIA basically asked him three questions over and over again, in different words:

1. Out of the four number plates found in the boot of the Scorpio, two belonged to Kuberia's security fleet. No attempt was made to hide this, whereas the chassis and engine numbers had been erased. Why?
2. Even the gelatin found in the car was not military-grade but commercial-grade, and no attempt was made to hide the details of its procurement. Why?

3. Neither the detonator nor the battery nor any assembling unit was found in the car. Doesn't it seem as though the so-called terrorists wanted the car, number plates, gelatin and letter to be found, but they did not want the owner of the car traced?

Hasmukh stuck to one response: how would he have answers to these questions when he himself was a victim. But the NIA refused to budge and told him that they would conduct a polygraph test. When Hasmukh googled it, he found that they were referring to a lie detector test where he would be hooked to a machine to see if he was telling the truth or not. His head had been in a jumble since then and he knew he had to meet Sathe urgently.

Nitya updated DIG Palande. The ATS team that had been deputed to keep a close eye on Hasmukh had informed Nitya that Hasmukh had left his house the moment the NIA team left. He had spent an hour a little distance from Aniket Housing Society, after which an SUV appeared and Hasmukh got in. The person inside the car could not be identified because the heavily tinted windows were rolled up. The SUV then drove off towards Bombay.

'Tinted windows! That's not allowed. Only police or agency officials use these,' Palande said. When he said 'agency', he was referring to the IB, R&AW, the Crime Branch and the Central Police Force.

'Sir, Yatin Sathe lives in Aniket Housing Society. I have been to his house,' Nitya said.

The two of them smiled at each other.

Once he got into Sathe's car, Hasmukh narrated the entire NIA interrogation to him. Hasmukh also mentioned to him the options of going underground or simply exposing the truth. Sathe was looking fresh, dressed in his white shirt and Ray-Ban sunglasses. He looked more like a corporate employee and less like a police officer. He was lost in thought when Hasmukh asked, 'Should I consider anticipatory bail?'

'What's the need for that? You are not a suspect. You are a victim, a witness. Remember you said no when I asked you to consider getting arrested as a suspect.'

'I don't want to rot in jail,' said a visibly frightened Hasmukh.

Laughing, and looking quite undisturbed, Sathe said, 'Don't worry so much. I have a better plan. Let's go to a lawyer right now.'

'Right now? As in just now?'

'Yes, right now.'

The ATS team that had been tailing Hasmukh had confirmed that he met Sathe. There was visual confirmation that Sathe was in the car with Hasmukh. The team requested further instructions.

'Tell the team to forget Hasmukh and follow Sathe instead. We will pick up Hasmukh tomorrow. He will talk like a parrot in custody. The case will be solved tomorrow and we will finally give Sathe the ATS sandwich,' said DIG Palande.

Having met the lawyer, Sathe dropped Hasmukh at an auto stand and took the Eastern Freeway to Mumbai. This was a seventeen-kilometre-long elevated road that ended two kilometres before the CIU office signal. It was usually traffic-free.

The moment Sathe hit the freeway, he spotted a car in the rear-view mirror. The Maruti gypsy was tailing him at a distance of hundred metres. Sathe could not recognize the people inside the car because they were wearing masks. After the freeway ended, Sathe turned towards Crawford Market. So did the gypsy.

Was he being followed, or was his mind playing tricks on him? And who could be following him? The ATS, NIA, some criminals or the media? Why would they follow him? And since when had they been following him? Did they see him with Hasmukh? Everyone knew where he lived ... so, was Hasmukh being followed? Had they stopped following Hasmukh and started following him after seeing them together? If the media had been following Hasmukh, they would not be so patient. They would have thrust a mike in front of his face by now. Then, was it the NIA or the ATS?

Sathe stopped his car, got down and started walking towards the Maruti gypsy, which too had stopped. Just then, two cars came from nowhere and stopped on either side of the gypsy. Armed men disembarked from these cars.

Because this filmi scene had unfolded near the commissioner's office, the media did not waste any time in getting there. Sathe had already sent the registration number of the gypsy to the CIU office, which had verified that the number plate was fake and belonged to a scooter. That was why, as per the plan, two armed units of the CIU now surrounded the gypsy and made two armed ATS men disembark.

Not long after this, the ATS chief found DIG Palande and Inspector Nitya in his office. Vishwajeet was trembling with rage as he spoke to Commissioner Tomar. Yatin Sathe was seated in front of the commissioner as this conversation unfolded. The ATS chief was defending his team saying that they were not following Sathe but Hasmukh, and that following Sathe had been a mistake. Because of the tinted windows, Vishwajeet said, they did not know Sathe was in the SUV. Also, the number plate was fake, which made them suspicious of the car. But the commissioner was not ready to listen to anything. He told the ATS chief that he would raise this matter with the home minister in the review meeting the next day.

The ATS chief slammed the phone down and glared at the two officers seated in front of him. The fear of facing the home minister the next day was clear on his face.

Before the chief could say a word, DIG Palande said, 'The cat is out of the bag. No point in delaying. We will arrest Hasmukh tonight. Tomorrow, he will be sitting in front of us and blabbering like a parrot. You can tell the home minister in the evening that the ATS has solved the case.'

'Or you both can be assigned the duty of telephone operators in the control room,' the ATS chief warned and ended the meeting.

Hasmukh ate his dinner hurriedly and started getting dressed. Seeing him don a formal white shirt at night, his wife asked him where he was off to. She was told that a police officer called Gavde had called from the Kandivali police station and asked to meet. Hasmukh's wife was surprised. Until now, the Vikhroli police, the CIU, the ATS and the NIA had been interrogating Hasmukh. *Why had the Kandivali police come into the picture*, she wondered. The station was located in the western suburbs of the city and was not connected to the Kuberia case at all. *Why was Hasmukh going there?*

She wanted to inquire, but seeing Hasmukh worried she let it go. She had been advising him to stay away from Sathe for months, and she held his friendship with Sathe responsible for the whole mess. She could see how her husband seemed to have aged a decade in just a week. She had decided that come what may, tomorrow she, along with her son, would convince Hasmukh to upload an honest statement on YouTube.

There was a lot of political pressure on everyone investigating the case. And now the fact that Sathe had deliberately hidden his acquaintance with Hasmukh had come out in the open. It added fuel to a raging fire. It became difficult for the government and the commissioner to defend API Yatin Sathe. The media, too, was berating him. Consequently, Sathe was strategically removed from the Kuberia case through a formal order.

The Kuberia case, which had been thought of as a straightforward case, would have been solved quickly had so many people not interfered. In a month's time, Sathe would have proven himself to be a supercop and absolved himself of all the allegations hurled at him seventeen years ago.

Sathe kept dwelling on the positive and negative aspects of the developments at the CIU office. He thought about the CCTV footage connected to this case. He was sweating so much that he could feel his white vest sticking to him, an indication that something bad was about to happen. He had had the same feeling seventeen years ago as well. He glanced around. The air conditioner was working optimally and no one else was sweating. The temperature outside was similar to the temperature inside, or maybe it was a little lower. Sathe put his mobile on charge, opened the door and stepped out.

2004

In January, one news item made the headlines. Wearing a white shirt, with a bandage on his head and purple bruises on his face, a young Yatin Sathe told the media that his team had been taking Nawaz, the accused in the bomb blast case, to Aurangabad when an accident happened and their jeep overturned. Many police officers, including Sathe, were injured. Taking advantage of the situation, Nawaz Salim disappeared. The next day, a woman spotted a man running across a field with handcuffs around his wrists.

That day, among the journalists present, was a young Sanjay Trivedi as well. He had just got a job and Sathe's story sounded like a scene straight out of a Bollywood film to him. There was no regret or guilt on Sathe's face when he spoke to the media, Trivedi noticed. The other reporters knew that Sathe was a member of the high-profile CIU, and that enmity or friendship with this agency could make or break their careers.

But that night, Sanjay Trivedi conducted his own investigation and filed a report, which refuted the entire '*accident mein farar* (escaped during the accident)' theory and exposed the drama that had been staged to hide something.

Present day

A few labourers reached the banks of the Thane creek to defecate. The dense green cover offered a natural toilet for them. There were proper toilets around, but according to them, nothing beat the feel of defecating in the open.

The mind is at its sharpest in the morning and every topic under the sun is discussed with great intellectual acumen. During one such discussion, the attention of one of the labourers went towards something white poking out of the sludge, from under the bushes. He inched closer and saw a white shirt that was dirty in patches. The body of the person who was wearing that shirt showed no signs of life.

Hasmukh Jain, the sole link, the sole witness and the supposed owner of the Scorpio involved in the Kuberia case, was dead.

4

It takes a thief to catch a thief

2004

A body lay on the wet floor. While Sathe insisted that Nawaz was unable to bear the water torture, his colleagues believed that Sathe's overconfidence had caused the death. Everybody agreed that Sathe had no experience when it came to sustained interrogation and that his imprudence had led to Nawaz's death. What was worse was that Sathe showed neither remorse nor guilt. According to him, the deceased was a terrorist, and the sooner the likes of him died the better.

Sathe, in fact, suggested to his DCP that they burn the body, wipe out all evidence and declare that Nawaz fled. Another officer suggested that they declare this as a custodial death so that the consequences were not as drastic, because if the truth came to light later, they could be in deep trouble.

Now, the DCP had foresight. In case of custodial death, the officer(s) responsible would be suspended and would have to face a department inquiry. Because it was the DCP who had sent Sathe to interrogate Nawaz, he would obviously be held responsible, as would all the officers who held ranks between the DCP and Sathe. He decided to give Sathe's cover-up plan the green signal, hoping this would keep the extent of the torture inflicted under wraps.

Present day

A police van and an ambulance stood on the banks of the Thane creek. With their feet submerged in sludge, the policemen thoroughly scanned the area for clues. No evidence had been found on the body or the clothes on it. The deceased was still unidentified. There was no wallet, no mobile phone and no identification document.

Incidents of people jumping into the Thane creek were not new. It was only because of the low tide that the body got stuck in the mangrove. If not, the high tide would have pushed it across into the Arabian Sea, where it would have floated undetected.

As the body was loaded into the ambulance for a post-mortem, the statements of the labourers who had discovered it were recorded one by one. The last among them was busy forwarding the video he had recorded on his mobile phone.

Awaiting his turn to speak in the Vidhan Sabha, opposition leader Jitendra Nagpure received the viral video of the body found in the creek. A WhatsApp message followed the video. Since it was important to verify the authenticity of the video and the message, Nagpure stepped out into the corridor to look at it again.

In the video, a few labourers could be seen removing the cover off a body. The moment the face was revealed, several handkerchiefs that had been stuffed into the mouth of the deceased fell out. The labourers could be heard in the background: '*Arrey bhenchod, dekho iske mooh ke andar kitne rumal* (Look at the number of handkerchiefs stuffed in his mouth).'

The moment Nagpure recognized the face of the dead man, he stopped watching the video and called IPS Naren Arya.

Yatin Sathe felt that good days were just around the corner, which was why he had made arrangements to herald them the night before. But the ringing of the phone roused him from his sleep. The hangover made his head feel heavy.

Upon the caller's instructions, Sathe turned on the television. The Vidhan Sabha was in session and its proceedings were being telecast on the local Marathi news channel. Jitendra Nagpure was speaking with gusto. Quite dramatically, he divulged the 'big reveal'.

'Hon'ble Speaker, I had mentioned earlier that a deep conspiracy lies behind the explosives-laden car found outside Kuberia. I had disclosed on this assembly's floor that API Yatin Sathe and the owner of the vehicle, Hasmukh Jain, knew each other. I had also asked for Hasmukh to be granted police protection. But the state's home minister paid no heed. He did nothing. Yesterday, Hasmukh disappeared suspiciously. This morning, his body was found near the Thane creek. His hands were tied and his mouth was stuffed with five handkerchiefs. No mobile phone was found. Despite these circumstances, the local police station has simply registered a case of accidental death. The NIA should investigate this matter because Hasmukh went missing suspiciously, and his body has been found under equally suspicious circumstances.'

Sathe's hangover disappeared the moment he heard 'missing suspiciously'. These very words had been hounding him for the past seventeen years.

2004

Missing Suspiciously

Sanjay Trivedi's news report, with this headline, led to two things: Yatin Sathe's downfall began at the cusp of his career and Sanjay Trivedi's graph as a journalist shot up.

In this report, Trivedi had torn into Sathe's 'missing under suspicious circumstances' theory in a sequential manner. He had even managed to get a statement from Dr Fatim, who had been in custody with Nawaz and now pointed fingers at Sathe.

Sathe had offered one explanation after another, but the distraught picture of Nawaz's parents broadcast by Trivedi had changed the entire perception of the case.

Sanchini Nayak was amongst the first senior journalists to congratulate Sanjay Trivedi. She was five years his senior and a crime reporter without any sizable breakthroughs to her credit. Trivedi was attracted to her, but the hierarchy had ensured he kept his distance. Sanchini, however, did not hesitate in approaching Trivedi. She did not like a horse that merely trotted, she preferred the ones that cantered. And Sanjay Trivedi was racing.

Sathe, on the other hand, felt like a lame horse. He was worried that his theory of 'missing under suspicious circumstances' would be replaced and propagated as the 'murder of Nawaz and the cover-up'.

Present day

Seated in his office at Vidhan Sabha, Home Minister Sardeshpande looked pale. He had been reprimanded by the chief minister for not keeping abreast with the advancements in the Kuberia case. *How was the opposition leader always one step ahead of him? Who was giving Nagpure regular updates?*

Sardeshpande knew that his credibility was being questioned. He had become the laughing stock in the assembly.

Nagpure, however, became a hero. The opposition had been presented with an opportunity to corner the ruling party. As an experienced politician, Sardeshpande knew that this would have far-reaching consequences. He called in the senior police officers and gave them a piece of his mind.

First, he made it amply clear to them that sensitive information pertaining to the case had to reach him first, especially with the Vidhan Sabha in session, so that he could be the one disclosing it and not Nagpure. Second, he asked them why the case had been registered as accidental death. Cowering under his rage, the officers apprised him of the recent developments and told him that the post-mortem report was awaited.

Normally, post-mortems are carried out by hammered ward boys, with the doctor merely writing the report. But in important and sensitive cases, like this one, the doctor himself dissects the body to ascertain the cause of death. The local police station, in all earnestness, had sent Hasmukh's body for a post-mortem.

Sathe knew that it was important for the doctors to understand that this was not a regular case. He had spent the last hour at the morgue, underlining this fact to them. He reminded them one last time that they should not forget who they were dealing with when they submitted their report.

He then headed towards Hasmukh's home. Cops from the local police station were already there and had been informed to not let the media inside. Clear instructions had been issued to ensure the media did not disturb Hasmukh's family in their moment of grief and turn his death into a show.

Sathe reached Hasmukh's house and offered condolences. In a voice heavy with sorrow he told the family that Hasmukh was extremely distressed because of all the interrogation and that he had felt harassed. Sathe then told them of his visit to the morgue and clarified that the family could collect the body in a few hours to perform the last rites. He also told some of Hasmukh's relatives that, based on the initial reports, it looked like suicide due to drowning.

Sathe had barely left Hasmukh's house when two ATS cars passed by. One was driven by Nitya Shetty himself. Sathe checked the newsfeed on his mobile and got to know that Sardeshpande had declared in the Vidhan Sabha that Hasmukh's death would be looked into by the ATS.

Sathe forwarded a letter to a few reporters.

The ATS team was in a conundrum. They did not know whether to curse their fate or the thirty-minute delay that had occurred the previous night. The ATS team had reached Hasmukh's house to arrest him, but Hasmukh had already left by then. The ATS was thirty minutes late.

His family members had informed the ATS that Hasmukh had gone to meet an officer named Gavde from the Kandivali police station. They tried to contact Hasmukh, but his phone was switched off. Its last location was traced to Vasai, which was thirty-five kilometres away from his home and in a direction opposite to the Kandivali suburbs, approximately thirty kilometres away.

The ATS knew something had gone horribly wrong when they called the Kandivali police station and discovered that no person by the name of Gavde worked there. After this, one ATS team was asked to wait outside Hasmukh's house for the rest of the night. The next morning, the ATS got to know about Hasmukh's death when the press splashed the news. The team left for the location where the body had been found.

When they got there, they were told that Yatin Sathe had just left the scene for the morgue. They found it unusual that Sathe had been present at the spot and then headed to the morgue, too.

It was unusual because the Thane creek area did not fall under the CIU or the Mumbai Police's jurisdiction. It was understandable for the local police to be present there, but why had Sathe got there so quickly? That too when he had been removed from the Kuberia case! What interest did he have in the post-mortem report that he could not wait patiently for it to be released?

When the ATS team reached the morgue, Sathe had already left. When they reached Hasmukh's house, Sathe had left from there too. He was ahead of the ATS. Everyone seemed to be ahead of the ATS, be it opposition leader Jitendra Nagpure, or the media that had splashed a letter over every channel and portal, apparently written by Hasmukh. The ATS team realized that they, too, were in the line of fire.

Hasmukh Jain had written the letter a day before his death. That it was not fake was confirmed when the 'received' stamp of the Mumbai Police, with the date and time recorded, was looked at. Along with that was an inward number, which is released only once the letter is officially received.

It was now clear that a day before he died, Hasmukh had sent this letter to the police commissioner's office. There was a date and time of receipt. The said letter had now gone viral and was being considered more a suicide note than a letter of complaint. Addressed to the Mumbai Police commissioner, the Thane Police commissioner, the Maharashtra chief minister and the state's home minister it read:

> *I have been staying at the above-mentioned address with my wife and children for the past seventeen years. I am forty-eight years old. Since the past twenty years, I have been in the business of high-end car accessories. I am a peace-loving citizen and bear no criminal record. On my way to south Mumbai a few days ago, the steering of the car (Scorpio) I was in got jammed. I left the car on the side of the road, on the Eastern Express Highway, and took an Uber taxi. The next day, when I went to retrieve my car, it was stolen. After that, I filed an FIR.*
>
> *A week later, two officers from the ATS came to my home with some disturbing news. They told me that my stolen Scorpio had been found outside Kuberia. Ever since, not a day has gone by when I have not been tortured. Questioning and interrogation*

at different police stations and by different agencies have left me completely frustrated and troubled. The CIU's Yatin Sathe and Joint Commissioner (crime) Nitin Bharadwaj have also questioned me independently.

In the last week, I have had to make numerous rounds to the ATS office and the local police station. The CIU and the NIA have also come to my house several times for questioning. I have been made to sit for hours, which is no less than illegal detention. One day, I was made to wait at the police station till 6 a.m. I feel humiliated.

This repeated questioning by different agencies has disturbed my peace. I am a victim in this case, but I am being treated like a criminal. A lot of reporters have also troubled me. One of them told me that I am a 'suspect' in this case. I am being harassed despite not having any information. The press and police agencies have no legal right to harass me and my family members and disturb our peace.

I humbly request you to step in and take the necessary steps.

At the bottom of the page was Hasmukh's signature, scrawled along with the date. The date on the letter and the date on the 'received' stamp were the same. The letter was received the very day it was written.

Forwarded several times over, this letter landed on Sanjay Trivedi's mobile and TV screen as well. He examined the letter thoroughly, paying attention to the language, formatting style, margins left on the sides, the numbers assigned to each point, the introduction and Hasmukh's signature at the end. He understood that it was not a normal complaint letter written by a victim. A lawyer had drafted it.

If he could find the lawyer who had drafted this letter, he would be able to understand Hasmukh's mental state. Exploring, and exposing, this angle had the potential of becoming an exclusive story.

The other issue that troubled Sanjay Trivedi was that the letter had been addressed to the Mumbai Police commissioner, the Thane Police commissioner, the Maharashtra chief minister and the state home minister, but the received stamp had only been collected from the Mumbai Police. The physical copy had been handed only to the Mumbai Police, while the rest of the recipients had received the letter via post. *Why?*

The Thane Police commissioner's office was closer to Hasmukh's home, then why did he go all the way to Mumbai to hand over the letter? And if Hasmukh had gone all the way to the Commissionerate, why didn't he also go to the office of the chief minister and the home minister that were close by?

'Nose for news' is a term often used in journalism. It works like a journalist's sixth sense where s/he can portend the arrival of some big news. Trivedi, sensing an important news item there, dialled ATS officer Nitya's number. He hoped that Nitya would shed some light on this angle, but the call went unanswered.

Trivedi read the letter once again.

2004

The moment Sanjay Trivedi read the letter, he said, 'This letter written in Marathi won't do. It has to be drafted in two ways: one for the media, where the letter should be written in a mix of Marathi, Hindi and English; and the other has to be in official-sounding language, like something a lawyer would draft. If the media and court put pressure, maybe we can achieve something.

This will be both complementary and supplementary to each other.'

Nawaz's parents were listening to him intently, but they did not understand the last bit because Trivedi had used English words. Trivedi, however, did not stop to clarify and continued to speak because he was already running late. He had decided to move in with Sanchini and had to meet the real estate agent to see houses available for rent.

'The more direct and easier the language used for the letter written to the media, the more heavy-duty the legal language used for the court should be. One point, however, should be made clear either directly or indirectly in both: That Nawaz was tortured and then his body was disposed of. If this was not the case, then Nawaz should be found and produced before the court, with step-by-step updates on the search for him being shared with the court periodically,' Trivedi said.

Nawaz's father asked, 'What's the point of this?'

'On the one hand, the media will raise questions, and on the other, the court will ask the police to file a reply. The police will then be compelled to give an official answer, which will be more believable than this dramatic story of him escaping.'

It was soon after this conversation that Sathe got to know about a fax Nawaz's parents had sent to all news channels and about a petition they had filed with the court. This meant that Sathe would face both a media trial and a court trial.

Present day

Both the ATS and the NIA were in a fix. The red tape involving the lack of clarity on the ownership of the cases was taking a toll on both the agencies. As far as the Kuberia case was concerned, initially, the CIU had been handed the case and the ATS had been granted permission to conduct a parallel investigation. Then the investigation had been taken away from the CIU and handed to the ATS, with the NIA allowed to conduct a parallel investigation. Then, through a notification from the central home ministry, the entire investigation was handed over to the NIA. The CIU and the ATS were asked to hand over all details to the NIA.

It was unintelligent to assume that the Kuberia case and Hasmukh's death were not connected. Even though the state home ministry had handed over the investigation into Hasmukh's death to an agency under its aegis, the ATS still wanted to look into it. So, through a back-door channel, the ATS managed to confirm that the investigation into Hasmukh's death had indeed been handed over to them. The agency then channelized all its resources into this case.

The ATS team went into a tizzy after Hasmukh's widow, Kamla, told them that Hasmukh and Sathe were not just acquaintances but good friends for years. Kamla also told them that her husband had given their son Sathe's number and told him to call Sathe if there was ever a problem. In fact, when Hasmukh was unreachable till eleven that night, his son called Sathe.

Sathe had told him that Hasmukh never went to meet any policeman without informing him, and that he was surprised at not being informed this time.

Now, the ATS had known about Sathe and Hasmukh's link since the time opposition leader Nagpure had hinted towards it, but there was a difference between being acquaintances and good friends. Why had Sathe hidden this fact? Did Sathe's seniors know about this?

It was with these thoughts that DIG Palande called Nitin Bharadwaj, joint commissioner (crime) of the Mumbai Police, the moment he left Hasmukh's house.

If you are wondering about the hierarchy in the Mumbai Police, it is like this: Right on top is the police commissioner, then come four joint commissioners, then the additional commissioner (crime), and then the DCPs and ACPs. Ranking below them are the CIU and other crime units.

Since Sathe was the head of the CIU and had been the lead investigating officer in the Kuberia case, DIG Palande called the IG, his senior and currently the joint commissioner (crime)—Nitin Bharadwaj.

Bharadwaj denied having any knowledge about Hasmukh and Sathe being old friends. He said that Sathe had never mentioned this to him and that he would get back to Palande after questioning Sathe.

Bharadwaj summoned Sathe. Even though he was the joint commissioner (crime), he was powerless. Until he took over as joint commissioner, the post was prestigious and powerful. In fact, after the commissioner's post, it was the most coveted rank. Top officers of the Mumbai Police had occupied this post in the Crime Branch, the Mumbai Police's attacking arm.

But since Mahavir Tomar became the commissioner, he had taken control of all sensitive matters concerning the Crime Branch—mostly to do with which unit would be headed by which officer and who would be assigned to which high-profile case. The officers reported directly to Tomar, bypassing Bharadwaj, who had no choice but to go along.

API Sathe was Commissioner Tomar's main man in the police department. Also, the commissioner had several contacts in the state government, which gave him a lot of clout. Bharadwaj knew that there was no point in complaining to the political bosses, because that would only invite the commissioner's ire.

As a result, the post of the joint commissioner (crime) was reduced to that of a paper tiger. Bharadwaj, however, maintained the dignity of his office and waited patiently for the tide to turn.

After some time, Sathe came into his office and saluted. Bharadwaj did not ask him to sit. He came straight to the point and questioned Sathe about why he had hidden his friendship with Hasmukh. Sathe responded by saying that he had never been asked about it. This answer was not only immature but also made the questioner sound like a fool. Sathe also said that his friendship with Hasmukh had no bearing on the investigation, which was why he had not mentioned it.

What arrogance and what impudence, thought Bharadwaj. He had understood that something was amiss. He had always been polite with Sathe—the commissioner's toady—but today he spoke in a stern voice and informed Sathe that the ATS had requested his permission to question Sathe, that he had given his approval and that Sathe needed to cooperate with the ATS. Bharadwaj gestured for Sathe, who looked bewildered, to leave.

Bharadwaj then called DIG Palande and offered his cooperation and support without being asked. He said that if the ATS wanted to question API Sathe, he had no objections. He promised to grant official permission if the ATS sent a formal letter requesting the same.

DIG Palande was well-versed in this tug-of-war for power. The joint commissioner (crime) had extended cooperation without being prompted. The ATS quickly faxed an official letter to Bharadwaj's office and received a 'no objection' letter within moments.

Yatin Sathe always desired to be in the limelight. Unfortunately, he often had his wish fulfilled, but for the wrong reasons. Today was no different. He was surrounded by the media. Hasmukh had left behind a letter, and the media considered it to be a suicide note.

'Hasmukh's letter mentions you. Why?' quipped a journalist the moment Sathe walked out after meeting the joint commissioner. He replied nonchalantly, 'How would I know? I did not write the letter.'

Sathe continued to walk, but the media kept up and threw a volley of questions at him: 'Hasmukh was tired of the investigation he stated in his letter.'

'I am no longer the investigating officer of the case,' replied Sathe.

'When you were the investigating officer—'

Before the journalist could complete his question, Sathe spoke up, 'He wrote in his letter that the police, investigating agencies and a reporter, in particular, were harassing him. Maybe that's why he decided to take his own life.'

'How can you say that Hasmukh committed suicide?'

Sathe quickened his pace and replied, 'The preliminary post-mortem report cites drowning as the cause of death.'

'So, a man stuffs his mouth with five handkerchiefs, dons a mask, ties his own hands and jumps into the bay. A little preposterous, don't you think? How many times have you heard of something like this in your twenty-five-year police career?'

Sathe was in his car by now. Even though the windows were rolled up, he could hear the din outside as the questions continued:

'You were the investigating officer of the Kuberia case, and Hasmukh was the sole lead to solving the case. Don't you think his death will bring that ongoing investigation to a dead end?'

'In case the investigation reaches a dead end, who do you think will benefit? Maybe the masterminds of this plan have a lot to gain.'

'Was Hasmukh a mere pawn in this big game?'

Sathe's car ambled along, leaving the media personnel behind, but the questions continued to reverberate in his ears. There was one question troubling Sathe, too: Was he also just a pawn in a bigger plot?

Pandemonium ensued at Hasmukh Jain's house when the news channels reported that Sathe had cited drowning as the cause of his death. Hasmukh's family, friends and relatives knew that he was a good swimmer; he often taught kids how to swim. But the more perplexing fact was that the creek where Hasmukh had drowned was barely hundred metres wide, which was not a great distance for a good swimmer.

Some of Hasmukh's relatives were doctors, too. They refused to believe the preliminary post-mortem report. If his mouth was stuffed with handkerchiefs, then how could water seep into his lungs and cause him to drown? This was like someone dying by holding his breath, a feat never accomplished by any human because it defies the basic principle of biology—that the brain has no control over reflex actions.

In fact, if Hasmukh was drowning, he would have tried to yank the handkerchiefs out of his mouth. People who read crime novels or liked watching crime shows understood this, as did the ATS, but they waited for the relatives to voice this in front of the media. They took a written complaint from the family so that these facts became public knowledge and could not simply be swept under the carpet.

The ATS also understood how pressure can be exerted from the plight of the doctors conducting the post-mortem. The doctors were under immense pressure and, after an interval of a few hours post the preliminary report, stated that the post-mortem report was inconclusive. This 'inconclusive' report was handed over to Hasmukh's relatives, who then collected his body from the morgue for the cremation.

Several crucial points came to light in Hasmukh's post-mortem report. His face and eyes showed signs of injuries. Two wound marks were seen on the back, about which the police had said nothing. But the question that remained was: How did Hasmukh get wounded?

The report did not elaborate on how the wounds were inflicted. The cause of death remained unclear, too. The only conclusive information was that Hasmukh had died twelve to thirteen hours before his body was found. The report did not confirm whether Hasmukh had been murdered or whether he had committed suicide.

When a death occurs under suspicious circumstances, a viscera report is prepared to ascertain the cause. The ATS had sent Hasmukh's viscera samples to Mumbai's Kalina Forensic Science Laboratory, as well as to a lab in Haryana. This was done to minimize the chances of the report being manipulated in Mumbai and to leave no room for doubts.

A diatom test was also undertaken to see if Hasmukh had died of drowning. Diatom is a common aquatic algae. If a person is alive when his/her body hits the water, diatoms trickle into the lungs as the person gulps in water. However, if a person is already dead when his/her body hits the water, no diatoms will be found.

The ATS also recorded the statements of both the doctors who had conducted the post-mortem and compiled their report under pressure from Sathe and Tomar. The agency left no stone unturned to ensure the case was watertight.

Even Sachin Tendulkar may not have faced as many back-to-back bouncers as Sathe was having to field from the ATS. Dilip Verma, who had been both Sathe and ATS Inspector Nitya Shetty's boss, was requested to mediate and stop the ATS from targeting Sathe.

Nitya met Verma but raised his hands in helplessness, saying that his boss, DIG Palande, would not agree to spare Sathe. Even Nitya did not want to let Sathe go scot-free, but he could not say no to Verma directly. Nitya knew that the ATS had made good progress on the case and was slowly but surely discovering the enormity of the mess. Given this, if the ATS was 'managed', then the NIA would waste no time in solving the case quickly. Nitya also understood that under such circumstances one false step could ruin their careers forever. He and DIG Palande had expected that someone would be sent to 'manage' them, and they were prepared to nip such advances in the bud.

When Verma got into his car, his black bag was as swollen as it had been before the meeting. Verma messaged Sathe to tell him that the ATS's kettle was hotter than its tea. On the other hand, Sathe had been trying to call the lawyer repeatedly, but the number was continuously busy.

At his modest two-bedroom house, where the front room served as the office, Rajeev Behl went through all his business cards. Ever since he started using a smartphone, he had stopped caring about these cards. Finally, he found the business card that belonged to an auto spare parts dealer for whom he had drafted a letter just the day before.

Busy at the court all day, Behl saw the news about Hasmukh's death only when he returned home in the evening. He dialled Hasmukh's number, but it was switched off. Then he called

Hasmukh's shop. The shop was closed, but the call was diverted to Hasmukh's residence.

Kamla picked up the phone. Behl apologized for calling so late in the night and then offered his condolences. He then informed her that he was the lawyer who had drafted the letter that was in circulation now. He told her that Hasmukh had approached him a day before his death.

Now, finding an opportunity in adversity is not the exclusive right of political parties. Identifying a business opportunity, Behl told Hasmukh's wife that if any will, house ownership transfer, insurance claim, etc. needed to be facilitated, she could call him without hesitation. He made her write down his name and number, and to prove that he was Hasmukh's well-wisher, he gave her Yatin Sathe's reference. He informed Kamla that Sathe had got Hasmukh to him the previous day and got the letter drafted in front of him.

After ending the call, Behl started calculating the money he could make if Kamla became his client.

Meanwhile, at Hasmukh's residence, a shocked Kamla dialled Nitya Shetty's number. She told Nitya about the phone conversation with Behl and gave him the lawyer's number. But Inspector Nitya was in for a bigger shock when Kamla told him that Sathe had been using their Scorpio for the past five months and had only recently given it to Hasmukh for repairs.

'The explosives-filled Scorpio that was found outside Kuberia had not been in Hasmukh's possession. Yatin Sathe had been using it for the past five months.'

5
The mystery of the white Innova

'Sathe had been using the Scorpio for the last five months. Ten days before it was found outside Kuberia, Sathe had returned the car to Hasmukh citing malfunctioning of the steering,' Kamla Jain told the ATS team. They couldn't believe it.

The ATS was bewildered. Why had Yatin Sathe hidden this fact? Sathe's friend's Scorpio, which Sathe had been using, was found outside Kuberia filled with explosives. Why then had Sathe been appointed as the investigating officer of the case? Was it a mere coincidence? Why did Sathe not recognize the car he had been driving, and why did he pretend to not know the car's owner, Hasmukh? Then, all of a sudden, Hasmukh is dead and Sathe pressurizes the doctors into manipulating the post-mortem report. Was this also a coincidence? Was Sathe a 'criminal in uniform'?

The ATS team reached Hasmukh's house at midnight. A second team had gone to Rajeev Behl's house, the lawyer who had drafted Hasmukh's letter. A third team was keeping an eye on Sathe's movements. After talking to Hasmukh's wife at length, the ATS team dropped enough hints for the family, hoping they would connect all the dots. Here was what the ATS had pieced together:

- Sathe had concealed the fact that he was friends with Hasmukh from everyone.
- Sathe was using Hasmukh for his personal gain. Hasmukh had been under immense stress because of Sathe.
- Hasmukh had fallen into this mess because of Sathe.
- Sathe had been using Hasmukh's Scorpio since the past five months.
- Sathe had asked Hasmukh's family to not disclose this aforementioned fact to anyone.
- Sathe had suggested to Hasmukh that he take the blame for planting explosives in the Scorpio and then parking it outside Kuberia, and that Sathe would ensure that he got bail. Hasmukh's family rejected this advice.
- Sathe took Hasmukh to the lawyer and got the letter drafted, which now sounded like a suicide note, and hid the fact that he had facilitated this.
- Sathe knew that Hasmukh was a good swimmer, yet he had declared that Hasmukh died due to drowning.

All these points were presented to Hasmukh's family in a sequential manner, which left no doubt in their minds that Sathe was responsible for their sorrow. Anybody would be able to put two and two together and identify Sathe as the villain. The grief-stricken family was emotionally vulnerable, which made it easier for the ATS to plant this notion in their heads. Often, the distraught family of a dead person wants to hold someone responsible for their grief and to avenge their loved one's death. Now they had a target—Sathe.

It was part of the ATS's well-thought-out game plan that the complaint indicting Sathe come from Hasmukh's family. DIG Palande and Inspector Nitya Shetty were aware that a lot of pressure would be exerted on them from different sources to save Sathe—from the ATS chief, from Commissioner Tomar and from Sathe's political bosses. The ATS would then have to prove, with the help of evidence and statements, that there was a legitimate case against Sathe, which would be a waste of time. This exercise would also give Sathe enough time and opportunity to file for anticipatory bail and his vicious mind would twist the investigation of the ATS to project it as a case of inter-departmental rivalry.

But if Hasmukh's family filed the complaint, Sathe's defence tactic of inter-departmental enmity would not hold any value. At the same time, public sympathy and the pressure created by the media through visuals of the weeping family would leave Sathe's so-called well-wishers no choice but to let the investigation take its natural course. It would ensure that they refrained from publicly obstructing the investigation to save their own skins. Also, an uproar would ensue in the ongoing assembly, placing Sathe's political bosses on the back foot.

The ATS gave Hasmukh's family time to think. Before leaving at 3 a.m. that night, the agency told the family that they could visit the ATS office any time after 10 a.m. and file an FIR. Even if they couldn't make it, the ATS would take suo moto action, which means action taken of its own accord, without any request by the parties involved. This would be done so that, in the interim, Hasmukh's family could hold a press conference if they so wished. The idea of the press conference was triggered by Sanjay Trivedi at the request of ATS. In turn, Trivedi had requested ATS to connect him with the lawyer who had drafted Hasmukh's letter.

After a few minutes, ATS Inspector Nitya dialled IPS Naren Arya's number.

Early the next morning, Sanjay Trivedi's news channel broadcast his report. It said that Sathe had taken Hasmukh to the lawyer to get the letter drafted. In no time, all information about this lawyer, Rajeev Behl, was flashing across all channels.

Based on this report, the opposition party created a furore in the Vidhan Sabha that was in session. Under Nagpure's lead, all members of the opposition party demanded Yatin Sathe's arrest. The chief minister was also blamed for saving Sathe, since Sathe was believed to be closely connected with the ruling party. The chief minister clarified that they had nothing to do with Sathe, that the ATS was investigating the case and that the culprit would not be spared.

To the opposition's demand of arresting Sathe, the chief minister said, 'Sathe is not Osama bin Laden. To first hang a man and then carry out an investigation will not be right.' The ruling party said that the opposition party had been agitated ever since the 'fraud TRP case', where Sathe had blown the cover of the news channel that literally worshipped the opposition party.

'Sir, is something really happening, or are we playing a game of charades?' the NIA SP (superintendent of police) asked his boss, IG Rohtagi.

Rohtagi, who had just seen the proceedings of the Vidhan Sabha, said, 'It seems like a game of charades to me. But in every game, there is a boss who decides what action will take place and when. It doesn't seem as if there is just one boss here.'

'Then?'

'The real bosses here are opportunity and timing. The person who uses an opportunity at the right time is the boss at that point. I have been the joint commissioner of the Crime Branch and understand their game very well.'

'What should we do, sir?'

'Nothing needs to be done. We are the NIA. We don't answer to the state government. Let them be at loggerheads with each other. That way they won't pay any attention to us. We will quietly do our job. When the time is right, we will show them what the NIA is capable of.'

There was silence in the office of the state's home minister, Sardeshpande. He was sitting with ATS chief Vishwajeet and DIG Palande. Sardeshpande had been attending the assembly session when a slip bearing an urgent message had been brought in. Sardeshpande exited the assembly immediately and headed towards his office in the same building, with Vishwajeet and Palande right behind him.

Though it was not the norm, the ATS chief wanted to keep the home minister in the loop regarding the proceedings against Sathe, given the sensitivity of the case. The intention was that the home minister should not be surprised in the assembly with any news pertaining to his department, especially from the opposition party.

The ATS chief was trying to kill many birds with one stone. On the one hand, he wanted to inform the home minister in advance to save him from any humiliation. On the other hand, if the home minister wanted to halt proceedings against

Sathe, then this would be his chance to tell the ATS. Third, if Commissioner Tomar went down with Sathe, then Vishwajeet could claim the post for himself. Lastly, if the investigation into the Hasmukh murder case proceeded unhindered, then the ATS would be able to solve the case and garner appreciation from both the public and the media.

Sardeshpande was lost in his own thoughts. If the ATS had spoken to him earlier, then he could have stopped the chief minister from saying that 'Sathe is not Osama bin Laden' in the assembly. He knew this statement would come back to bite them. He also knew that Sathe had direct links with the chief minister, but the circumstances had changed now. The investigation into the Kuberia case had been handed over to the Centre's agency, the NIA. Even if it was as a consolation prize, the home minister wanted to take the credit for solving Hasmukh's murder case and save whatever remained of his self-respect.

The home minister gave the ATS the go-ahead and left to meet the chief minister.

The NIA team had gone through CCTV footage of the areas surrounding Kuberia, covering both government and private buildings. They were sure that before parking the car filled with explosives, a recce would have been conducted. But since the area right outside Kuberia had a lot of private and government security personnel stationed, the culprits would have identified at least two to three probable parking spots. Also, the recce would probably have been carried out sometime in the previous month. They needed to scour the entire month's CCTV footage.

Considering the Scorpio had been reported stolen only a week before it was found outside Kuberia, and given that it was taken to Thane and then brought back into Mumbai, footage from all cameras positioned at the three toll plazas that connected Mumbai to Thane had been called for.

In total, over one lakh hours of CCTV footage had been obtained. It had been three days since the NIA had been going over it, but a lot still remained.

'We were told that five to six handkerchiefs were found in his mouth. My husband was a very good swimmer; he could not have drowned. His belongings—his gold chain, purse, etc.—were not found on him. It seems he was murdered, by Sathe.' Hasmukh's distraught widow's video led to an uproar across the country.

When it comes to news broadcast on TV, technical points and legal arguments are valid, but nothing tops the impact a weeping widow and her children have. Kamla's heaving sighs were proving to be heavy for the ruling party, the opposition, the CIU, the ATS and the NIA.

The video went viral in a few minutes and started trending on social media. It was forwarded several times over on WhatsApp, causing a public outcry.

Sathe, meanwhile, tried to clarify. He said he was not connected to the Scorpio in any way and that he had not been using it. What Sathe, an encounter specialist who thought the sword was mightiest, did not expect was to become India's most hated man. The man whose very name induced fear in the most seasoned of criminals had been branded as one himself. The video had an impact that no amount of damage control could undo.

A while later, Yatin Sathe received a call from the headquarters and was told that he had been transferred to the LA (Local

Arms) division and asked to report for duty in the next twenty-four hours.

2004

Yatin Sathe marked his attendance at the LA division. Till the day before, he had been a member of the CIU, a glamorous and powerful division of the Mumbai Police. And now he was left to rot in the LA division on a punishment posting, a posting where officers facing controversies were sent. If the situation escalated, the officer concerned was simply suspended.

It was after Nawaz's controversial death, which was presented as a disappearance, that he had been given this posting. Until now, Sathe had been relying on the narrative that linked the death of a suspected terrorist to patriotism, but the dismal picture of Nawaz's weeping parents had subverted the entire plot.

The Court had asked the state's CID to conduct an investigation into Nawaz's case. Sanjay Trivedi's reporting in this case, right from the big reveal to its conclusion, had made him a star in the world of journalism.

Sanchini, his senior and live-in partner, a beautiful woman, began thinking that she might soon become Sanjay's side posting. Her insecurities were not uncommon given the way Indian society normally functioned.

The day after Sathe was transferred to the LA division, the CID registered an FIR against him based on a complaint filed by Nawaz's parents.

Present day

Based on Kamla Jain's complaint, the ATS filed an FIR that included charges under various sections of the IPC—murder, tampering of evidence, criminal conspiracy and common intention.

The CIU's erstwhile assistant police inspector, Yatin Sathe, was back in the LA division. He now lived in terror, expecting the ATS to arrest him any day. Sathe, who was very cautious about his image and loved the media attention, thought about how humiliating and insulting it would be to stand in court like a common criminal. More than being worried about being convicted under Section 302 of the IPC, which would mean life imprisonment, he was worried about his image getting defiled. He had spent a year building it and all his effort would go to waste, not to mention that jail was not a pleasant place to be in. Sathe had been in jail before and knew the hell that awaited him there. He knew he had to do something. The ATS had already summoned him for questioning, but he would go after taking care of one last thing.

'Sir, see this. First, the Scorpio arrives at midnight and is parked. After some time, a white Innova arrives. The driver of the Scorpio disembarks, boards the Innova and leaves,' the NIA SP told his boss, IG Rohtagi.

They were looking at CCTV footage of the road leading to Kuberia on a big screen. The driver of the Scorpio could not be identified. In the backdrop of the coronavirus pandemic, it was not unusual to see this man wearing a surgical cap, a face shield and a mask. His face was entirely covered. There were gloves on his hands, and his shoes were covered too. He seemed to be wearing what initially looked like PPE (personal protective equipment) covering the entire body that was usually worn by healthcare workers. But this PPE was unusual; it seemed to reach the knees. On zooming in, the NIA discovered that the man was actually wearing a long white kurta.

Rohtagi said, 'It's clear that at least two people were involved. They knew about the CCTVs and made all arrangements to conceal their identities. Good. At least we know where to begin.'

The NIA SP added to this. 'Something interesting happens roughly two to two and a half hours later. The white Innova arrives, a man gets off, walks towards the Scorpio and peeps in. He opens the door and places a tiny object inside the Scorpio and leaves. This man is also fully covered.'

'Play the footage once again,' Rohtagi said. He wanted to see what the man had put inside the Scorpio. When they zoomed in, the image got pixelated. The item placed inside the car was so sleek that it could not be seen clearly. The NIA team went over the things found in the car once again and guessed that it might have been the threat letter.

It was concluded that maybe the suspects had forgotten to place the letter, which was why they had to make another trip. What was interesting was that the number plate of the Innova that had come back was different from that of the first. Given the clothes, the style of walking and the height and appearance, the NIA estimated that the man who had got down from the Scorpio could be the same as the one who had alighted from the Innova the second time.

After hours of going through the footage from different angles, in slow motion and by scanning each frame, the NIA decided the course of its investigation.

- The opinion of a body language expert would be taken to discern whether the person who got down from the Scorpio and the Innova was the same.

- Private and government CCTV camera footage would be scanned from 1 a.m. to 6 a.m.
- What transpired in those two to two and a half hours between the Scorpio being parked and the arrival of the second Innova to drop off the letter?
- Were cars with the same number plate moved in and out of Mumbai one week prior to the Scorpio being found outside Kuberia? The CCTV footage of the three toll plazas needed to be scanned.

The NIA wanted to see if a similar Innova could be spotted in the CCTV footage. This task, however, was like looking for a needle in a haystack, given how common white Innovas are in Mumbai. To add to this, the suspect was likely to be wearing a mask because of the pandemic.

Sathe was hopeful that he would be granted anticipatory bail and not have to face the humiliation of going to jail. He was okay with being interrogated by the ATS, but not with being put behind bars. He had already spoken to his lawyer, got him to draft a petition for anticipatory bail two days ago and filed it with the court the next day.

Sathe's lawyer presented the argument that the ATS was targeting him because of a personal vendetta and the allegations levied against him were baseless. No evidence had been found against him. There was no reason for him to be arrested since he was assisting with the inquiry. The lawyer shocked everyone by declaring that, during the duration in which Hasmukh disappeared, Sathe was leading a raid on a bar that was roughly forty kilometres away in Dongri, close to the CIU office. His mobile phone records proved that Sathe was far away from where Hasmukh was believed to be on the night he disappeared.

Sathe seemed to have his tracks covered right from the evening of the disappearance till the next morning. Many police officers and employees of the bar were witnesses; Sathe had led the raid.

This alibi shocked the ATS. Sathe believed it would work in his favour and that he would be granted anticipatory bail.

Opposing the petition, the counsel for the ATS argued that because Hasmukh's wife had directly accused Sathe of murder, and because Sathe and Hasmukh were in constant touch with each other, Sathe's involvement in the case was quite obvious.

The court reserved its order on the bail hearing. It would announce its decision after an interval.

The CCTV footage from the toll plaza located on the Mumbai–Thane road was being assessed in the NIA office. The white Innova had to have crossed the toll at some point.

The NIA had started by noting the time when the Scorpio had been parked and the arrival of the second white Innova. They matched this with the CCTV footage obtained from the camera on the road leading to Kuberia. The NIA found that between 1 a.m. and 1.15 a.m., the Innova entered Mumbai from Thane. Forty-five minutes later, it picked up the driver of the Scorpio outside Kuberia. After one hour, the Innova crossed Mumbai and headed towards Thane around 3 a.m. Then, after another hour or so, the same Innova entered Mumbai from Thane again. A man got out, placed the letter inside the Scorpio parked outside Kuberia and left. But after that, there was no evidence of the Innova going to Thane. This implied that for the next few hours, or days, the Innova was in Mumbai.

In the CCTV footage, the driver's face was covered at all times, making it impossible to confirm the identity. But even the smartest of criminals leave at least one clue behind. Here, it was an imported tissue-paper box seen inside the Innova. Another important clue was that the car's left headlight was dimmer than the right headlight. Leaving the conspicuous tissue-paper box in the car was a foolish mistake. To add to this, the driver seemed unaware that one headlight was brighter than the other, probably because the road from Mumbai to Thane is well-lit.

Armed with this information, the NIA knew its next challenge was to ascertain the location of the Innova in Mumbai.

Sathe could not believe his ears. The sessions court had given its ruling on his anticipatory bail plea. The judge's words reverberated in his ears: 'Sathe's interrogation in custody is necessary because serious sections of murder, tampering of evidence and criminal conspiracy, along with common intention, have been levied in the case. Because the deceased's wife has directly indicted Sathe, and since Hasmukh and Sathe were together for days before Hasmukh disappeared, anticipatory bail cannot be granted in the initial stages of the investigation.'

Sathe was in trouble. It was Friday and the high court would be closed on the weekend. His appeal against the order of the sessions court would only be heard on Monday. He knew the next two days would be critical. He would now have to report to the ATS office for questioning today.

By now, the NIA was sure that Sathe had been using the Scorpio. Hasmukh's wife had informed them that Sathe kept the Scorpio parked in his housing society. It was possible that both the Scorpio and Innova had entered Mumbai from Sathe's housing society. One NIA team went to Aniket Housing Society and asked the society office for the DVR containing CCTV footage. They were told that Sub-Inspector Haji of the CIU had taken the footage away a couple of days ago. There was no copy. The team was also shown a letter from the CIU, bearing Sathe's signature. The date on the letter was the last day of Sathe being the investigating officer in the Kuberia case.

The case was slowly unravelling before the NIA. Since Yatin Sathe was no longer with the CIU, getting the unit to cooperate would be straightforward. They had to go to the CIU office, collect the footage of Aniket Housing Society and question Haji. The NIA was sure the loose ends of the case would begin to tie up after this.

The other important task before the NIA was to locate the mysterious white Innova that had entered Mumbai the day the Scorpio was parked outside Kuberia and disappeared mysteriously thereafter.

Sathe was aware of the means of interrogation adopted by the police forces. He had spent twenty-five years in the force and had put those techniques to use on numerous occasions. The moment he entered the interrogation room, he was told that he would have to leave his mobile phone at the reception. Sathe was unaware that a hacker had been called in to recover deleted data from his phone. Getting Sathe to surrender his phone would ensure he did not know what the ATS was up to.

He had been waiting for two hours already. He also knew that no one would show up for another hour or two. This was a technique used to exert psychological pressure. The logic was that the suspect, while waiting, would lose control of his thoughts and feel terrorized, that his/her self-confidence and mental preparation would begin to slack during this long wait. It was purely a mind game.

Ploys like this were generally used when the suspect could not be subjected to third-degree torture. Sathe knew that he was being watched from another room. He was prepared for this. He knew he had to somehow make it until Monday, which was when the high court would hear his anticipatory bail petition. He had already hired one of the best lawyers in town.

Sathe thought about the questions he would have asked if the roles were reversed. He also thought of answers to those questions, when to answer, when to keep mum, which questions to avoid, when to lie and to what extent.

What Sathe did not know was that both the NIA and the Mumbai Police were in a quandary. The NIA had thoroughly searched Sathe's CIU office and found no trace of the DVR from Aniket Housing Society. No official entry had been made for the DVR that held footage of the Scorpio's movement before it was parked outside Kuberia, as well as the white Innova's movements, which would have offered crucial leads. The NIA suspected Sathe, but thought that the entire Mumbai police had joined forces and was trying to derail their investigation. Consequently, the agency confiscated the hard discs of many CIU computers, along with papers related to the case.

For the Mumbai Police, this was a shock, a blow to their self-respect. For the first time in its history, another agency had raided the Commissionerate's premises. The country's most recently formed investigating agency had raided the premises of one of the oldest forces of the country. Many Mumbai Police constables who were on the threshold of retirement were moved to tears at the sight.

The raid at the CIU office had piqued the interest of officers from the other departments, too, and they began to peep through their windows. Videos began circulating on WhatsApp. Sathe was being criticized for bringing shame to the Commissionerate.

The NIA, meanwhile, had demanded the CCTV footage from inside the CIU office, and from the parking lot, too. The agency hoped this would offer a clue about when the DVR was brought in and where it was taken.

It was at this point that both the Mumbai Police and the NIA got a shock. All CCTV footage for the CIU office had been deleted from the main server three days ago. Crucial evidence had been erased. Someone was a step ahead of the NIA and had stolen from right under the nose of the Mumbai Police.

API Yatin Sathe looked up and saw DIG Palande enter the room he was in and place a packet on the table.

'*Bhosdi ke, seekha nahin kya apne seniors ko salute karna* (Dickhead, haven't you learned to salute your seniors)?' DIG Palande thundered.

Because both Palande and he were not in uniform, Sathe did a civilian salute. DIG Palande reminded Sathe of the incident outside Kuberia, where he had not saluted an officer four ranks his senior. Adherence to discipline and hierarchy was the backbone of any organized force, but Sathe was not prepared for that lesson today. He regretted what he had done in the past and knew it would come back to bite him.

DIG Palande opened the packet, took out a sandwich and began eating. Sathe had done the same thing outside Kuberia.

There was a sandwich between them again, but the roles had been reversed. That day, as it was today, the sandwich was a symbol of power. Only the power holder had changed. Sathe felt as if Palande had put his self-respect, reputation and ego in between the two slices and was attacking it with gusto.

'*Purush bali nahin hot hai, samay hot balwan. Bhillan looti gopika, wahi Arjun wahi baan*,' DIG Palande recited from the Mahabharata. 'The battle of Mahabharat ended. Krishna understood that the victor, Arjun, had become arrogant. He told Arjun, "Some of my gopis (Krishna's eternal consorts) are here with me. I want you to take them to the neighbouring town tomorrow morning." The next morning, Arjun left with the gopis. The moment he approached a settlement of the Bhils, they blocked his way. A battle ensued between Arjun and the Bhils, which Arjun lost. The tribals abducted the gopis and tied Arjun to a nearby tree. Then Krishna said to Arjun, "A person is not powerful, time is powerful. Your time was good during the Mahabharat, so you won, but today you lost to ordinary tribals because your time was not good."'

DIG Palande bit into the sandwich, paused and said, 'What I am trying to tell you is that your time is over, shitbag. You are in trouble.'

In the other room, Inspector Nitya Shetty was listening to this conversation. Because he had worked with Sathe, he understood his mindset well. Nitya knew that Sathe would have come prepared for the standard questions, which was why the ATS had decided to target his ego. The strategy was working. Sathe was not prepared for this assault, just as he was not ready for what was to happen in the next few hours.

The NIA's suspicion turned into belief in the Kuberia case. Immediately, a summon was issued to question API Yatin Sathe.

He was asked to report to the NIA office at noon the next day. The NIA had obtained CCTV footage of all the roads on which the gates of the Commissionerate opened. The contract for maintenance and responsibility of the CCTVs on these roads was with a private company, so it was easy to get the footage from their servers.

No corners were being cut in this investigation. After all, it involved Kuber. After speaking to the central home ministry, the NIA flew in additional staff on a BSF (Border Security Force) plane from Delhi to Mumbai. The team got down to work to sort through the mountains of footage.

The NIA was desperate for the DVR from Aniket Housing Society. All they wanted was a clue about the whereabouts of this crucial CCTV footage, but what they found was beyond their expectations. They had found big fish in a small pond. They had got Las Vegas at 'Bangkok' rates.

The mysterious white Innova that they had been looking for had been found. It was the car that had made the second round of Kuberia. There had been no clue about its whereabouts initially, but here it was finally.

The CCTV footage showed it entering and leaving the Commissionerate. A vehicle involved in the crime had been at the Commissionerate many times!

6

The investigation race

2004

Televisions across the country broadcast images of Sachin Tendulkar heading back to the pavilion, with the cricketers continuing to applaud him, even those from the other team. Respect from your opponents is truly a rare thing. Some members of the CID (Crime Investigation Department) were also watching this on the TV in the office.

In the next room, a meek and subdued young Sathe sat on a chair. The case about the mysterious disappearance of Nawaz had come back to haunt him. As per the orders of the court, the CID had been ordered to investigate. For the first time in his police career, Sathe was going to be questioned like a suspect. He was aware of the CID's cruel techniques of interrogation; he had heard many stories and was petrified.

After some time, the CID officers came into the room. They were very gentle with Sathe because they had instructions from the home minister: 'handle with care'. This was all thanks to the years of goodwill and trust that the seniors backing Sathe had shared with the then home minister, the boss of both the CID and the Crime Branch.

Now, the CID had to strike a balance between the court orders and the home minister's instructions. Till the time the court directive was followed, they could prioritize the home minister's instructions.

This was Sathe's first experience with a higher-level game. He had begun to believe that no matter what the level of investigation, something or the other could always be managed.

The CID began questioning Sathe.

Present Day

Whoosh! First, the sound resonated in his ears and then the heat began to spread across his face. This was totally unexpected. Sathe's self-confidence was turning into fear. This was not the gentle behaviour he expected from a fellow police officer, but it was happening. This time the 'handle with care' instructions issued by the home minister to the ATS were based on the recent but out-of-compulsion 'goodwill'.

A balance had to be struck between the court orders and the home minister's instructions. For the time being, the home minister's instructions were given priority. Sathe had understood that these big-league games were like the IPL matches, where the tables could turn at any time.

The NIA had managed to spot the white Innova in the CCTV footage obtained from the camera positioned on a road outside the Commissionerate. It was seen entering and exiting the Commissionerate several times. The agency ran the number plates: two of them were bogus, but one was legitimate. When they checked the government records, they were in for another shock. The car was registered as the official vehicle of the CIU and had been doing the rounds of the city bearing false number plates.

They had been unable to trace the car so far because it had been parked in the Commissionerate, a place where no investigating agency would think of checking. Also, because the Innova was the CIU's official car, no one suspected anything when they saw it entering or leaving the premises, or simply being parked there. The NIA had not expected this. By now, they had also traced the Scorpio's movement.

The challenge now was to piece together the movement of the Innova, with its ever-changing number plates, between Kuberia, the Commissionerate and Thane.

Sathe was still at the ATS office. DIG Palande continued to grill him. A police officer from the Maharashtra cadre would have probably handled Sathe with kid gloves, thinking that the roles could be reversed in the future, but that was not the case with Palande.

Palande was from the Bihar cadre and in Maharashtra for five years on deputation, after which he was to return to his parent cadre. His father-in-law had been a minister in the Maharashtra government, so he was not worried about political backlash. DIG Palande also had a massive ego that had been bruised by a mere assistant inspector. He was out for blood and didn't care much about the 'friendly equation' between the ATS chief, Commissioner Tomar and former encounter specialist Dilip Verma.

DIG Palande threw tough questions at Sathe: about the Scorpio outside Kuberia, his friendship with Hasmukh, hiding that friendship, his interaction with Hasmukh in his last days, the WhatsApp chats, taking Hasmukh to the lawyer to draft a letter, pressurizing the doctors who had conducted Hasmukh's post-mortem, instructing Hasmukh's family to keep mum about the Scorpio, interfering with the work of the local police with whom Hasmukh had registered a missing car report, etc., etc.

While Sathe answered some of these questions, he lied about others.

DIG Palande had underestimated Sathe. He was under the impression that he could get Sathe to confess all, but he had been unable to breach his junior's shield.

Despite the insults, pressure and tension, Sathe was adamant about one thing: that he had been forty kilometres away from Hasmukh's last known location on the night that he disappeared. He insisted that he was in the Dongri area close to the CIU office, conducting a raid on a bar. He had witnesses to back up this claim. He declared with confidence that the ATS could corroborate his statement with the location on his mobile phone.

The ATS had no counter to this defence, which was why they hadn't arrested Sathe. Of course, if they wanted to they could still arrest him, but the court would not only grant him bail but also pull the ATS up for jumping the gun.

Consequently, Sathe was detained at the ATS office for hours under the garb of questioning. The ATS's second team needed some time to think of a way to breach his defence. A while later, the team let the office know that they would have more evidence against Sathe in the next twelve to fifteen hours. The

ATS, not having any more reason to hold Sathe, let him leave. He had already spent twelve straight hours at their office.

The NIA, too, had been trying to reach Sathe to summon him for questioning, but his phone had remained switched off. Later, through the media, the NIA learnt that Sathe was being interrogated by the ATS. It wasn't difficult to guess that the ATS had held onto his phone.

The NIA had put into sequence the footage from the Commissionerate, Kuberia, Thane and Aniket Housing Society. The agency only needed Sathe to clarify a few links. They were apprehensive now because if the ATS had arrested Sathe today in the Hasmukh murder case, then he would be in their custody for fourteen days. The NIA would have to wait that long to question him regarding the Kuberia case.

The last twelve hours had been the worst for API Yatin Sathe. He was mentally exhausted. His police honour had been blown to pieces, but he had somehow managed to hold on to his last defence. Sathe knew that he could not sustain such rigorous questioning for another day. He had to make it to Monday anyhow, which was when his anticipatory bail plea could be filed in the high court. Friday was already over. Sathe had two more days to survive.

The ATS had let him go after a full day of questioning and with instructions that he would have to come to their office the next day again. Sathe had no choice but to agree. He had only gone a short distance when he braked suddenly. He had missed hitting the car in front by a whisker.

The car had sped up from behind, overtaken Sathe and screeched to a halt in front of him. Sathe's hand had almost reached into the glove compartment for his pistol when he spotted the NIA sticker on the car. He withdrew his hand. Two people got out of the car and gestured for Sathe to roll down his window. The moment Sathe did that, they slipped a piece of paper inside. It was a summons. The NIA wanted Sathe in their office on Saturday for questioning.

The NIA team had been waiting a little distance away from the ATS office to serve Sathe the official summons. The moment he left the ATS office, he had been followed and blocked.

The NIA inspector waited for Sathe to sign the summon. Sathe was in a dilemma. The ATS had also called him on Saturday and he could not be in two places at the same time. He had to think quickly. His day had not gone well at the ATS and he wasn't expecting tomorrow to be any different. With the NIA, it would be his first day of questioning. DIG Palande would not be there to wage a personal war against him.

Sathe debated in his head. He had both the Hasmukh murder and the Kuberia case to consider. The ATS had moved ahead in its investigation. He could spend a day with the NIA. Weighing all his options, Sathe chose to sign the NIA's summon.

While DIG Palande interrogated Sathe, the ATS team recovered deleted data from his mobile phone. They identified some numbers Sathe had been in touch with in the last couple of days. Amongst these numbers, five had been activated recently. The SIM cards for these five numbers had been bought on the same day, at the same time and from the same place. A little bit of digging told them that all five numbers had been bought under one family's name in Daman, a city in the union territory of Daman and Diu, located one hundred and seventy kilometres away from Mumbai.

An ATS team left for Daman the same night. Four out of the five numbers had been switched off since the night of Hasmukh's murder, but the one number that was still active had been traced to several sensitive places associated with both the Kuberia case and Hasmukh's murder case: the NIA office, Sathe's house, the Commissionerate and the ATS office. It could not be a coincidence.

Besides the NIA and the ATS, the IB and the media frequented these places, but they worked in teams. Who was this lone wolf? And then the ATS had a lead. The phone's location had been near the ATS office for the past two hours.

Sathe stopped his car at the GPS location sent on his mobile phone. He had made sure that no one was following him by taking the long route, stopping a couple of times, taking U-turns and reducing the speed. He had put to test all the ruses that he knew to confuse anyone who might be following him. The location had been carefully chosen. The streetlights in this lane were not working and the car's lights had been switched off as well.

Sathe lit a cigarette and awaited the arrival of his confidant.

A while later, the passenger door of Sathe's car opened and a man sat inside. He explained to Sathe in a clear sequence what had transpired outside the ATS and NIA offices when Sathe was being questioned. Finally, he passed on Dilip Verma's message. Upon hearing it, Sathe trembled with anger and started his car. The man got off quickly and Sathe sped away.

A little distance ahead, the man was about to get on his bike when his mobile phone vibrated in his pocket. He took it out and saw that it was an unknown number. He disconnected the call and placed the phone back into his pocket.

The ATS officers who had been tracing the number had found their man. Before he knew it, the ATS had nabbed him under the cover of darkness.

The moment the man was brought to the ATS office, people began asking him how he had managed to get out of jail. Gajanan Jhende was a suspended policeman; his peers believed that he had nerves of steel. He had been a constable in Dilip Verma's squad, and because he had been in the Crime Branch, he had a good network of informers. His squad had carried out a fake encounter for which he had been given life imprisonment.

The ATS threatened Jhende and told him that if he didn't come out with the truth, his parole would be revoked. He would then be sent back to jail and never get parole again because he had violated the conditions once.

Just then, the state's home minister, Sardeshpande, called the ATS for an update. He was eager to know what progress had been made in the Hasmukh murder case. The NIA had taken away the Kuberia case from Maharashtra, but the Hasmukh case was still with the state's ATS. The home minister did not want to waste this opportunity to prove his efficiency.

One hundred and seventy kilometres away from Mumbai, the ATS team knocked incessantly on the door of a palatial bungalow in Daman. One by one, the windows lit up. The servant opened the door to five men who looked like government officials. Five ATS officers barged in. The head of the Damania family, Sethji, came out of his room with a lungi tied around his jiggling tummy.

Once a Portuguese colony, Daman was now a union territory known for its coast. The Damanias were one of the richest families in the city.

The five SIM cards had been bought under the Damanias name, of which one had been found with Sathe's friend Jhende. Sathe had been in close contact with all five numbers. Sethji was stunned when he heard this. He clearly told the ATS that his family had not bought the SIM cards and that normally the servants bought SIM cards for them. Because the Damanias were well known, the local seller had probably not bothered to verify their details or asked for identification. After all, no one expected such a rich family to be involved in such a crime.

When the servants were questioned, one of them revealed after a few slaps that he had bought the SIM cards and given them to one Mahesh Bhor. He claimed to have no clue about why these SIM cards had been bought in the first place. He also told the ATS that Bhor lived in Mumbai and came to Daman only to 'amuse himself'.

The slap that followed was the ATS's way to get the servant to elaborate on what he meant by 'amuse himself'. Sethji, meanwhile, called the local SP because no local policeman had accompanied the Maharashtra ATS team. But before he could disconnect the call, the ATS had left with the servant.

The NIA's forensic experts were examining the white Innova. A small piece of paper peeked out from the floor mat in the rear seat. The forensic experts carefully picked the paper up with tweezers and held it up for perusal. An illegible four-digit number was written in pencil in the top right corner and then scratched out.

The agency then proceeded to tow the Innova from the Mumbai Police Commissionerate to its own office. A thorough examination was undertaken to find more clues and leads.

IG Rohtagi examined the paper. There was a logo on top and the words 'Bombay Belmonte' at the bottom. Bombay Belmonte was a five-star hotel, and often such hotels leave a monogrammed writing pad and pencil in the rooms for their guests to use. Rohtagi wondered if this piece of paper was a part of that writing pad.

A mere five kilometres separated Bombay Belmonte from the NIA. Minutes later, an NIA vehicle was headed towards the hotel.

The almost-thirty-year-old woman, believed to be Mahesh Bhor's mistress, sat squashed between two ATS men in the middle seat of the car. Their body odour made her nostrils twitch and their hairy arms pricked her recently waxed skin.

They had picked her up from her small, beachfront house and shoved her into the car. She had gone to bed in a knee-length, transparent negligee and they had not even given her time to change. Every bit of her body was on display.

The men kept turning around to check if they were being followed by the local police. They relaxed the moment the car crossed the Daman border and entered Maharashtra. Sitting in the last row, the servant of the Damania household had been beaten up quite a bit by the ATS officer seated next to him.

Half an hour after they had entered Maharashtra, the car stopped on the side of an isolated road. The ATS officers pulled out the good-looking woman from the car. They did not bother to ask her name and simply called her randi (whore) before starting to question her and hit her. With each slap, she felt as if her skin was peeling off.

The ATS had picked her up from Mahesh Bhor's love nest based on information received from the Damanias' servant. She had met Bhor as a customer in the dance bar she worked at in Mumbai. Bhor was involved in money laundering and she had contacted him for employment after the dance bar closed.

Bhor also ran a youth club where individuals who had long crossed the threshold of youth gathered to gamble and play cards. She had been appointed as the hostess of that club. In his office, Bhor had installed a special couch which offered heightened sexual pleasure to its user depending on his or her position. His secret, however, could not remain hidden from his wife. When she found out, Bhor shifted his mistress to the house in Daman and made at least one trip a week to see her. Since the ATS did not have time to wait for his weekly trip, they nabbed his mistress to lure him in.

Bhor and his mistress were not in a committed relationship, so some slaps and the threat of tearing off her flimsy clothes was enough to make her tell all. She was used to being naked, but violence frightened her. And very rarely did men get her to open her mouth to speak.

The shift in-charge at Bombay Belmonte was available. Between midnight and 5 a.m. not much work needed to be done, and the in-charge very patiently and in great detail gave the NIA all the information they needed for the requested time frame. Before long, Sathe showed up on the CCTV at the reception. Upon checking the hotel records, the NIA discovered that Sathe often stayed there under a false name and submitted a fake Aadhar card. Clearly, it was not difficult for a CIU officer like Sathe to obtain a fake ID. But to put one's own photo on a fake document was plain stupid, according to the NIA. He could have used the photo of someone he resembled a little. A booking for hundred days had been made at the hotel, with the payment being made by a famous jeweller of Mumbai. Once the NIA googled the jeweller's name, everything began to fall into place. The jeweller was being investigated by the Mumbai Police.

Security measures at the Bombay Belmonte had been beefed up considerably after the terror attack on the city. Every public area of the hotel was under the surveillance of high-quality CCTV cameras. The floor where Sathe's room was booked was covered by a CCTV camera, too. A lot of people were seen entering and leaving his room in the footage. One woman was seen particularly often. In one video she was seen leaving the room with a cash-counting machine. She was seen arriving and leaving the hotel in a black BMW, the number of which was clear in the footage. She had a toned body and was young and attractive, but she didn't seem to be the person who could drive around in a seventy-five-lakh-rupee beamer.

In one footage, she was even seen arriving with Sathe on a Harley Davidson worth twenty lakhs. Now, neither Sathe nor the woman seemed to have the means to own these luxury rides. The woman, in fact, had goofed up once by submitting her original Aadhar card at the hotel's reception. That this Aadhar card was not fake was proved when her driving licence, PAN card and social media profile matched the details on the card.

Interestingly, both the BMW and Harley bore fake number plates and were anonymously owned. But it was easy to spot their movement and last location on the CCTV.

The ATS team saw Mahesh Bhor's mistress leave. She was wearing the dirty old burkha that was always kept in the ATS car to cover the faces of criminals. Since no shops would be open that early, the burkha was her only option. A lot of women wearing burkhas came to the Chowpatty Sea Face for a morning walk, so she did not stick out. In any case, the dirty burkha was better than the knee-length transparent negligee that left nothing to the imagination. In the dark of the night, the negligee would have caused little trouble, but in the daylight, her milky white body would have attracted unwanted attention.

The ATS had managed to reach Mumbai from Daman in just two and a half hours. And thanks to Bhor's mistress, the agency had him in custody. He had come running after receiving a distress call from her in the wee hours of the morning. Had the ATS called him directly, Bhor would have had an opportunity to alert Sathe. Their statements recorded, Mahesh Bhor's mistress and the Damanias' servant were sent back to Daman with the minimum return fare in hand.

Now, the ATS had managed to arrest two people in the Hasmukh murder case—Sathe's confidant and the owner of the youth club, Mahesh Bhor; and convicted constable Gajanan Jhende.

The NIA did not have to struggle much. They already knew that Sathe was too overconfident and would make mistakes. The sun was just beginning to turn the sky red when they found the black BMW in a parking lot on the same road as the Commissionerate.

The NIA recovered five lakh rupees, a cash-counting machine and Sathe's diary from the car. They even found the original number plate of the Scorpio that had been parked outside

Kuberia and a half-empty ten-litre can of kerosene. The agency suspected that the kerosene was used to burn the PPE kit, white kurta and other evidence pertaining to the case. If that was the case, then some fragments of the PPE kit or kurta were still likely to be in the BMW, which the forensic team could pick up. Of course, the car was towed to the NIA office.

Post that phone call from ATS, after many days, Home Minister Sardeshpande's morning was good in the literal sense. A little while ago, he had been reading the headlines of the morning newspaper and casting a cursory glance at the important bits. His attention was focused on any news pertaining to the Kuberia or Hasmukh murder cases.

The newspaper carried information that had been out up until 9 p.m. the previous night. There was nothing there that he had not already heard during the morning briefing of the state intelligence department. The news item that he was looking for was not in the newspaper.

Yatin Sathe and all news related to him had not only embarrassed the government and the home department but had also put Sardeshpande's political career on the back foot. In the internal meetings of the government and the ruling party members, the blame fell on his head for not being able to control the mess. After all, news pertaining to his department had been reaching the opposition before him; he had become the butt of all jokes.

His assistant brought in the phone and said that it was the ATS. Sardeshpande took the phone and listened attentively for a very long time. The last bit almost blew his mind: 'The Hasmukh murder case is almost solved. We have arrested two people in the last ten hours. Today, the mastermind will be arrested as well. After that, you can hold a press conference to break the news.'

Both Sardeshpande and the ATS were under the misconception that since their morning had been good, the rest of the day would be fine too. Neither of them was prepared for the hell Sathe was about to unleash.

7

The scapegoat

1986

Kolhapur

For fourteen-year-old Yatin Sathe, the cricket kit was heavy to lug around. But he was sure that he wanted to be the next Syed Kirmani. All through the day, he would be worked to the bones on the cricket ground. In the end, he would drag his weary body and bulky kit into Shivaji Colony.

The most troubled player on the field is often the wicketkeeper, which was Yatin Sathe in this case. While other players get a chance to rest their weary muscles from time to time, the wicketkeeper has to be alert and in position for each and every ball. As a result, the back often gives trouble.

Dumping the kit at home, Sathe left immediately without paying any heed to his mother's summons. There was a godown at the end of Shivaji Colony which moonlighted as the office-cum-printing press for the local newspaper—*Kolhapur Express.* Sathe's uncle, a Kolhapur based part-time correspondent for a big newspaper headquartered around four hundred kilometres away from Mumbai, was also the reporter-cum-editor-cum technician-cum-clerk of the two-page *Kolhapur Express*. In the small town of Kolhapur, the readership for crime stories was high, and Sathe's uncle was a master when it came to crime reporting.

Early morning, Sathe had left for the match and had not been able to read the newspaper. Grabbing a copy of the paper from his uncle, he returned home hurriedly. He maintained a file of newspaper copies that reported his cricket performance. The newspaper was carrying a write-up about his performance that day, but it was hidden in a small box. Half the newspaper was filled with articles about the internationally wanted criminal Charles Sobhraj, who had been arrested the day before. The paper was bursting with praises for Inspector Madhukar Jhende, the man who had nabbed Sobhraj.

Yatin took out some of the old newspapers from his file. In a paper from 1984, alongside his cricket performance, was a write-up about the encounter of mafia gangster Rama Nayak. Again, the newspaper was filled with stories of praise for Inspector Rajan Katdare who had led the encounter. In one edition of 1982, there was news of the encounter of the notorious criminal Manya Surve. Inspector Isak Bagvan had led the encounter, which was considered the first encounter involving a member of the underworld.

Sathe thought of asking his reporter uncle why crime news overshadowed all other news, and what was an encounter. Sleep engulfed him before he could dwell more on these thoughts.

Present day

With great difficulty, Sathe woke up to the alarm. He saw the time on his mobile; he had only managed to get four hours of sleep.

He made a call to his political guru-cum-friend-cum-political handler, Pranil Sanap. He was told that the minister was busy and could not talk. Sathe had been allowed entry into the Mumbai Police, after a gap of seventeen years, only because of Sanap's efforts, because Sanap was close to the chief minister.

Of course, nothing is free or for charity in politics. In return, Sathe had carried out a lot of illegal work and done vasooli (money recovery) for them. When it came to these things, Sanap was his political handler. But the minister had been avoiding Sathe's calls for the past few days. Sathe had an idea about why this was happening. Of late, he had embarrassed the state government, the chief minister and the home minister. It was fairly obvious why Sanap had started maintaining a distance from him. This call had been Sathe's final attempt at reaching out to Sanap. His hope that the political leadership would come to his aid was shattered.

Later, he updated his WhatsApp status: 'The CID arrested me under false allegations in 2004, and that case is still pending. History is being repeated again. My fellow officers are trying to implicate me. But the circumstances in 2021 are different from that of 2004. I was young then and had years of hope, restraint, life and career in front of me. But now, keeping my age in mind, I do not have another seventeen years to make a comeback, nor do I have the patience. I think the time is close to bid farewell to the world.'

Sathe got ready and left his house. The moment he exited his society, he felt as if a VIP convoy had been awaiting him. His car was immediately tailgated by the ATS, the NIA and dozens of media vehicles. The cars were driving bumper-to-bumper behind him. And there was a convoy of the local police waiting at the boundary of its jurisdiction.

Sathe knew that given the media presence, neither the ATS nor the NIA would try to take him forcefully. They would not try to pull him like a Buzkashi goat in the middle of the road, surrounded by so many cameras, and offer an embarrassing spectacle that needed to be avoided at all costs.

Sathe had seen on Discovery channel that Buzkashi was a famous and old sport of Afghanistan, in which horse-mounted players divided into two rival teams competed to snatch a goat carcass that was placed in the centre of a field.

His latest WhatsApp update, meanwhile, had been enough to alert everyone and to give a message to a select few. Sathe welcomed the media presence because they were like a temporary shield against possible arrest.

Some media personnel hung out of their cars dangerously and reported live, stating that Sathe's status update was an indicator of probable suicide. It was because of this that the ATS and NIA were following Sathe, but unlike the media, they were not hanging out of their cars.

Where will Sathe go: NIA or ATS?

This was the headline flashing across news channels. Thirty minutes later, the ATS team was in for a surprise when they saw Sathe drive past their office and seemingly head towards the NIA's office. Tailgating Sathe, the ATS team informed its seniors and awaited directions on what was to be done next.

In the interim, the news channels told their viewers that Sathe was going to the NIA office. The NIA team following Sathe was also surprised: why was he heading towards their office two hours in advance? They informed their senior officers. After some time, Sathe's vehicle drove past the NIA office as well. He had two options now: to go to the home ministry or the Commissionerate.

Everyone else was also wondering where he was headed. On the left side of his speeding car was Azad Maidan, which had brought him to Mumbai for the first time thirty-three years ago.

1988

Mumbai

Azad Maidan was where a lot of cricket matches took place simultaneously, on numerous pitches. Amongst all the matches being played that day, everyone's eyes were focused on two school boys who were making history with the longest batting partnership. Sathe had not heard of Sachin Tendulkar and Vinod Kambli before, but sitting on the side, he was seeing them play in the flesh. He was disappointed because he had not made the cut as a wicketkeeper.

Mumbai was considered the nursery of cricket. Children from small towns and cities, who had limited exposure in their hometowns, came here to train and hoped to make it big. His reporter uncle, who had got him to Mumbai for the selection, was engaged in a squabble with the selection coach, blaming him for accommodating the less-deserving son of an encounter specialist and ruining the career of a talented player like Yatin Sathe. It was that day that Sathe got his first glimpse of the power commanded by an encounter specialist.

Until that moment, cricket had been his life. But Sathe was now wondering if it was time to start afresh.

Present day

During the time that Sathe was inside the Commissionerate, his WhatsApp status received a lot of attention.

In fact, his 'probable suicide' was trending on social media. Panel discussions and debates between psychologists were being held in news studios to discuss Sathe's mental state. Reporters telecast live from outside the Commissionerate and doled out unwanted advice.

Sathe emerged from Commissioner Tomar's office armed with a lot of information—some of it came from the commissioner and some of it was self-realization.

Commissioner Tomar, who lived by the principle of 'kill or die', had created and destroyed dozens of officers like Sathe. Tomar had understood the signal Sathe had tried to give through his presence in the office and through the WhatsApp status. He intended to convey his intentions, too.

Commissioner Tomar first berated Sathe about how his wrong-handling, mismanagement and over-confidence had triggered this whole fiasco and landed the force in a soup. He then expounded on how he had attempted many feats in his career, but he had not made the mistake of leaving behind so many clues. He told Sathe that he had saved him on every occasion in the past, but that Sathe was probably not built for the big game.

Sathe patiently heard the commissioner out and then requested that whatever money was owed to him be given to his family, consisting of his brother and wife, dependent on him.

But the commissioner made no commitment regarding this. The commissioner believed that Sathe, despite being arrested and tortured, would not open his mouth on account of his greed for money. On the other hand, Sathe thought that once he was arrested, he would no longer be in control and would not know what was to follow, which was why he wanted the money immediately.

Sathe had the option to blackmail. He could choose to spill the beans before the NIA and the ATS. Yes, that would mean he would go down, too, but he would take the others down as well. Tomar, meanwhile, seemed to have no option but to keep Sathe quiet. Through his WhatsApp status, Sathe had made it clear that he would take everyone down if push came to shove. But Tomar had made it clear to Sathe that he would simply eliminate all links leading to him. In the end, he repeated to Sathe what he had said thirty-three years ago: 'There is tremendous power in a ...'

1988

Mumbai Police Commissionerate

After ending his cricket career at Azad Maidan, a sad Yatin Sathe accompanied his reporter uncle to the premises of the Mumbai Police Commissionerate. They were standing outside the press room. Azad Maidan was just five hundred metres away. His uncle, with the help of a few reporter friends, had complained to the chief of the Crime Branch about the encounter specialist who had used his clout to get his son selected. But, as expected, the complaint had been of no use.

The reporters were drinking tea outside the press room when a young, influential and well-built IPS officer dropped by. He was introduced as Mahavir Tomar, an officer from the IPS batch of 1988 who had maintained the record of standing first throughout his training. He was posted in rural Maharashtra and had come to the Commissionerate for some work. Sathe's interest was piqued when he was told that Tomar had played cricket for his university in Haryana and was currently the captain of the Maharashtra IPS cricket team.

The reporters told Sathe about the officer and hoped that Tomar would offer some words of encouragement to the disappointed boy. But Tomar's way of viewing the world had changed over the years. He touched the revolver resting in the holster on his hip and said, 'There is tremendous power in a gun vis-à-vis a cricket bat.'

That day, a young Sathe decided to join the police force.

Present day

When Sathe's car left the Commissionerate at 11.30 a.m., the convoy of ATS, NIA and media vehicles followed him. Sathe was expecting even the IB to have joined the bandwagon by now. Maybe even Commissioner Tomar would have sent someone after him. Once out of the Commissionerate, the NIA office came before the ATS office. He had to decide where to go: the NIA or the ATS. There was no third option.

At the Commissionerate, the moment the media vehicles left after Sathe, a waiting Dilip Verma entered the commissioner's office after receiving a message from him. Former encounter specialist Dilip Verma and Commissioner Tomar were secretly strategizing their plan for the future. They knew they would be in trouble if Sathe opened his mouth in front of the NIA or the ATS. They were also worried about Sathe committing suicide and blaming them. But if Sathe disappeared without leaving any names or links behind, then they would be safe.

Here, the word 'disappear' meant two things: flee abroad to never return, or leave for a place where no man has ever returned from. Tomar and Verma kept both options—especially for Sathe, who had not hesitated to put his dear friend Hasmukh in the line of fire. They decided that the moment Sathe returned after being questioned they would talk to him and give him the option of disappearing himself.

Sathe's WhatsApp message had already set the stage. His disappearance could now be passed off as him having committed suicide. Even the media would get busy with the upcoming elections in five states. Everyone would forget.

Tomar asked Verma to make arrangements. He also told him that if Sathe did not agree to the first option, of disappearing himself, Verma knew what needed to be done.

Sathe, too, was thinking about the future as he drove. He knew that for Tomar and Verma, the safest option would be to pull a Hasmukh part two on him. Having worked with them for so many years, Sathe knew what they were capable of. They were the two most dangerous, evil and conniving officers of the Mumbai Police. Under the current circumstances, the safest bet for Sathe would be to flee to a foreign country and settle there with a new identity, just like the most wanted criminals of the underworld.

Expecting that he might have to flee overnight, Sathe had already laundered money out of India two days ago. The remaining cash had been converted into dollars. He had also obtained a fake passport under the alias of Ahmed Sheikh.

Seventeen years ago, Sathe had learnt his lesson the hard way. He knew that in these dangerous games the tide could turn anytime, without a warning. After joining the police force, he had been able to do what others before him had only thought of doing. In just one year, he was handling the top five high-profile cases, including the fake TRP case and the biggest car designer's scam. Be it collections from the nightclubs and luxury bars that were open till late in Mumbai to cash recovery from the syndicate of government tenders, Sathe was everywhere.

But when a batsman tries to hit a six of every ball, the chances of his wicket falling also increase, even if the batsman is Sachin Tendulkar himself. Sathe knew this and, during the last year, he had made arrangements to disappear in a way that no one would be able to find him unless he wished to be found.

Sathe had used his latest girlfriend, Nina Dias, to get all the arrangements done bit by bit. Nina was an escort and had met Sathe when she was a prostitute. She had been a victim of her circumstances—she had married a man from another religion for love, but when the going had got tough, he had pushed her into prostitution to meet their financial needs.

Sathe was under suspension when he met Nina. He had kept his real identity and profession hidden from her. But after frequent meetings, he had begun to reveal all. The difficult phase the two of them were going through seemed to have forged a bond. Soon, Nina became a means for Sathe to release pent-up frustration and offer some sadistic respite.

Often, a prostitute falls for a not-so-perfect man: be it a thief, a thug, a corrupt politician, a dishonest policeman or a hooligan. Nina was no different. She had devoted herself to Sathe. After divorcing her husband, she sent her son to a boarding school. When Sathe was reinstated into the police force after a few years, he took advantage of her credibility and financial expertise. He made her quit prostitution and kept her on as his mistress-cum-accountant for fifty thousand rupees a month.

Sathe needed someone like Nina. She was fifteen years younger than him and had proven her prowess both in the bedroom and finance and accounting. Since Nina was not connected to the police department in any way, he had put her accounting skills to use. Nina was aware of Sathe's alternate arrangements and Sathe knew that keeping her with him was a risky proposition.

Seventeen years ago, after the Nawaz case, Sathe had understood that a secret remained a secret only if it stayed with one single person. The moment it was shared with another person, the chances of it being revealed went up by fifty per cent.

Nina had been attracted to Sathe's money, power and position. And Sathe knew that if you had money, you could have any girl in the world. He had not wanted to cause Hasmukh or Nina any harm, but the changing circumstances had left him no choice. He was not the person he was seventeen years ago. Today, he was smarter and stronger and had managed to make his own arrangements, without anyone catching a whiff.

The state home minister's call operator connected to the ATS and immediately asked for an update on the Hasmukh murder case. Hasmukh, whether living or dead, made no difference to Home Minister Sardeshpande. All he was interested in was the adulation that would follow if the ATS solved the murder case. The embarrassment he had suffered in the last two weeks would be forgotten if that happened. He would be able to leverage the situation to his benefit and use it as a launch pad to bounce back.

The ATS informed Sardeshpande that Sathe had met the police commissioner in the morning and not reached the ATS office yet, but a team was following him. Sardeshpande's sixth sense told him that if Sathe had gone to meet the commissioner, then it had to be important. And Tomar had not given him an update about this meeting. There was already enough trouble because of Tomar covering up for Sathe. Sardeshpande was beginning to suspect that he was actively involved in this entire case, that he had made a grave mistake by appointing Tomar as the commissioner of Mumbai.

Sardeshpande disconnected the call after instructing the ATS to give him regular updates.

All news channels were offering live telecast on the Sathe situation. In fact, people in betting dens were placing bets on where he would go: the NIA or the ATS.

Sathe, too, was weighing the pros and cons in his head. Given the progress the ATS had made in the Hasmukh murder case, his chances of being arrested were high. Also, his cheek was still smarting from the slap DIG Palande had planted. If he just had to make it past one more day, the NIA seemed to be the better option. He expected the agency to take more than a day to interrogate him in the Kuberia case and verify the facts against the evidence. He just needed to get past one more day.

Sathe inched along with the convoy trailing behind him. On his right was the NIA office. His car went past it. The press had just begun to break the news about Sathe heading towards the ATS office, and the ATS had just breathed a sigh of relief, when Sathe took a U-turn from the signal at Jaslok Hospital.

Sathe's car entered the NIA office exactly at noon, followed by the vehicle carrying the agency's team. The ATS's car stopped where it was and the media was not allowed to enter. Before getting off his car, Sathe sent a message to the ATS officers saying that he would not be available because the NIA was questioning him today.

The media broadcast visuals of Sathe disembarking from his car and entering the NIA office.

Looking at his TV screen, Sardeshpande dialled the ATS office. He asked them what was to be done about the press conference that had been announced. The ATS suggested that it be postponed by a day, and that Sathe would be arrested the moment he left the NIA office.

Agitated and angry, the minister asked why Sathe had not been arrested before he entered the NIA office. Calmly but firmly, the ATS told him that indulging in any drama would have reflected badly on them. But more importantly, the home minister was told, the NIA would have considered this as interference in their work. It would have sent the message that the ATS, the state's agency, was protecting Yatin Sathe from the NIA, the centre's agency.

The minister was aware of this conflict between the central and state officers. He accepted the logic, but not entirely. He rebuked the ATS officers for not thinking on their feet and slacking before disconnecting the call.

Yatin Sathe was sitting alone in the NIA's interrogation room. He knew that when he left the office, three possibilities awaited him:

- He would have to disappear immediately.
- Someone else would have made arrangements to make him disappear forever.
- The ATS would be waiting to arrest him.

No matter what, it was Sathe's last day as a free man. It felt like a T-20 cricket match where the outcome remained undecided till the last ball was played.

When the door opened, Sathe lifted his head to look at the investigating officer who had entered. His face turned as white as a ghost. Something told him that coming to the NIA was his gravest mistake. He thought that DIG Palande's questioning, even if accompanied by slaps, would have been better than this.

8

The hunter gets hunted

A year ago

Commissioner Mahavir Tomar and Joint Commissioner (crime) Rohtagi, amidst a gathering of top police officials, could not decide whether Yatin Sathe should be reinstated into the police force or not.

Maharashtra was the most affected state in the country due to the coronavirus. And because the police force was on the frontline, thousands of policemen and their families got infected and many deaths were reported. Barring a few key positions, officers and constables above the age of fifty were asked to stay at home or given non-active duty. There was a 20 per cent shortage of personnel. Under these trying circumstances, it was decided that suspended officers, or officers awaiting posting, would be reinstated. The records of such officers were checked and a list of those eligible for reinstatement was drawn up. All of the names on that list had received a general consent, except Sathe, who had been suspended seventeen years ago in the Nawaz case.

Sathe, meanwhile, eagerly waited outside the building where the meeting was being held. Anxiety had got the better of him and he was smoking one cigarette after another. He had been off active police duty for seventeen years. He could have been reinstated earlier as per the rules, but previous commissioners had not let that happen because of personal prejudice.

This time, however, Sathe had pinned his hopes on Mahavir Tomar. He knew Tomar from before and his political handler, Minister Pranil Sanap, had got the chief minister to recommend his name directly. But Sathe knew he couldn't get his hopes up until the official announcement was made. He knew that Joint Commissioner (crime) Rohtagi did not like him one bit and would be adamant against his reinstatement.

A member of the review committee, Rohtagi objected to Sathe's reinstatement, but it did not hold because of the raging COVID19 outbreak and its impact on the police force. Besides, Sathe was reminded that officers who were reinstated were generally given non-important postings with divisions like local arms, control room, reserve police, traffic police, etc., mostly to monitor their work. Important postings were not handed out in the first year of reinstatement.

Post lunch, when the meeting resumed, Commissioner Tomar announced that Yatin Sathe would be brought back to active duty as the head of the prestigious CIU. Joint Commissioner Rohtagi was shocked. The CIU fell under his domain and it had always been headed by a senior inspector, not an assistant police inspector who had been off active duty for seventeen years. He was stunned that the notorious Sathe would lead the CIU, the Mumbai Police's attacking arm.

Rohtagi refused to accept Sathe as the CIU head. He knew that he alone exercised the authority to appoint its head. Commissioner Tomar, however, was prepared for this. He revealed the ace up his sleeve and showed Rohtagi a new order, according to which the rights pertaining to the posting of officers in the Crime Branch had been taken away from the joint commissioner (crime) and given to the commissioner. Interestingly, this order had been issued just an hour before the meeting.

All members present in the meeting were experienced officers. They understood that the rules had been twisted in favour of Yatin Sathe—it was like asking a cricketer who had not played for seventeen years to become the captain. Everyone also realized that without high-level political backing, Commissioner Tomar would not have been able to pull this off. They kept quiet, but Rohtagi got up and left the meeting. He had decided to ask for a transfer outside Maharashtra.

Sathe, who had been waiting outside, saw Rohtagi leaving in his car. For a fleeting moment, their eyes locked. Instead of saluting Rohtagi, who was his senior, Sathe smiled. All Rohtagi saw was arrogance, shamelessness and an utter lack of respect.

Present day

Sathe clearly saw the need for revenge on Rohtagi's face as he sat in front of him. It was just the two of them in the NIA interrogation room: Yatin Sathe and the agency's newly appointed officer, IG Rohtagi.

Karma, put simply, is a verb. There is no menu card for good or bad karma where you get to choose. When it comes to karma, you are served what you deserve. Always treat others the way you want them to treat you because whatever goes around, comes around. If someone hates you or fights with you, know that it's your own karma.

Rohtagi was in front of Sathe, as the in-charge of the investigation, making him wonder if he would have been better off with the ATS. For a while, Rohtagi simply looked at Sathe, who did not have the courage to look him in the eye. Rohtagi called his junior officers, instructed them to install a TV in the room and left. He told Sathe that he had ten hours to confess.

2004

The news across all TV screens in the country was the same: Sub-Inspector Sathe arrested for the murder of Nawaz, a suspect in the bomb explosion case.

The allegation was that Sathe had tortured Nawaz, killed him and got rid of his body. He had then spun stories about Nawaz fleeing from custody. Sanjay Trivedi was taking credit for his reportage, enunciating during the live telecast each injustice Sathe had committed.

Present day

News channels across the country screamed the same news: Assistant Police Inspector Yatin Sathe arrested in connection with the explosives found outside Kuberia.

Standing apart from other reporters, Sanjay Trivedi linked this arrest with Sathe's arrest from seventeen years ago, amplifying the police officer's notoriety quotient.

Sathe, who had not left the NIA's interrogation room, was flummoxed to see the news of his arrest. It had been ten hours since his arrival at the agency's office and he had not been questioned at all. He had simply been made to wait. *How had the NIA announced his arrest?*

The state's home minister, Sardeshpande, who had just seen the news, let out a volley of expletives on the ATS. The ATS officers themselves were baffled at their plan to arrest Sathe going awry. They could not understand how the NIA had managed to pull off the arrest so fast. As far as the ATS knew, the investigation into the Kuberia case was way behind the one in the Hasmukh murder case.

Equally as frustrated as the ATS officers were Dilip Verma and Commissioner Tomar. All their plans and arrangements had been in vain. They were aware of every law pertaining to crime, but they had forgotten Murphy's Law, according to which whatever can go wrong in a situation will go wrong. Basically, what you don't want happening will definitely happen.

'You haven't even begun questioning and you have announced my arrest to the media?' Sathe said the moment IG Rohtagi entered the room. 'This is not the way. You are tampering with the law, rules and regulations.'

Rohtagi sat down and calmly replied, 'A year ago, if the law, rules and regulations had not been tampered with, you would not have been sitting here. You would be rotting in some side posting, warding off flies. But you are here now. Your godfather, Commissioner Tomar, cannot come to lobby for you. If you had worked within the purview of the law, you would not have been arrested today or seventeen years ago.'

Memories from a year ago flashed across Sathe's eyes. He asked in a loud voice, 'On what basis have you arrested me? Without any evidence?'

Laughing, Rohtagi replied, 'You and the Mumbai Police think that only you know how to investigate cases, that other police officers are incompetent. On account of your proximity to Bollywood, you all have got into the habit of making up filmi stories. It's what you did in this case as well.'

Rohtagi then asked an officer to play a video on the TV screen and started narrating a story. 'The main character of this story is Yatin Sathe, who has a friend called Hasmukh in the business of auto spare parts. A customer approached Hasmukh to get his Scorpio repaired in October. The bill was so high that the original owner of the car and Hasmukh got into an argument. Hasmukh refused to return the car till the bill was cleared. Sathe decided to back Hasmukh, so that he could throw his weight around and not return the car, thus becoming its de facto owner. Now, we must establish Sathe's connection with the Scorpio. In November, when Sathe went to arrest the owner of a news channel in the "abetment to suicide" case, he was using the same Scorpio. Footage of the same was recorded by the cameras of the news channels.'

Here, Rohtagi gestured to his subordinate who played another footage for Sathe to see.

Rohtagi continued. 'After that, Yatin Sathe continued using the Scorpio, parking it outside his residence in Aniket Housing Society. In the interim, Sathe's Kuberia plan was finalized. He removed the chassis and engine numbers so that the car's owner cannot be identified. But the plan required more than one car. Sathe then decided to use the official car allotted to the CIU. He didn't expect anyone to suspect that car; after all, it was a white Innova. Next, Sathe got several fake number plates made from a shop close to his house. He knew he would have to use different number plates at different times on both the Scorpio and Innova. Sathe then had to get the explosives. The easiest explosive to obtain is gelatin. Being used industrially also, it's easier to obtain compared to other explosives. Sathe used his contacts to obtain some gelatin sticks from a factory in Nagpur. However, gelatin does not become an explosive unless there is a detonator. There was no detonator in this case because that would have been too risky. After this, getting hold of Kuber's cricket team's jersey was easy.

'The spot where the Scorpio filled with explosives had to be parked was identified. Then, Sathe, in cahoots with the Mumbai Police chief, ensured that the investigation into the Kuberia case was handed over to the CIU, of which Sathe was the head. All arrangements had been made and Sathe began to execute the plan.

'Now, Sathe involved Hasmukh in the plan, but he did not reveal anything about Kuberia. Hasmukh agreed for friendship's sake. Sathe returned the Scorpio to Hasmukh. Based on Sathe's instructions, Hasmukh took the car from Thane to Mumbai. The car didn't give him trouble, but Hasmukh still parked it on the side of the highway after entering Mumbai and booked a taxi to head towards the Commissionerate. Later, Hasmukh lied about the location to the investigators because Sathe had told him to do so.

'The NIA found the taxi driver through the cab company's app. He told the team that Hasmukh was talking to someone on the phone, someone he repeatedly addressed as 'sir'. We know that Hasmukh always addressed Sathe as 'sir'. The taxi driver gave us the exact location where Hasmukh was dropped off close to the Commissionerate. The NIA then obtained CCTV footage of that traffic signal.'

IG Rohtagi signalled and another video was played.

'In the CCTV footage, it is clearly visible that Hasmukh got off on the opposite side of the road. Sathe's BMW was stationary in the middle lane of the road, amidst heavy traffic, but on the other side. Even when the signal turned green, Sathe did not budge. The cars behind him drove around to move ahead. By then, Hasmukh crossed the road, got into the car and they drove off.'

Rohtagi paused the video here but continued to speak.

'In the BMW, Hasmukh handed over the keys of the Scorpio to Sathe and went back to Thane. Sathe, or one of his men, used that key to pick up the car from the highway, take it back to Thane and park it in Aniket Housing Society. The next day, as per plan, Hasmukh filed a complaint about a stolen car at the local police station. Now, this proved to be a loophole in Sathe's planning. If the steering of the Scorpio was faulty, then how was it driven off? Obviously, you would need to get the steering fixed before driving the car. Since both these scenarios are improbable, the lie about the faulty steering was exposed. After that, the Scorpio crossed Mumbai and entered Thane. The footage of the driver in a mask entering Thane was caught on the CCTV footage of the toll plaza. Lastly, the day arrived when the plan was to be executed. The gelatin and the jersey were placed inside the Scorpio. To confirm this, we got CCTV footage from the roads near the toll plaza, Kuberia and the Commissionerate. We placed the footage in serial order to make the picture clear. Final showdown please.'

The images began to play on the TV screen. Its corresponding audio reverberated in Sathe's ears.

'On Wednesday, Sathe's man left the Mumbai Police Commissionerate in a white Innova. The car crossed the toll plaza and was seen entering Thane. After a few hours, in the middle of the night, the date changed to Thursday. A few minutes past midnight, Sathe, first with a fake number plate on the Scorpio and after a few minutes with a fake number plate on an Innova, crossed the toll plaza from Thane and entered Mumbai. First, the Scorpio was parked near Kuberia. After some time, the white Innova arrived and Sathe, who was driving the Scorpio, got into the Innova. Sathe was completely covered. The Innova left and crossed into Thane. Sathe then remembered that he had forgotten to place the threat letter inside the Scorpio. So the Innova, with another fake number plate, crossed the toll plaza again and re-entered Mumbai. Around 4 a.m., the Innova reached the road leading to Kuberia. A CCTV camera near Kuberia captured a fully covered man, Yatin Sathe, disembarking from the Innova, placing the threat letter inside the Scorpio and leaving in the Innova. Now, because he had to get to his office in a few hours, and since his office and Thane are in the opposite direction from Kuberia, Sathe took the Innova and went straight to the CIU office in the Commissionerate's premises. But here, Sathe committed a mistake. He did not change the number plate of the Innova after leaving Kuberia. The car was seen entering the Commissionerate with the fake number plate.'

API Yatin Sathe was officially arrested on Saturday night. Since an accused needs to be presented before the magistrate within twenty-four hours of the arrest, the NIA produced him before a holiday court. For emergency cases that happen on a holiday, a single judge presides over the court, which is colloquially called a 'holiday court'. Of course, there was a lot of media presence, and among it was Sanjay Trivedi.

'From there on, everything went according to plan. The local police station, the Bomb Squad, the CIU and the ATS descended on the crime scene. Sathe, ironically, was made the investigating officer of the case. And although Sathe had removed the chassis and engine numbers, he made yet another mistake. He did not notice the fine imprint on the window of the car that had details of the car's loan. This was spotted by the investigating officers, after which it was easy to reach Hasmukh and establish a link with Sathe. Seeing the situation slip from under his control, Sathe panicked and began to get rid of all evidence. He managed to get rid of the DVR of the CCTV footage of his housing society and the CIU office. Those DVRs would have established a link between the Scorpio and the Innova. Sathe did the same with the DVR of the shop from where he had got the fake number plates, but getting rid of all footage from Mumbai was not in his hands.'

Here, the public prosecutor stopped for a breather and took a sip of water. He went on to show the court all the relevant footage in a sequential manner, after which he turned off the TV screen and said, 'Your Honour, accused Yatin Sathe possesses a very dangerous mind. Despite being a police officer, he has committed this grievous crime, which makes it all the more serious. The prosecution demands that API Sathe be placed under the custody of the NIA for fourteen days so that more information can be obtained.'

The judge then asked the defence lawyer to present his argument. Sathe's lawyer requested the court that since the accused was a police officer and had in-depth knowledge of the law, he wanted to present his own defence. The court granted permission for the same.

Sathe thanked the court and requested for the footage played by the prosecutor to be replayed. He asked for it to be stopped at the point where, on the road leading to Kuberia, a man is seen getting off from the Scorpio and getting into the Innova.

Clearing his throat, Sathe spoke. 'Two cars can be seen in this video, a Scorpio and an Innova. The Innova arrives after the Scorpio, and the man from the Scorpio sits inside it. Now, this was obviously driven by someone. This means that at least two people were present. In that case, where is the second man? Why hasn't the NIA found the second man? In fact, in its remand application, the NIA has not even bothered to declare the second man as wanted. This implies that this entire investigation is to trap one man, Yatin Sathe. This second man alone can confirm if one of these two men on the screen is Yatin Sathe or not. But there is not even a mention of this second man. It means that, by hook or by crook, the intention is to put API Yatin Sathe behind bars. That seems to be the sole objective of the NIA.'

On a roll, Sathe requested for another video to be played. Getting it paused midway, he said, 'The NIA has presented this video as evidence. This footage is of the toll plaza from where the Innova entered Thane. According to the NIA, the Innova picked up the person who had exited the Scorpio before entering Thane from this toll plaza. Please look at the paused video carefully. In the CCTV footage, only the man seated in the driver's seat can be seen. No one is seen riding shotgun; the passenger seat is empty. If it's the same Innova, then where is the second man? Was he dropped off somewhere, or did he hide behind the backseat? If he was hiding, then why? Or is it possible that this is not the Innova that the NIA is claiming it to be?'

The judge noted this point and looked at the public prosecutor, who did not seem to have an answer. He then gestured for Sathe to proceed.

Sathe got all of the NIA's videos played once again, pausing at several places. He said, 'You have seen, whether it is the Scorpio or the Innova, that there are eight CCTV footage of both. In every footage, the driver has donned a surgical cap, a surgical mask below a face shield and a PPE kit. I want to say two things: First, all of you know that the twin cities of

Thane and Mumbai are separated by a toll plaza. Thousands of frontline medical workers wearing exactly this gear cross the toll plaza every day. Thousands of Innovas also cross the toll plaza each day, in which the driver's face is covered with a mask or face shield. In that case, how did the NIA differentiate between Sathe and the others? Second, when the person's face, head and body are totally covered, we cannot tell whether the person is fair or dark, bald or has a full head of hair, fat or thin, young or old. Nothing can be deciphered except the height. In that case, how has the NIA singled me out? I am a police officer myself. I was the former investigating officer in the case and, as far as my understanding of technology goes, there is neither an artist nor any software that can sketch someone's face on the basis of height alone. The NIA, in its remand application, has not mentioned the recovery of any PPE kit, cap, mask, etc. Given this, the public prosecutor should throw light on how the NIA came to believe it was Yatin Sathe.'

The judge looked at the prosecutor, who in turn looked at the NIA officers seated next to him, and shook his head. The judge noted this point and looked at Sathe.

Sathe felt boosted. His defence was going well and the media was hanging on to his every word. Emboldened, he spoke with confidence, 'Now the question remains about the identity of the Innova and having a particular brand's tissue paper box on its dashboard. Please note that this is only corroborative evidence, the work of which is to support the main evidence. The question is: Where is the primary evidence that proves indisputably that the man in the footage is me? As far as the BMW is concerned, and the cash and currency counting machine that was found in it, its connection to this case is yet to be established. Discovering a half-used kerosene can does not prove that it was used to burn evidence. Kerosene is an easily available commodity. It was in the car so that it could be used to light a bonfire for a picnic. If the evidence was burnt, then the NIA should show at least some remains. Also, kerosene's sole purpose is not to burn. It serves other purposes. Before this, seventeen years ago, a murder investigation was started against me. That body has not been found till date, which is why that case is still pending.'

Sathe bowed slightly to show his respect for the court and continued, 'I respect this court and, without challenging its authority in any way, want to state that as far as the matter of my expensive lifestyle and use of luxury cars is concerned, the anti-corruption bureau can interrogate me for the possession of disproportionate assets. This is certainly not the platform or forum for that, and neither is that case being heard today.'

Not sensing any discontent or anger on the judge's face, Sathe heaved a sigh of relief. He added, 'Since I was arrested on Saturday, I have been produced before this holiday court. The fourteen days remand sought by the NIA is too much and outside the scope of this holiday court.'

The judge looked at his watch and urged Sathe to wind up.

An encouraged Sathe said, 'The NIA's investigation is incomplete. I have been caught in the middle of a tussle between different investigating agencies and a political tug-of-war between the Centre and the state. I am merely an assistant inspector, not even a complete inspector. I have become a pawn in this game where bigger powers are at work. In the last one year, I have handled high-profile cases such as the fake TRP scam and the car designer's scam, as a result of which I have several enemies. I am being made the scapegoat. I request the court to immediately grant me conditional bail. I will assist the NIA in its investigation and be present whenever I am called for questioning. I want to repeat that a fourteen-day remand is too much and out of the scope of this holiday court.'

The judge shot back. 'Based on that logic, granting bail must also be beyond the scope of this holiday court?'

'Your Honour, bail is a rule, jail is an exception. The Supreme Court, in the case of *State of Rajasthan vs Balchand* in 1977, gave a landmark judgment and established a legal doctrine based on fundamental rights, the guarantee of which is enshrined in the Constitution of India. Because this is related to a man's freedom, based on my limited legal information, I can safely say that every court has the right to protect the freedom of a person. I would like to end my argument with this,' Sathe concluded.

Sathe's argument was powerful. It almost seemed as if the tables would turn in his favour.

The NIA lawyer stood up to speak after a quick discussion with the NIA officers. 'Your Honour, the way Mr Sathe has presented the defence is commendable. It is obvious that he is well-versed in the laws of the country. He has put this knowledge to use in destroying evidence, which is why the NIA wants him to be in custody. Before being arrested, this API destroyed the CCTV footage of his housing society and the CIU office, which were important evidence. Seventeen years ago, too, he was tried for destroying crucial evidence. If he is granted bail, he will tamper with evidence again. What could be the reason, other than causing destruction, for planting a car full of explosives? In this case, sections of the Explosives Act have been imposed, which are serious. Granting bail under such circumstances won't be right. Yatin Sathe should not be granted bail.'

The judge interrupted the prosecutor here. 'You are telling me why bail should not be granted. You are not telling me why custody should be given.'

'The honourable court knows that the accused was arrested only last night. After the arrest, the medical examination, etc., and other processes took time. The NIA needs custody so that it can answer the questions the accused raised in court today. Scene recreation needs to be carried out to see if it matches the images seen in the footage. Also, more information needs to be collected on the accused's so-called accomplice. The evidence destroyed by him needs to be recovered, which includes the DVR of the housing society and the CIU and footage from the shop where the fake number plates were made. Information pertaining to the evidence that has been burnt also needs to be gathered. The accused is not cooperative, which is why the NIA needs custodial interrogation. If custody is not granted, then last night's arrest will become meaningless.'

With both sides done with their arguments, the judge announced his order. The court rejected Sathe's bail application and granted the NIA custody for two days. The judge said that since the investigation was in its nascent stage, bail could not be granted. Also, since this was a holiday court, the accused needed to file his bail plea with a regular court. In conjunction, the court also told the NIA that after two days they could present the accused before a regular court and request for further remand.

However, even though Sathe's bail plea had been rejected, he appeared relaxed and the NIA officers looked tense. IG Rohtagi knew that today Sathe's plea might have been rejected, but he had shown the power of reasoning. Years of experience told him that if the NIA did not show significant progress in the case in the next two days, things would get difficult in the next hearing.

The next forty-eight hours were going to be very crucial for the NIA. The cunning and conniving Sathe had to be broken. And the agency had one last arrow left in its quiver. Sathe, on the other hand, did not know that the next forty-eight hours were going to be the most humiliating moments of his life.

9

Embarrassment in a PPE kit

'You fucking piece of shit, stop acting so smart.'
'Walk the way you walked that night.'
'Come back a little and then walk again.'
'Be consistent with the way you are walking.'
'Don't come up to the front so much.'
'Stop where the mark has been made.'
'Now pace yourself. First walk slowly, then fast.'
'Cooperate, or we will kick your ass again.'
'Do it again.'
'Fucking prick, we will make you do it till you do it right.'

For many hours, these voices ordered and insulted Sathe. His ears were ringing and his vision was hazy. He was dressed in a kurta that looked like a PPE kit and a surgical cap, exactly like the man in the footage. The NIA also placed a camera at the same height and angle as the original CCTV that had recorded the footage.

Thanks to the mask and face shield covering his face, no one could see his eyes brimming with tears. He felt as if the weight of his body had multiplied manifold. Every step seemed as if he was dragging a huge weight along.

He had been made a complete spectacle, like a bear in a circus dancing to the tunes of its trainer; like a stripper repeatedly stripped of his respect; like a prostitute asked to lift her skirt for a customer.

Barely two weeks ago, he was the lion of the Mumbai Police. And now he was the NIA's pet dog. His voice had been confident and firm a few hours ago in court, but now his throat was choked and he repeatedly had to swallow his spit laced with phlegm. The fact that it was humid outside and he was fully covered made the sweat drip from his bald head, mixed with the tears streaming down his eyes and reached his lips, leaving a salty and bitter taste in his mouth.

Before making him don the entire get-up, Sathe was made to wear an adult diaper. He had understood right then that this drama would go on for hours. He had already peed in the diaper once and his bladder was full again. His mind and heart told him that committing suicide would have been better than this abject humiliation. He also knew that this was happening because he had challenged the NIA in court. The agency was affronted.

Sathe, who had never faced something like this, felt sorry for himself. He had not felt this self-pity when he had been arrested seventeen years ago. Staying outside the police force for so many years, he had faced a lot of hardships, but not once had he felt so despondent. The consecutive blows from the ATS and insults heaped by the NIA did not make him feel as sorry for himself as he was feeling at that moment.

The NIA was trying to recreate the crime scene as accurately as possible. They intended to match the original footage with the one being recorded just then to determine if the man exiting the Scorpio was Yatin Sathe or not. To ensure that they got the height, gait, etc., right, they made Sathe repeatedly walk up and down the road leading to Kuberia.

IG Rohtagi had already made it clear to Sathe that if he did not cooperate, he would be dragged disgracefully in front of everyone and forced to do as told. Sathe knew people were peeping out of the windows of neighbouring buildings; some had even stepped out onto the road and were recording videos on their mobile phones. The local police had been summoned for security and they, too, were watching this spectacle unfold. At a distance, cameramen from various media houses zoomed in to click pictures. Sathe recognized Sanjay Trivedi in that crowd, reporting live with gusto.

Always conscious about his image, Sathe knew that his images in this get-up would have gone viral on social media by now. WhatsApp messages with memes on him were probably in circulation, too. For years to come, this image of Sathe would remain etched in the minds of people.

Sanjay Trivedi was making the most of the live telecast. He stated that he had known Yatin Sathe for almost two decades, and that initially, he thought that he was the only reporter who believed that Sathe lied with finesse, but later his belief was affirmed by other reporters as well. He told his audience that Sathe had been nicknamed 'jhuttad', or a compulsive liar. Trivedi added that returning to the force after seventeen years, Sathe had seemed humble for a few weeks before his body language had changed suddenly. According to Trivedi, Sathe's head was in the clouds. He claimed to have a strong apprehension that Sathe would go back to his old ways again. He ended by saying that his apprehension had turned to reality, which was much worse than what he had conjured in his mind.

Sanjay Trivedi had never seen any policeman be humiliated this way in his twenty-year journalism career. He had seen many police officers and people from other professions get arrested, but such a spectacle was new. This was a lesson not only for policemen, but also for all people.

While Trivedi berated Sathe, there were people who felt sorry for him as the NIA had made a spectacle of him. People who had been apathetic to his plight earlier now felt sorry for him.

The CIU's Sub-Inspector Haji, Sathe's associate, was visibly terrified. Watching Sanjay Trivedi report on his TV screen at home, Haji knew that an example was being made out of Sathe. He thought about how Sathe had already spent more than twenty-five years in the police force and how his innings was almost over. Haji, meanwhile, had just started out. His entire police career lay in front of him. He had heard about Sathe's misfortunes several times, directly from Sathe. All those stories made Haji believe that police officers who were suspended and expelled for serious crimes could not get a job anywhere else. Kuber's name carried so much weight that no corporate house would entertain him. The question of getting a government job, too, did not arise. He knew that whatever he had done had been based on Sathe, his senior officer's, instructions. Had he refused to follow Sathe's orders, he would have been facing action for insubordination. In that case, there would have been no point in complaining to his super seniors also because the top boss, Commissioner Tomar, was sheltering Sathe.

Haji, who had to report to the NIA office in a few hours for questioning in the Kuberia case, could feel himself going numb.

All night, Yatin Sathe was made to recreate the Kuberia scene. In the morning, the NIA started to question Sub-Inspector Haji. The agency did not have much time. Sathe had to be produced before the court on Tuesday to request for an extension of his remand. There was immense pressure to gather enough evidence.

IG Rohtagi knew it won't be easy to question a trained police officer; Sathe had already shown him that. He expected the same with Sub-Inspector Haji, but he was in for a pleasant surprise. Haji declared at the outset that he would confess all if the NIA made him an approver, which would assure him of some leniency and probably reduce his punishment.

IG Rohtagi, who had not expected this, said, 'An approver is not some object placed on a shelf in a mall that can be picked up at will. Nor is a court anything like what you have seen in Bollywood films. You've just about finished your police training and become a sub-inspector, so you must know what an approver is and what it takes to become one.'

Passing a small bottle of water to Haji, he continued to speak. 'If more than one person is involved in a crime and if one of the perpetrators testifies and helps in gathering evidence, then he is called an approver. However, not anyone can turn into an approver. A lot of things need to be considered before that. If the prosecution wants to make someone an approver, an application has to be filed with the court. The court then determines the extent of the role played by the accused in question. The main accused can never turn into an approver. If someone has played a small role in the crime, then the judge can use his/her discretion to decide. As per Section 306 of the CrPC, a provision for pardoning an approver exists. Remember that an approver *can* be exempted; it's not compulsory.'

Haji was restless. 'What's the best deal you can offer me?'

'I've already told you that we are not in a shopping mall. Whether you cooperate or not, we will find all the missing pieces related to this case and put the picture together. You do not have much of a choice. Sooner or later, you will be arrested. Yes, if you understand the analogy of a shopping mall, then you tell me what you have to offer and then we can discuss what it is worth.'

The ball was in Haji's court.

At noon on Monday, the bridge situated over the River Mithi in the Bandra Kurla Complex had been cordoned off for the public and vehicular movement. People were asked to take a diverted route. There was no major impact on traffic because the BKC mostly houses offices that were closed because of the pandemic.

The Mithi River is hardly a river. Its width is no more than that of a sewer. Using its water for drinking, bathing or even washing means inviting diseases. More than water, the river carried filth, excrement, garbage and industrial waste, as a result of which the flow was never strong. Given this, the NIA had managed with great difficulty to convince four divers to enter the river.

The divers dove into the water one by one. Spectators began to gather. Media vans also arrived in droves. It was after their arrival that Yatin Sathe was made to parade in front of them. The NIA had understood that the mental angst Sathe would experience because of this humiliation would be far more hurtful than any physical torture. Sathe had revealed his weak point to the NIA by requesting that he be given the respect due to a police officer, especially in front of the press.

For the next six to seven hours, the divers continued to scan the river and mostly came up empty-handed. But the times they did find something, made Sathe's face lose colour. They had retrieved two number plates, a computer's CPU, a hard disc and two DVRs.

The faces of the NIA officers brightened. The fatigue that had started to take over them seemed to be dissipating. Until a few hours ago, they had no idea about where to gather the evidence from. Now, thanks to Sub-Inspector Haji's revelation that he had handed over the DVRs of Aniket Housing Society to Sathe on the bridge across the Mithi River, the NIA saw some light at the end of a dark tunnel.

This also tied up with why Sathe had taken the long route home, via BKC. The NIA had been hoping to recover this evidence from the river, and they were not disappointed. Sathe had tried to destroy evidence.

Sathe, meanwhile, knew that his special junior, Fakhruddin Haji, had opened his mouth in front of the NIA. Also, being a technocrat police officer, he knew that if not all, at least some data or video would be retrieved.

IG Rohtagi ordered for the damaged equipment and other evidence recovered from the river to be sent to the forensic lab where an attempt at data recovery could be made. Rohtagi was not expecting to recover everything, but he was hopeful of finding something.

Sathe, who was also apprehensive, realized that only mens rea could save him now.

1992

Mens rea. The professor enunciated the phrase and then stopped to glance at the recruits seated before him. It was a class on law as part of police training for the recruits who had been selected recently. It was clear from the recruits' expressions that the words closest to the phrase in their heads were 'Men's Riya'.

Smiling, the professor spoke again. 'Don't take it literally. Mens rea is a Latin phrase which means "guilty mind". It is a person's intention to commit a crime; or the knowledge that one's action, or lack of action, would cause a crime to be committed. Mens rea is embedded in the fundamentals of law and judicial systems around the world. It is a measure to gauge the intentions of a person who commits a crime. What was the intention or motive of the accused behind committing the crime?'

The professor rested his hand on Yatin Sathe's shoulder. 'Consider this. If Yatin sends an anonymous threat letter to someone's house and gets caught, then we have to determine if he sent the letter in jest or intended to commit a serious crime by sending it.'

Yatin Sathe felt uncomfortable at this example. When the professor removed his hand, Sathe felt as if a burden had been lifted.

The professor continued to speak, 'When you investigate, the criminal's motive and intention both need to be assessed. If someone has committed a crime and gets caught, then the prosecution has to prove his motive in court. If the motive cannot be established and proved, the case becomes very weak. Consequently, the accused is either acquitted or let off with light punishment.'

Present day

That morning, the courtroom was packed. Besides the media, a lot of lawyers who were not even connected to the cases scheduled for hearing that day were in attendance as spectators.

Accused Yatin Sathe was produced before the court. IG Rohtagi and the other NIA officers seated themselves behind their attorney. Sathe's lawyer presented an application saying that his client wanted to argue the case himself. All this time, Sathe's face was drawn in a smile.

Speaking on behalf of the NIA, the public prosecutor informed the court about the progress made in the investigation in the last two days, about the NIA recovering evidence that the accused, Sathe, had thrown into the Mithi River with the objective of erasing it. He added that the evidence found in the river had been sent to the central forensic lab for data recovery. Also, since the objects had been recovered only the previous evening, the lab would need time. The NIA also informed the court about the reconstruction of the scene outside Kuberia. With this as context, the public prosecutor requested that Sathe's custody be extended.

The judge looked at Sathe, gesturing for him to present his argument.

'Your Honour, during police training we were told about mens rea, which is vital in every case. Behind every crime is a motive and intention. If a crime has been committed, there must be a motive. This is my second hearing before a court, and even in its second remand application, the prosecution has not been able to tell the court what my motive was behind committing such a crime. If they have no idea about the motive, why am I being kept in custody unnecessarily? A few months ago, in September 2020, criminal appeal number 1121/2016, in *Anwar Ali vs state of Himachal Pradesh*, the Supreme Court's bench of three judges expounded on a very important point. It said that circumstantial evidence, meaning not being able to prove the "motive" behind a crime, is a factor that falls in favour of the accused,' Sathe said.

He then glanced at the reporters in the court and continued, 'Before this, in many other cases, this fact has been established.

It is the second hearing. The prosecution should at least be able to enlighten the court about my motive. If not, why keep me in custody?'

Here, the public prosecutor interrupted. 'Objection. The demand for custody is not unnecessary. Because the accused has attempted to get rid of evidence before, it is important for him to stay in custody, or else he might tamper with evidence again and maybe even influence witnesses. He has already murdered the one witness and link of this case, Hasmukh. Yes, his motive remains unknown.'

'Sustained,' responded the judge and looked at Sathe. This was a signal for Sathe to respond.

'If Hasmukh was the sole witness and link in this case, why wasn't he granted police protection? Did the investigating agency not think that if the sole witness disappeared, the case would hit a roadblock? Before he was murdered, did Hasmukh give a statement holding me responsible?' Sathe spoke to the judge.

The spectators began whispering. The reporters understood that this hearing would take time because Sathe had linked the issue of custody with a Supreme Court order and also the Hasmukh murder case. The case would unfurl; it was not as straightforward as it looked.

The public prosecutor said, 'Your Honour, actually there are two cases being investigated by different agencies. The NIA is looking into the case of the explosives-filled vehicle found outside Kuberia, for which it is seeking custody of the accused. The second case is that of Hasmukh Jain's murder, which is being investigated by the ATS.'

Sathe had a reply ready. 'According to the NIA, if I killed Hasmukh, then the ATS should have arrested me by now. They should have filed a remand application with the court requesting my custody, which they have not done. The NIA has my custody at the moment, but they still have no idea about my alleged motive in the Kuberia case. Does the ATS have any theory about why I murdered Hasmukh? If it did, an application for custody would have been filed by now. No motive has been established in either case. The NIA should at least ask the ATS about their investigation and what they think my motive was.'

1992

Amongst the new police recruits attending the law class was Nitya Shetty. Seated at the back, he was feeling relieved because, a few minutes ago, the professor had presented Yatin Sathe as a criminal in an example. Shetty raised his hand and asked, 'If Yatin Sathe has to be proven as a criminal then what?'

The way he took Sathe's name, with emphasis, made the entire class erupt in laughter.

Shetty's idea of pulling a fast one on Sathe had paid off. He contained his laughter and phrased his question better this time. 'What I meant is, what needs to be done to identify the accused's motive and intention? Is it always massive wealth, a fancy car, a bungalow, expensive tastes, girls and fame because of which a crime is committed?'

'Yes,' the professor replied, 'these factors are not out of the purview of a crime. In the next class, we will discuss this in detail, but for now please understand that even the cleverest of criminals leave some evidence or clue behind. First and foremost, based on the evidence, find the criminal and then find the motive.'

Present day

'We have identified the motive in the Hasmukh murder case. First, we began to work on the clues. Then we started collecting evidence. The arrested co-accused Jhende and Mahesh Bhor have also indicted Sathe in their statement. Even the victim's wife accused him of murder,' said Nitya Shetty.

ATS chief Vishwajeet, DIG Palande and Nitya Shetty were at Home Minister Sardeshpande's residence. Shetty was the lowest-ranking person in the room, so he had been made to sit on a separate chair while the others sat on a couch.

DIG Palande saw his WhatsApp messages and held up his mobile screen. 'Right now, the ATS lawyer has filed an application for Sathe's custody. He is currently under the NIA's custody.'

The lawyer representing the ATS asked for permission to intervene. After getting a go-ahead from the judge, he sought a hearing on the application he had filed with the court. The ATS was saying that it was close to solving the Hasmukh murder case and had arrested a few people as well. They had evidence, witnesses and motive. All they needed now was the prime suspect, Yatin Sathe, in their custody so that they could interrogate him further.

Sathe was shocked. Composing himself quickly, he went for a new approach. He told the judge that if the court thought it appropriate, he could be sent to judicial custody, i.e., jail, where the NIA and the ATS could come and interrogate him as and when needed.

Sathe knew that if the NIA or the ATS got custody, he would have to stay in their lock-up. In judicial custody, he would be in jail as an undertrial prisoner. In any of the two agency's lock-ups, he would be tortured and interrogated round the clock. But the jail in Maharashtra came under the purview of a separate division. Jail rules would apply with the time for sleeping, eating, etc., predetermined. The NIA or the ATS would have to take permission from the court or the jail administration before questioning him.

Also, compared to being interrogated continuously by an agency, in jail he would be interrogated only for a few hours. Jail would also be more convenient when it came to meeting his lawyer and filing a bail application. Sathe also thought of the underground system in jails where, in return for money, some facilities could be obtained illegally. Although not a good place to be in, he felt that jail would be better than being with any of the two agencies.

Both the NIA and the ATS objected to Sathe being put under judicial custody. On receiving permission from the court, IG Rohtagi got up to speak. He told the court that the forensic lab had sent in the report about the scene reconstruction from outside Kuberia. According to it, the man who was seen covered head to toe in the CCTV footage was, in fact, API Yatin Sathe of the CIU.

The judge announced that the court would break for lunch. The NIA, meanwhile, was asked to bring a certified copy of that report and present it in court.

'The court will resume post lunch. The hearing may go on till late evening,' Shetty said, turning off his mobile phone and looking at his seniors seated on the couch.

The state home minister took a few seconds to think and then asked, 'Is your investigation in the Hasmukh murder case complete? Do all the dots connect?'

The ATS chief nodded in agreement.

'Story?' Sardeshpande asked.

'It adds up, and it is dangerous and sensational. We even have a motive, which the NIA does not. We are ahead of them in our investigation. The media will lap this up,' the ATS chief said.

'This is some relief. At least we will be able to save face this way before people start thinking that the state machinery is useless and the Centre does all the work. This mess was created by the state's police, and we should be seen cleaning up after ourselves.' With this, the home minister asked his personal assistant to call a press conference urgently in the next thirty minutes. The assistant immediately got to work. The home minister then turned to address the ATS team.

'Tell me the complete story without leaving out any details. Right from Sathe's mobile location, which placed him in the CIU or its vicinity around the time of the murder. Sathe claims that he was raiding a bar far away from the murder spot. How could he be in two different places at the same time? If he has an alibi, how did he kill Hasmukh?'

10

The revelation

ATS officer Nitya Shetty began telling Home Minister Sardeshpande the sequence of events. 'By now you know that Yatin Sathe and Hasmukh were good friends. Hasmukh was in the business of auto spare parts. He had a Scorpio that Sathe had been using for many months. About a week before the Kuberia debacle, the Scorpio's chassis and engine numbers were erased and it was returned to Hasmukh. Now, Hasmukh was told to leave the car and file a theft report. He was assured that Sathe would investigate the case and everything would be settled easily. Then, as per the plan, the two of them planted a car filled with explosives outside Kuberia, and the Mumbai Police commissioner handed over the investigation to Sathe.

'The investigation seemed to have reached a dead end because without the chassis and engine numbers it would not be possible to find the owner of the car. But the ATS spotted what Sathe missed. On the window of the car, in very small and inconspicuous letters, was information pertaining to the car's loan. The ATS used this to find the original owner who led them to Hasmukh. This is where Sathe's plan began to derail. Hasmukh panicked when the ATS suddenly showed up at his door for questioning. He met Sathe and told him what had happened. There is footage available of the traffic signal, which corroborates that Hasmukh did indeed meet Sathe, who was in a BMW. A few days before this, they had met at the same spot. This was the day the Scorpio was allegedly stolen. We have CCTV footage to confirm this.

'Hasmukh lied to the ATS and Sathe lied to his senior, the joint commissioner (crime), about knowing each other. When the matter began to slip out of his hands, Sathe told Hasmukh to take the blame for parking the car filled with explosives outside Kuberia, vouching to get him out on bail soon. Hasmukh did not agree to this. His family, too, was not on board with Sathe's plan. In fact, they began to consider Sathe a villain.

'Sathe called Hasmukh to his CIU office once again, where he and some former and serving encounter specialists pressurized Hasmukh. A paranoid Hasmukh came out of the office for a few minutes and started muttering to himself about the plan. The owner of a bar, who was seated outside after being called by Sathe to pay his weekly protection money, overheard this muttering. Hasmukh had been grumbling to himself about why he should take the blame when he had not done anything and why was he being pressurized. The owner of the bar confirmed this.

'That day, despite all threats and pressure, Hasmukh refused to give in to Sathe's demand and returned home. The next day, Sathe met Hasmukh with an alternate plan. He took Hasmukh to a lawyer and got a letter drafted. With Hasmukh's name, date and signature, he sent it to the Mumbai Police commissioner, the Thane Police commissioner, the chief minister and the state's home minister. Sathe himself took the stamp of delivery and receipt for the letter at the Mumbai Police Commissionerate. He assured Hasmukh that with this the interrogation would cease. Hasmukh believed his friend.

'The interesting thing here is the contents of the letter. The bottom line was that Hasmukh was being harassed as different police stations, the CIU, the ATS, the NIA and the media were hounding him and trying to prove he was guilty. The letter was drafted in a way that it could appear both as a complaint as well as a suicide note. Sathe had lied to Hasmukh about the letter; his real plan was totally different. At this point, Sathe and his accomplices had understood that Hasmukh was the sole link in the Kuberia case. If Hasmukh was removed from the picture, then the crime would not be traced back to them.

'By now, Sathe, through his bookie friend Mahesh Bhor, had procured five SIM cards under the name of one family from Daman and distributed them to his friends to help execute the final part of the plan. Sathe called Hasmukh on WhatsApp one night. And because Sathe knew that Hasmukh's wife would get angry upon hearing his name, he instructed Hasmukh to tell her that he had to step out to meet a policeman named Gawde from the Kandivali police station. Hasmukh lied and left his house, telling his son to call Sathe in case of an emergency.

'Sathe, meanwhile, left his mobile phone on charge at the CIU office, so that his mobile phone location would reflect that. He did not leave the office through the main gate of the Commissionerate, as there are CCTV cameras there. He jumped over a wall behind the office. Wearing a mask, face shield and surgical cap, he reached the nearby CST railway station. From there, he got into a train heading towards Thane.'

Here, Shetty took out his iPad and showed Sardeshpande the footage of Yatin Sathe boarding the local train, with his face and head covered. He also showed the home minister footage of Sathe disembarking at Thane station.

Then, Shetty spoke again. 'Yatin Sathe got down at Thane and bought half a dozen handkerchiefs from a vendor outside the station. One of his accomplices picked him up in a car and they reached Ghodbunder Road, where Hasmukh also reached in an auto. Picking up Hasmukh, the car headed to a deserted location outside Thane. Another car with Sathe's accomplices followed. Then, at an abandoned spot, these people first tied Hasmukh's hands. Then, they shoved the handkerchiefs into his mouth while two people held him tightly to keep him from moving. Soon after, they killed Hasmukh. The body was thrown into the nearby creek. After getting rid of the body, one car took Hasmukh's mobile phone thirty-five to forty kilometres away, to the outskirts of Vasai, and dumped it there. This way, when Hasmukh's disappearance was investigated, his last location would show up as Vasai.

'In another car, Sathe reached the Thane railway station, boarded a train and got off at Sandhurst Road station, which is two stops ahead of CST station. From there, he went to the local police station. Sathe has already made a plan to create his alibi there. He told his junior, Sub-Inspector Haji, to retrieve his mobile phone from the CIU office. Then, along with the local police, he raided a famous bar under the pretext of investigating illegal activities. According to Sathe's plan, there were now many witnesses to vouch for him.

'The raid itself was interesting. Nothing was found and a nil panchnama was prepared, which is done only if no illegal activity is noticed. This is very rare because, normally, a raid is carried out after the police receive credible information. However, the raid on this bar led to nothing. Post this raid, Sathe first went to the CIU office and then headed home. His accomplices also left. All of them got rid of their fake SIM cards, except one.

'Sathe had taken the train so that he could save time and also remain inconspicuous in the crowd. Essentially, the raid and the phone being left at the CIU office were to create the premise that he was far away from the spot where Hasmukh was murdered. But he made one mistake. There was no CCTV footage of him leaving the Commissionerate to conduct the raid, but there was footage of him returning. This offered a clue about Sathe having used another exit, which led to the discovery of how he had taken the train to and from Thane.

'Sathe and his accomplices had thrown Hasmukh's body into the creek, where an estuary connecting it to the sea was close. They thought the corpse would float towards the sea. But because of the handkerchiefs stuffed into Hasmukh's mouth, water did not fill his lungs. Sathe had not expected the corpse to surface so soon. And even if it did surface, he thought it would be at a spot far away from where it was dumped because the sea would have carried it away.

'But luck did not favour Sathe. Hasmukh's body got stuck in the sludge right before entering the estuary. The mangrove prevented it from moving ahead. In the morning, when some labourers arrived there to relieve themselves, they found the body. Before the local police could reach, the labourers had pulled the body out of the sludge. One labourer made a video of the handkerchiefs being pulled out of the corpse's mouth. It was strange: the tied-up hands, the stuffed mouth under a mask. The video went viral and it wasn't long before the corpse was identified as Hasmukh Jain. Sathe hadn't expected this. He was the first to reach the spot after the local police.

'When Sathe got to the spot, the local police were taking the statements of the labourers. He was informed that the body had already been sent for post-mortem. Sathe raced to the hospital and pressurized the doctors to mention drowning as the cause of death in their report. Sathe was hoping to encourage the suicide theory with that report. He was already in possession of the letter signed by Hasmukh, which could be understood as a suicide note. He WhatsApped photos of that letter to several reporters friendly with him, so that news about Hasmukh supposedly committing suicide, because he was fed up with the media and investigating agencies, could be broadcast.

'But before sending the letter to the media, Sathe went to Hasmukh's house. After offering condolences, he told Hasmukh's wife to not divulge the fact that the Scorpio had been with him, or that he and Hasmukh were friends, to the ATS and the media. After leaving the house, Sathe astutely pushed the suicide theory to Hasmukh's relatives waiting outside the building. Subsequently, he gave a statement to the media saying that Hasmukh had died of drowning, and that it was a suicide as the result of the harassment.

'The ATS had followed Sathe everywhere that day. They were surprised because the case was outside the CIU's jurisdiction. By then, the investigation into the Kuberia case had also been taken away from Sathe. Why then was he hopping from one place to the other? Why was he declaring the body found under suspicious circumstances to be a suicide, without the post-mortem report? Hasmukh's family members, too, gave their statements to the media and the police. They mentioned how Hasmukh had been called to meet by a policeman named Gawde. His phone had been switched off after that.

'When the ATS checked, they got to know that there was no Gawde serving at the Kandivali police station. Hasmukh's last location, as per his mobile phone, was in the suburbs of Vasai, far from where his body was found. The investigation was about to hit a dead end. But then three developments took place. First, Hasmukh's family refused to accept that he had drowned because he was a good swimmer. Second, the family expressed surprise that despite knowing that Hasmukh was a good swimmer, Sathe had declared that he had drowned. Third, the lawyer who had drafted Hasmukh's letter called up his wife and told her that just the day before, Sathe had brought Hasmukh to him. This was information that Sathe had hidden.

'The family also found it suspicious that Sathe wanted to hide the fact that he had used the Scorpio, and that he and Hasmukh were friends. They also remembered that Sathe had earlier tried to push Hasmukh into taking the blame in the Kuberia case. They put two and two together and held a press conference to accuse Sathe of Hasmukh's murder. As a result, the post-mortem report was not made public and viscera samples were sent for further investigation. This was the first signal that Sathe's suicide theory was likely to be rejected. The second was Sathe's transfer out of the CIU.

'Seeing the situation worsen, Sathe filed for anticipatory bail, which was rejected. The ATS registered a case of murder and summoned Sathe for questioning. Until then, the ATS had no evidence. But Sathe's phone had been collected before he was questioned. The ATS recovered some deleted data from his mobile phone. Using that, they found out about the five SIM cards that had recently been purchased and that the maximum number of calls had been made to those numbers on the day of the murder. Also, all those numbers were switched off, barring one. Even that number was intermittently switched off. The ATS narrowed down on the location at a time when the number was active and arrested the user, Gajanan Jhende. He had been loitering around the ATS office and other locations connected to the case. Jhende was a constable who had been sentenced for carrying out a fake encounter and was out on parole.

'Since all the SIM cards had been bought from Daman, under the Damania family's name that lives there, it was the next stop for the ATS. They reached Daman, one hundred and seventy-five kilometres from Mumbai, that very night. Without informing the Damania family, one of their servants had bought the SIM cards at Mahesh Bhor's request. The owner of a youth club in Mumbai, Bhor's location was unknown, but the servant knew his mistress who lived in Daman. The ATS then brought both the mistress and the servant to Mumbai. In Mumbai, Bhor stepped out in response to a distress call from his mistress and was arrested by the ATS.

'Basically, while Sathe was sleeping, two of his men were taken into ATS custody: Mahesh Bhor and Gajanan Jhende. They revealed to the ATS all the secrets related to Hasmukh's murder. Now only Yatin Sathe had to be questioned again and arrested. But Sathe chose to go to the NIA office where, contrary to everyone's assessment, the agency unexpectedly arrested him. It was a premature arrest because the NIA had not found Sathe's motive for leaving an explosives-filled vehicle outside Kuberia. The ATS, however, knew why Sathe had murdered Hasmukh.'

'The motive behind Hasmukh's murder was to destroy the only link, the only witness in the case of the explosives-filled vehicle found outside Kuberia, so that the investigation came to a standstill and no more details surfaced,' Sardeshpande said and finally paused after half an hour.

He had addressed a press conference and sequentially laid out how the case was investigated and solved. He felt relieved. Despite all the humiliation the state government and his department had faced, one good thing had happened: the ATS had solved the Hasmukh murder case.

Looking at the ATS chief seated next to him, Sardeshpande said, 'I would like to congratulate the ATS team on the exemplary work done. They worked day and night to solve this case and are trying to get custody of Yatin Sathe through the proper court process.'

A round of questions and answers followed. Sanjay Trivedi waited for the lackey reporters to exhaust their stock of feel-good questions. When enough backs had been patted, he raised his hand. Everyone knew that, as usual, he would pour all the bitterness and negativity of his personal life into the question.

Trivedi shot out several questions rolled into one. 'Hasmukh was murdered to cover up the Kuberia incident. You even arrested a few of Sathe's companions in connection with this murder. But the question is whether Yatin Sathe alone pulled off two big crimes. The Kuberia case, for example, comes under the geographical jurisdiction of another unit of the Crime Branch, but Sathe's unit was assigned the investigation. Initially, Sathe was made in-charge of the case, not the ATS. As per the NIA's investigation, it is evident that even before the Scorpio was parked, it had been decided that CIU's Sathe would handle the investigation. Is there another senior officer involved in all this with Sathe? Is it possible that an API alone can carry out not one but two big crimes all by himself? Who gave Sathe unlimited power? Are Sathe and his accomplices mere pawns in some high-ranking official's game? Will you investigate this?'

11

The monkey's leap

Sanjay Trivedi was troubled. He wanted a temporary and quick fix, but the psychiatrist was suggesting a permanent, partially risky and long-term solution. Trivedi had been under treatment and on medication for many years now. The medicines had been helping him sleep, but of late his troubles had mounted and they had become ineffective.

Trivedi attributed his troubles to depression. Whenever he came face to face with Sanchini, his brain seemed to strain against his skull, threatening to explode. He would often make an excuse to avoid facing her. The entire media fraternity was aware of this. Trivedi also saw the sarcastic smiles and the hushed whispers that began whenever he and Sanchini found themselves in close proximity. But Sanchini was not in the same predicament as him. She appeared nonchalant and gave off a I-have-moved-on vibe. But in Trivedi's mind the incident was fresh, as if it was only yesterday that he had started living with Sanchini.

At one point, they were the power couple of journalism. For Trivedi, it was the peak of his career as an investigative journalist. His reportage had been credited with sending Yatin Sathe and other policemen to jail. Compared to Trivedi, Sanchini's success and youth both were on the decline. She was five years older than him.

Trivedi, who kept breaking one sensational incident after the other, was surprised when Sanchini broke some news of her own. She was pregnant, but Trivedi was not the father. It was an old managing editor of a news channel, whom she married soon after. In the media fraternity and on social media, Trivedi became the laughing stock. Everyone was talking about how an investigative journalist who gathered inside news had been oblivious of the man inside his girlfriend's bedroom.

After this episode, Trivedi slipped into depression. He took a break from journalism and had recently embarked on his second innings. It was a joke destiny played on him, he thought, that his success lay in Sathe's ruin. This time, too, he had exposed Sathe's exploits one after the other and regained his lost prestige. His health, however, remained questionable. The psychiatrist treating him had told him that his problem was probably not mental but a neurological disorder given the symptoms he was displaying: weakness, unclear speech, difficulty swallowing food, muscle stiffness, etc. If the situation worsened, the psychiatrist had warned, Trivedi could lose his memory.

The psychiatrist wrote him a prescription for some new medication and referred him to a neurologist.

After his session with the psychiatrist, Trivedi turned on his mobile phone to see what had transpired in the world in the past thirty minutes. With great difficulty, he managed to make it to a prescheduled appointment, but half an hour late. The home minister had called for an impromptu press conference, which Trivedi knew he had to attend. This was why he had left the court proceedings against Sathe midway, too.

The answer to the question that Trivedi had asked the home minister during the press conference did not come clearly but in a roundabout way; it was actually a deferred political response. But Trivedi knew that his question had created a premise for a new narrative. The focus had shifted from Sathe to the bigger players.

A WhatsApp video got delivered to Trivedi's phone, in which opposition leader Jitendra Nagpure was saying, 'We have just seen the home minister's press conference. He has taken credit for solving the Hasmukh murder case but avoided answering an important question. We think that Yatin Sathe is a small pawn in a big game. The people who handed him this case should be investigated and those who brought him back into the police force and made him the head of the CIU by ignoring all rules should be questioned.

'Who are these big players who have protected Sathe at every step? Who is attempting to protect them now? Both the Kuberia case and the Hasmukh murder case are connected. Why then are two different agencies investigating the matter? This matter cannot be investigated impartially by the state. We demand that the investigation be handed to the central agency, the NIA, so that it can conduct a neutral investigation. We will write to the central government about this.'

After seeing Nagpure's statement on the TV, Aman Choudhury noted the droplets of sweat forming on the forehead of Commissioner Mahavir Tomar who was seated in his air-conditioned office. He went ahead and handed him a bouquet of flowers, along with a birthday wish in Kuber's handwriting.

'Flowers in this state? What a joke! But if it's from Kuber, I accept,' said Commissioner Tomar.

Aman said, 'Actually, Kuber Sir was of the opinion that a bouquet would not be appropriate under the current circumstances, but you know Dhruv Baba.'

Commissioner Tomar knew Kuber's son, Dhruv. He was trying to remind Tomar through the bouquet. With a forced smile, Commissioner Tomar thanked Aman and said, 'You already know ... what's happening ... my position ... I paid so much money for this post and have recovered only half the amount.'

Aman Choudhury nodded in agreement. He knew Mahavir Tomar, who was a friend of Kuber's, was the kind of policeman who believed in fighting it out till the end without caring about whether he was in the right or wrong.

'Benjamin Franklin had said, "Out of adversity comes opportunity." In Indian politics, this principle has been used successfully many times in the past few years. I don't know why policemen have not been able to take advantage of this. See how your junior officer, Arya, is playing the game,' Aman said and got up. He once again wished Commissioner Tomar a happy birthday and left the office.

Commissioner Tomar's brain, through the Wi-Fi of Aman Choudhury, had plugged into the network of despicability and got activated. He knew that he was no longer under the patronage of the home minister and that he was the next target. He had to do something, and he had to do it quickly. With agonizing helplessness, the powerful Commissioner Tomar called up the central government's favoured officer, IPS Naren Arya. The two did not like each other.

After taking the credit for solving the Hasmukh murder case, Home Minister Sardeshpande had regained some lost prestige, but he was still on a slippery political plane. He knew that the opposition would go all out to target the commissioner. This time he did not want to lag behind. He wanted to be proactive and take the wind out of the opposition's sails.

Sardeshpande was no saint. He was as corrupt as the rest of the ministers. The practice of taking money from police officers in lieu of important posts had been prevalent in Maharashtra for the past twenty-five years. What had pinched him this time was the fact that despite having no role to play in both the Kuberia case and Hasmukh Jain's murder, he had been targeted the most. It was the worst he had seen in his political career, and Sardeshpande held Commissioner Tomar responsible. Not only had Tomar hidden information from him, but he had also fed him wrong information. Tomar had encouraged Sathe, a man with a tendency to do the wrong things, and had broken the traditional systems of the Mumbai Police by running it like a dictatorship.

When Sardeshpande went through the ATS report, he discovered that the Scorpio that had been left outside Kuberia was reported stolen a few days before the incident. The theft complaint was registered at Vikroli police station. As per Mumbai Police protocol, all police stations fall under the joint commissioner (law and order). The investigation into the Kuberia case had initially been handed to the CIU, which came under the purview of the joint commissioner (crime). Both the joint commissioners reported to Commissioner Tomar. Both were senior IPS posts.

The home minister thought that maybe the joint commissioners knew something about the case, but had kept quiet because of the commissioner's dictatorial attitude. Now, because the state government had lost faith in Commissioner

Tomar, perhaps they could reveal some facts about their boss so that there would be strong grounds based on which action could be taken against him. Immediately, he summoned both the joint commissioners for a meeting.

Commissioner Mahavir Tomar did not have much of a choice. He had to take a decision about the condition IPS Arya had placed before him when he had asked for help. Arya had pointed out that if a branch becomes weak, then a smart monkey jumps to a stronger branch. Tomar now had to choose between the devil and the deep blue sea. He had to decide if he wanted to continue swinging from one branch—the state government—or jump on to another branch—the Centre. The ruling party at the Centre would not let go of any opportunity to humiliate its rival in the state. Tomar knew he would have to choose his new boss wisely.

It's easy to choose between the good and the bad, but choosing between two wrongs is difficult. When time is of the essence, you end up taking a chance rather than making a well-thought-out choice. Tomar speculated that if he stayed with the state government, he would probably be let off lightly in the Hasmukh murder case—investigated by the state's ATS—but would not be spared by the centre's agency, the NIA, in the Kuberia case. If he sided with the ruling party at the Centre, then the NIA would grant him some respite, but the ATS would give him a tough time in the Hasmukh murder case.

Commissioner Tomar couldn't help but wonder that his decision would become easier if both cases were investigated by one agency. He was weighing the pros and cons when he received the news that Home Minister Sardeshpande had called his subordinates—joint commissioner (law and order) and joint commissioner (crime)—for a meeting. He smelt danger. Neither the home minister nor the joint commissioners had bothered to inform him about this meeting. However, this made Commissioner Tomar's decision easy. He called up IPS Arya and informed him that the monkey was ready to swing onto a new and stronger branch but on one condition.

It was evening by the time the court was about to adjourn the day-long incomplete hearing until tomorrow. The NIA's IG Rohtagi stepped out of the courtroom to receive an urgent call. He came back almost running and informed the court that the central home ministry had just issued an order as per which the Hasmukh murder case was being transferred to the NIA for investigation. He added that the order was being faxed to the court as well.

Everyone was stumped, including Yatin Sathe and the lawyer for the ATS. Because the court had to study that order and the ATS lawyer had to take instructions from the state government, the judge announced a thirty-minute break, after which the court proceedings were to resume. It was clear that the court would now be in session for a longer period than usual.

Joint Commissioner (law and order) Namit Vikhe and Joint Commissioner (crime) Nitin Bharadwaj had been waiting for the moment when the political leadership would ask them about Commissioner Tomar's modus operandi. They knew by now that the commissioner no longer had the blessings of the state government. It was their time to be heard.

Both Vikhe and Bharadwaj were senior and capable officers. For decades, joint commissioner-level officers commanded respect and exercised influence. But the moment Tomar took over as commissioner, he took away the joint commissioner's crucial rights, especially Bharadwaj, and reduced them to being glorified clerks. This led to an officer who was five ranks junior to the joint commissioner, an assistant police inspector like Yatin Sathe, poking his nose in every department. The order of rank was bypassed completely. Officers like the additional commissioner, the DCP, the assistant commissioner and senior inspectors had to take orders from Sathe.

The CIU, headed by Yatin Sathe, and the rest of the Crime Branch units came under the joint commissioner (crime). But last year all high-profile cases had been allotted to Sathe, as if no other capable officer existed in the force. Sathe, in turn, reported directly to the commissioner and did not update the joint commissioner (crime) on the progress made.

Overstepping his boundaries, Sathe had also got into the habit of thundering orders at the personnel in the police stations that fell under the joint commissioner (law and order). He carried out raids on bars and nightclubs and extorted money from them. He also collected heavy sums of protection money from builders. His extortion tactics were an open secret in the police department, but everyone kept quiet because he was the commissioner's special man.

Sathe had started functioning as an independent unit within the Mumbai Police, overrunning established procedures whenever he wanted. He was like an animal freed after being chained for seventeen years, one that pounced on anyone and anything it saw. Only Commissioner Tomar could keep Sathe in check.

Both the joint commissioners spoke openly with the home minister. However, they did not mention the name of Sathe's political handler, a member of the ruling party and a minister.

They thought that it was better to not mess with the political leadership of the state. Their targets were Commissioner Tomar and Sathe only.

Both the joint commissioners expounded on how both Sathe's reinstatement and appointment as the CIU head had met with objection. Despite a written objection submitted by the joint commissioner, Rohtagi, Commissioner Tomar had used his special privileges to support Sathe. In fact, the commissioner had scolded any complainant and ignored all objections against Sathe being given high-profile cases and interfering with the work of other departments.

The joint commissioners added that both in the Kuberia and Hasmukh murder cases, the commissioner had repeatedly instructed the two joint commissioners to not take any action. They were also verbally asked not to cooperate with the NIA and the ATS.

When the home minister had heard the two joint commissioners and was satisfied, he called the chief minister. The three of them then left for the chief minister's house.

Before leaving for the chief minister's house from the court, Aman Choudhury observed the journalists reporting live from outside the gates. It was dark. The extended session had finally ended at 8.30 p.m. Choudhury's gaze rested on Sanjay Trivedi.

Trivedi had reported the maximum breaking news stories and exclusive information in this case. But compared to what he looked like on TV, Trivedi was pale and sickly in person. He was leaning against a pillar for support and it appeared as though he would collapse without it. Choudhury attributed his tiredness to the long hours.

Trivedi, meanwhile, noticed a white Range Rover go by behind the camera. He could not see the face of the person inside, but he caught the shine of a locket. He continued to report without being distracted. 'The NIA informed the court that because the Kuberia explosives case and the Hasmukh murder case are connected and dependent on each other, as per the instructions of the central home ministry, the NIA has decided to take over the investigation in the Hasmukh murder case as well. The lawyer representing the ATS objected to this and said that law and order are state subjects, and that the ATS has in fact already solved the case. The NIA, however, told the court that since the central home ministry's notification has already been issued, it will prevail over the state's jurisdiction and the ATS should let the NIA take over the Hasmukh murder case. This led to a showdown between the NIA and the ATS. Finally, the judge announced his decision in favour of the NIA and instructed the ATS to hand over all evidence, paperwork and the custody of Sathe's arrested accomplices to the NIA. This is a huge setback for the ATS. In fact, it's a huge setback for Maharashtra as well, whose home minister had vouched just this afternoon that the state had cracked the Hasmukh murder case.'

While speaking, Trivedi had managed to glance at his mobile. He could not read the entire message, but he did see 'CM HOUSE' in capital letters.

On the way to the chief minister's house, Home Minister Sardeshpande got to know that the Hasmukh murder case had been handed over to the NIA. Despite the disappointment, he was relieved that he had called a press conference in time to take credit for solving the case. But his political sixth sense warned him that the central government would create trouble for the state government through the NIA. He wanted to share this apprehension with the chief minister. He decided to meet the chief minister alone before calling the joint commissioners inside.

Commissioner Tomar was not surprised when the chief minister summoned him late that night. His sources had informed him about the home minister and the joint commissioners meeting the chief minister earlier that day. He knew he could be called any time. He was not just the Mumbai Police commissioner. He was first and foremost a policeman, which was why the head of the state police, the DGP (director general of police), had also been summoned. Before getting ready to leave, he read the reply ACP Mahesh Phalke had sent to his message. He then drafted and sent an answer himself.

Sanjay Trivedi, along with other media personnel, waited outside the chief minister's bungalow. They had not been granted entry. A while ago, Commissioner Mahavir Tomar and the Maharashtra DGP, Nagesh Dixit, had reached the chief minister's residence. Speculations were rife. It was midnight. With a throbbing headache, Trivedi stood against a tree and waited.

After the meeting with the chief minister, Commissioner Tomar came out with panic evident on his face. He saw Aman Choudhury in the waiting room but left without greeting him. After some time, DGP Dixit emerged. He sat in his car and drove off as well. Like Tomar, he did not talk to the waiting media.

Choudhury had been waiting patiently for a while now. His appointment had been fixed in advance, but he had been made to wait despite arriving on time. The DGP and the commissioner had arrived after him, but they were sent in straight to the chief minister.

Moments later, the chief minister's secretary informed Choudhury that the minister would not be able to meet him. Kuber's son, Dhruv, had sought the appointment. Despite this, Kuber's special man, Choudhury, was denied an audience. This was unprecedented. Getting up, Choudhury picked up the file labelled 'Kuberia Helipad'.

The next morning, the first thing Sanjay Trivedi did was go to a hospital. He had been avoiding the tests prescribed by the psychiatrist for some time, but the increasing pain and his deteriorating health had forced him to reconsider. He had just left the hospital when a video of Home Minister Sardeshpande's statement was released on social media.

'We have removed Mahavir Tomar from the post of the Mumbai Police commissioner. He has been transferred to the welfare department, and this is not a routine transfer. The investigation of the NIA and the Maharashtra ATS have brought some facts to light. With Tomar as the chief of the Mumbai Police, some officers working under him made serious mistakes that cannot be forgiven. He is also being removed so that the investigation can be carried out properly and without obstructions. Junior or senior, if found guilty, no one will be spared,' Sardeshpande said.

This message went viral everywhere. It was circulated everywhere: on social media, within the police fraternity and the political world.

Normally, the government would have explained such a change as a routine transfer. This was the first time that a home minister had openly spoken against a senior officer.

A dishonoured Mahavir Tomar did not bother to complete the handover formalities and drove off within a few minutes of Sardeshpande's video being released. Barely five minutes after he left, DGP Nagesh Dixit entered and took over as the new commissioner of Mumbai. It was all over before the media could get to the Commissionerate.

In most states of India, the most prestigious post in the police is that of the state DGP. However, in Maharashtra, even though the DGP may be the highest in terms of rank, the most prominent post is that of the Mumbai Police commissioner. All of the state's IPS officers carry the ambition of holding that post. The post of DGP ranks second.

Interestingly, in terms of seniority, the posts of commissioner and DGP are the same. Formally, however, the DGP is considered to be senior.

Mumbai is the country's entertainment and commercial capital. It is also the hub of the underworld. The glamour, power and networking that the Mumbai Police commissioner enjoys is unparalleled. It was with this in mind that Nagesh Dixit left his post as the DGP of the whole of Maharashtra and agreed to become the commissioner of Mumbai.

The headlines, however, did not proclaim who the new commissioner was. They flashed the news of how Mahavir Tomar had been disgracefully removed from the post. For a person like Tomar, who had had a controversial but magnificent career, this was utterly shameful and humiliating.

Rumours were abounding. They ranged from Tomar's interrogation to possible arrest. Some news channels kept Tomar's role confined to that of a mentor to Yatin Sathe, while others called him the mastermind of the Kuberia incident.

Meanwhile, Home Minister Sardeshpande had shown that he was in control and that politicians held the real power.

And then suddenly, there was an explosion. A bomb seemed to have exploded.

12

The letter bomb

The 'letter bomb' from Mahavir Tomar caused a major political explosion in Maharashtra. Disappointed at being disgracefully removed from the post of commissioner and dumped into a lousy posting, Tomar wrote a letter to the chief minister and then leaked it to the media.

In that letter, Tomar shamelessly declared himself honest. He claimed that he had been made the scapegoat so that the attention could be diverted away from the real culprit. He wrote that the allegations made by Home Minister Sardeshpande regarding the Kuberia case were false. In fact, he indicted the home minister.

Citing a recent meeting he had had with the chief minister, Tomar wrote: 'In that meeting, I told you, the deputy chief minister and other senior ministers about the disturbances the home minister was creating in the Kuberia case. Home Minister Sardeshpande was interfering with the work of the police by bypassing me, the police commissioner, and giving orders directly to the junior officers.'

And then Tomar mentioned an alleged order from the home minister about recovering hundred crore rupees, which also involved Yatin Sathe. 'In the past few months, the home minister had been calling API Yatin Sathe to his house, and ACP Mahesh Phalke had been given the target of extorting money to the tune of hundred crores. The home minister had told Sathe that Mumbai has over three thousand big bars, nightclubs, restaurants, shops and hookah parlours, from where at least three lakh rupees from each such bar could be collected monthly to meet the target. Sathe informed me about this incident the day it happened and I forbade him from doing the home minister's bidding. Sathe's call records can be checked for confirmation.'

In support of his statement, Tomar shared WhatsApp chats between him and ACP Falke, which had information pertaining to this allegation. Tomar alleged that he was also pressurized into targeting the ruling opposition party at the Centre. He used the context of a case in which an MP from a neighbouring state had committed suicide in Mumbai. The home minister wanted to run the case in Mumbai on the basis of the suicide note, but Tomar had refused, saying that the state he was a representative of should look into it.

This letter sparked a scandal not only in Maharashtra but also in the entire country. For the very first time, a high-ranking police officer had openly indicted a state home minister for such a big crime.

The opposition wasted no time in grabbing this opportunity and demanded Home Minister Sardeshpande's resignation. Sardeshpande, meanwhile, denied Tomar's allegations and accused the former commissioner of venting his anger over his dismissal. He, in turn, accused Tomar of dancing to the tunes of the opposition party and the Centre.

Interestingly, Sardeshpande and Tomar had had each other's backs till a week ago. The home minister had been Tomar's guardian and Tomar had been his most favoured officer. But now swords had been drawn.

The NIA had collected all evidence and information pertaining to the Hasmukh murder case from the ATS. Sathe had got to know about Tomar's letter when the NIA officers came to interrogate him after collecting evidence from the ATS.

Sathe felt sadistic pleasure at the thought that though he was in the NIA's custody, outside another incident connected to him had taken a peculiar turn. Suddenly, Sathe could see a sliver of light at the end of this dark tunnel. His cunning mind got to work on how he could take advantage of the letter.

The media now had a third case to focus on. It was all connected: the Kuberia explosives case, the Hasmukh murder case and now the extortion case. At the Mumbai Press Club that night, a lot of senior journalists were heard contributing their two bits to the situation.

The journalists who covered the crime beat said that Mahavir Tomar calling himself honest was as unbelievable a claim as someone having a fifty-six-inch chest. These were the same journalists in whose eyes Tomar was a corrupt but effective police officer. On the other hand, the journalists covering politics were heard saying that money reaching ruling politicians through systematic recovery chains was an established truth and an open secret. According to them, Tomar had raised the issue about the money only because he was going to be labelled as the mastermind in the Kuberia and Hasmukh murder cases. For the business reporters, who had unearthed major scams, hundred crores was a paltry amount. The entertainment beat reporters, meanwhile, saw a tremendous plot for a web series. Some saw Yatin Sathe as Pablo Escobar from *Narcos*, while others wanted Pratik Gandhi of *Scam 1992* fame to essay the role of Sathe.

Sitting alone at a table in a corner, drinking Old Monk and swiping right on Tinder, Sanjay Trivedi had a hunch. He matched the timing of Tomar's dismissal as the commissioner with that of the WhatsApp chats between Tomar and ACP Mahesh Phalke. He drained his glass in one go, placed the money on the table and left immediately.

On his way out, he met some speculating journalists who told him that only this news would trend for a week and nothing else. They were right.

It started trending from the next day, i.e., Thursday.

Thursday

The Mumbai Police had probably never acted so fast. The new commissioner, Nagesh Dixit, had completed the inquiry into the extortion scandal in just twenty-four hours. His report highlighted, on the basis of statements from the joint commissioners, the mistakes that Mahavir Tomar had committed while he was the commissioner. This included the irregularity of reinstating Yatin Sathe into the police force and making him the head of the CIU despite written objections from senior officers.

Bypassing the rules, Tomar was working directly with API Yatin Sathe. The internal intelligence report was made public. It clearly stated that, on Tomar's instructions, Sathe had extorted money. Here, ACP Mahesh Phalke's U-turn astounded people. Changing his stance, ACP Phalke said that Tomar had pressurized him into creating a fake WhatsApp chat with the home minister pertaining to the extortion scandal. He added that all information in the chat was false.

The report gave Home Minister Sardeshpande a clean chit and dealt a heavy blow to Mahavir Tomar.

Even Yatin Sathe was hit when he was produced before the court after his two-day remand. The NIA told the court that they were going to apply the UAPA, the Unlawful Activities (Prevention) Act to the case against Sathe, in addition to Hasmukh's murder charge. The court extended the NIA's custody of Sathe by five days. Being a policeman himself, Sathe knew that the UAPA did not have a distinct definition of terrorism. This meant that the NIA could torture him for a long time using an arbitrary interpretation.

Sanjay Trivedi had noticed Yatin Sathe's face turn a ghostly white. He read up about the UAPA till late that night. As per the UAPA, an organization or person can be declared a terrorist based on suspicion alone. Under this Act, it is not necessary to establish a connection between the accused and any terrorist organization. It has stringent provisions, which when applied gave the NIA the right to take action in a state without informing the state police. Also, it meant that an accused's time in custody of the police or the NIA would go up. Yes, s/he could get bail, but it was rare.

Under the UAPA, if the NIA chief wanted to, he could get the property of the accused confiscated and have him/her sentenced to at least seven years in jail. So far, the UAPA had been used against the terrorist organization Jaish-e-Mohammed's chief Masood Azhar, Lashkar-e-Taiba's chief Hafiz Saeed and terrorists Zaki-ur-Rehman Lakhvi and Dawood Ibrahim.

Trivedi's eyes darted outside the window. What he saw turned his suspicion into belief. His journalistic sixth sense told him that he was being monitored.

Friday

Reporter Sanjay Trivedi was in earnest pursuit of a gentleman since the morning, taking care about not being spotted. In the afternoon, he saw the man enter a mosque in a Pathani suit and was stunned. He had guessed the man's connection to the case, but not once had Trivedi fathomed that the man posing as a Hindu for the world would be offering Friday prayers in a mosque like a devout Muslim.

A lot of questions began to arise in Trivedi's mind. *Why would a Muslim man pose as a Hindu? Or why would a Hindu pretend to be a Muslim and go into a mosque?*

Concurrently, Mahavir Tomar went straight to the high court as soon as he landed in Mumbai that afternoon. He had left for New Delhi early that morning for a purpose unknown to anyone else. His lawyer was already in the court. The moment he signed the petition, it was submitted. The hearing was scheduled for two days later, on a Monday. The famous lawyer whom Tomar had hired charged ten lakhs in cash for an appearance. This sparked a debate all over social media: How could a government employee, an IPS officer, afford such an expensive lawyer?

The same night, a message began circulating amongst the Maharashtra police officers. It said that anyone who wanted to register a complaint of harassment or corruption against Mahavir Tomar could write to the Maharashtra Home Ministry in the next two days.

Saturday

Early morning, former commissioner Mahavir Tomar reached the NIA office for questioning. He was there for hours.

After Tomar, former encounter specialist Dilip Verma marked his attendance at the NIA office. Verma was associated with Sathe as a troubleshooter, a spin doctor and sometimes a companion during his recent exploits. Verma was also detained at the NIA office for ten hours in the name of interrogation.

Till the time Tomar and Verma were in the NIA office, the media kept speculating that they would be the next ones to get arrested. But both Tomar and Verma left the office smiling, as if they had just returned from a vacation. The NIA, too, changed its stance and informed the media that both Tomar and Verma had been questioned as witnesses. The question that was raised was why were the two of them, who should have been arrested after being questioned as suspects, now being considered witnesses.

After Tomar and Verma left, Sathe, who was in the NIA lockup, started thinking about his meeting with the two and the questions that had risen in his mind. *Should he become a part of the new equation? Should he accept the offer of NIA, Tomar and Verma? If Tomar and Verma had accepted the offer, was it based on the condition that they would not be arrested? Should he consider enmity with the state government or continue to suffer at the hands of the Centre's NIA? Now, with the UAPA being applied to the case, his getting bail looked difficult. Which deal would work in his favour? Instead of being considered a supercop, would he have to live with the tag of a terrorist? Tomar and Verma knew many of his other dark secrets, the disclosure of which could lead to new cases being registered against him. Given this, did he have any option except to support Tomar?*

Sunday

A letter leaked by the NIA ruined everybody's lazy Sunday morning.

Yatin Sathe had written a four-page letter in his own handwriting, reaffirming the allegations Tomar had levelled against Home Minister Sardeshpande. Based on the premise set by Tomar's letter, Sathe said that Sardeshpande had given him a target of extorting hundred crores. He named a cabinet minister, Pranil Sanap, as his political handler and added that Sanap had given him verbal instructions to extort an additional fifty crores from other sources.

The people who were well-versed with Tomar and Sathe's corrupt nature could not believe that Sathe had written that Tomar had asked him not to do the minister's bidding. Sathe added that he, too, had chosen not to do it because he knew it was a crime. The opposition party, however, was convinced.

Till yesterday, the opposition leader who had called every word uttered by Sathe and Tomar a lie, who had considered all their actions to be wrong, was now proclaiming their statements to be true. The opposition demanded the resignation of both Sardeshpande and Sanap.

While Sanap resorted to the drama of swearing on his children's heads in front of the media, Sardeshpande decided to handle this matter in a different way.

A bureaucrat in the Maharashtra home ministry, that was located in the Mantralaya, was wasting away his Sunday. Till late in the evening, he sorted through the most incriminating complaints received against senior IPS officer Mahavir Tomar.

That night, when Tomar went to a police station to file an FIR against Sardeshpande, the station-in-charge refused to register it. The policeman who trembled at the sight of Tomar till a week ago was refusing to file an FIR to his face. Tomar had expected this.

Sanjay Trivedi reached home around midnight after an entire day of reporting. When the date changed at midnight, he filed three Right to Information (RTI) applications online. He knew that the civil aviation department, the municipal corporation and the state home ministry would not disclose any information directly on such a sensitive issue. But, given the legal compulsion, all three departments were bound to respond to the applications eventually, even though they may do so after a delay of a few days.

Monday

Sanjay Trivedi was sitting with his doctor who was going through his reports. Trivedi was told that if a surgery was not done soon, his nerves could explode and put his life at risk. It was a specialized surgery. Trivedi calculated the amount of money he would need to get operated on in a good private hospital, by a good neurosurgeon and his team. He also worked out the post-recovery costs. The total amount he reached was higher than two years of his salary put together. He did not have so much money, and the medical insurance would also cover only a portion of it.

When the doctor asked when he wanted to get the procedure done, Trivedi did not have an answer. He left the hospital and went straight to the high court.

Mahavir Tomar had filed a petition in the high court, asking for the CBI to question Home Minister Sardeshpande in the extortion case and for arbitrarily taking the decision to remove him as the police commissioner. The state government's lawyer strongly opposed this petition. The biggest ground for the objection was that, sometime last year, the Maharashtra government had withdrawn the consent given to the CBI to conduct investigations in the state. The CBI no longer had the right to investigate any matter in the state of Maharashtra.

The CBI faced a roadblock that other central agencies, like the ED (Enforcement Directorate) and DRI (Directorate of Revenue Intelligence), did not have to worry about. In the distribution of powers between the Centre and the states, the police came under the state governments. So, the first right to investigate belonged to the state police. The CBI, on the other hand, was formed under the Delhi Special Police Establishment Act of 1946, as per which it had to seek permission from a state government before conducting an investigation.

In the last decade, the ruling party at the Centre had increased its meddling in the affairs of states ruled by opposition parties. Because of the apprehension about the Centre using the CBI for its own political gains, eight opposition-ruled states (Rajasthan, West Bengal, Jharkhand, Kerala, Maharashtra, Chhattisgarh, Punjab and Mizoram) had decided to withdraw the common consent initially given to the CBI to investigate cases in the respective states.

Tomar's lawyers argued that under Article 226 of the Constitution, the high court had the right to order a CBI inquiry into the matter and that the consent of the state government was not required in such a case.

The court, however, reprimanded Tomar's lawyers. It said that since Tomar was such a senior police officer, he should have known the law. As per the rules, he should have filed an FIR first.

Tomar's lawyers then presented evidence to the court that Tomar had tried to do so last night, but the officer-in-charge at the station had refused to register one. The state government's counsel had no information about Tomar's move and thus could not offer a satisfactory answer.

The court heard both sides and then announced its order. It took note of the fact that the FIR was not registered despite a complaint being filed at the police station. The court then stated that since the allegation was against the state's home minister, the circumstances were unusual. The police, which came under the state's home ministry, could not carry out a neutral investigation, which was why the CBI would look into the matter.

The home minister would now be questioned by the CBI, a matter of great shame for the state government.

With a CBI inquiry ordered, Sunil Sardeshpande resigned on moral grounds.

Ultimately, the NIA was now investigating both the Kuberia case and the Hasmukh murder case. The CBI was to investigate the extortion case. And both the NIA and the CBI came under the aegis of the central government.

The investigation had turned into a competition with everyone wanting to one-up the other. But the day had not ended.

Tomar had not even been able to celebrate his small victory when, based on the complaints received against him, the state government announced separate investigations. It wasn't just a matter of revenge any more; the misdeeds of Tomar and his henchmen were out in the open. They were safe till they were serving the state government. But now the circumstances had changed with numerous complaints being received. What followed was expected as per retaliatory proceedings.

1. An FIR was filed against Tomar and the officers close to him because a troubled police officer had alleged that, during his previous tenure, Tomar had pressurized him to shield some of the accused. When he did not agree, he was physically tortured and a false case was lodged against him.
2. Another officer said that he had filed an FIR against an influential person. When he did not help this person as instructed by Tomar, he was suspended. Tomar had allegedly demanded two crores to revoke the suspension.
3. One builder had alleged that Tomar and former encounter specialist Dilip Verma, in cahoots with each other, had extorted four crores from him in lieu of a false case. Apart from him, two other businessmen accused Tomar of extorting fifty lakh each from them by threatening to indict them in a false case.
4. Tomar was accused of having ties with the underworld, after which the DGP of Maharashtra ordered an investigation into the matter.
5. To investigate the allegations of corruption levelled against the home minister in Tomar's letter to the chief minister, the state government constituted an inquiry committee headed by a retired high court judge and gave the powers of a civil court to this committee.

Tuesday

Mahavir Tomar went to the CBI office and got his statement officially recorded.

At the same time, a new drama unfolded at the court. In every hearing so far, Yatin Sathe had either sought to be kept in jail or be granted bail, all to avoid the NIA custody. But today, he turned around and asked the court to send him to the NIA's custody, so that the CBI could reach him there and record his statement. Sathe's plea was accepted.

The CBI, infamous for its slow pace of investigation, took off at warp speed. Sathe found CBI officers waiting for him in the NIA lockup after the court hearing. They went ahead and recorded his statement in the capacity of a witness. Sathe corroborated Tomar's allegations and reiterated that Sardeshpande and Pranil Sanap had instructed him to extort crores of rupees.

In the evening, after recording Sathe's statement, the CBI team left to question former home minister Sardeshpande. The questioning, which began at sundown at Sardeshpande's residence, went on till late in the night. An army of renowned lawyers stood guard inside Sardeshpande's residence, while the media waited outside. When the CBI team left, thousands of Sardeshpande's supporters could be seen outside his residence, indulging in furious sloganeering against the CBI and the central government. The police, too, had deployed additional forces to deal with any untoward incident and to exert mental pressure on the CBI.

Sitting in a white Range Rover a little away from Sardeshpande's residence, Aman Choudhury was repeatedly scrolling through his iPad to see the copies of the three RTI applications filed by Sanjay Trivedi, which Kuber's son, Dhruv, had forwarded to him. Choudhury had guessed that Kuber's well-wishers in the departments concerned would have leaked copies of these applications to Dhruv. On Dhruv's instructions alone, he had come to meet Sardeshpande. He waited patiently for the crowd of supporters, the media and the lawyers to disperse so that he could go in and meet the former home minister. On the back seat lay the Kuberia Helipad file.

Wednesday

The next morning saw the ED (Enforcement Directorate) jumping into the extortion scandal. An agency under the central government, the ED's job is to monitor and investigate financial crimes in the country. The ED also has the power to make seizures and arrests and conduct searches against those indicted on charges of money laundering.

The ED, in its sixty-five-year-old history, had not received the amount of media attention that it had got in the recent past. In recent years, the ED had also begun to dive into matters in which it was not approached directly by the complainant. From the suicide case of an actor to targeting the leaders of opposition parties, the ED's interference was increasing. Like the CBI, it was also accused of working for the benefit of its political masters.

The ED registered a case of money laundering against Sardeshpande on the basis of the CBI's FIR. The ED team then went to the NIA office to record Yatin Sathe's statement. After that, the team left to question Sardeshpande.

Given the ED's recent history, the state government was prepared for this manoeuvre by the Centre. In response, Tomar was questioned twice that day—by the Anti-Corruption Bureau (ACB) and by the home secretary.

The ACB immediately started investigating the allegations of corruption against Tomar and also the possession of disproportionate assets by him, which involved twenty acres of land purchased in a nearby district and owning expensive apartments in Mumbai. Along with this, Tomar was also accused of forcibly taking gold biscuits from subordinate officers on Diwali.

The home secretary, meanwhile, started an inquiry into Tomar's simultaneous use of two government accommodations, which was in violation of government rules.

Yet another interesting incident took place that evening. The NIA, which had been seeking Yatin Sathe's custody all this while, told the court that he should be sent to jail. The agency, explaining why it no longer needed Sathe's custody, said that its investigation was complete and that the motive in the Kuberia case had finally been identified after Sathe had explained his intent.

This was sensational news. New love seemed to be blossoming between Sathe and the NIA. Sathe had disclosed his motive in the Kuberia case and the NIA was now mollycoddling him. However, this gave rise to new questions.

The media camped outside the NIA office all night long. Everyone knew how an assistant inspector of the Mumbai Police, Yatin Sathe, had executed the Kuberia incident. People were curious about why Sathe had parked a car filled with explosives outside Kuberia, the house of Asia's and India's richest man. Also, it became important to know what was the connection between Sathe's sudden confession of his motive and the events of last week.

13

The myth of the supercop

Sanjay Trivedi's experience told him that an internal settlement had been reached. He had reasons to believe this was the case. Long hours awaited him as he prepared to delve deeper to understand what was unfolding behind the scenes.

Today, the ever-increasing pain in his head was unbearable. To ease the throbbing, he took a double dose of the pills. The doctor had strictly instructed him to take a double dose only in case of an emergency, but a single dose offered no relief. In fact, he had taken a double dose for the second consecutive day to ensure illness didn't come in the way of his work.

The medicine took thirty minutes to kick in. Trivedi collapsed in his chair, shut his eyes and began to think. He began to assess the entire episode. After the developments of yesterday, two camps emerged. In one camp was the state's ruling party, former home minister Sardeshpande, the state's

ATS, the Mumbai Police, the Anti-Corruption Bureau and the journalists supporting the state. The other camp comprised the Centre's ruling party, the NIA, the CBI, the ED, former Mumbai commissioner Tomar and the journalists supporting the central government.

As the case progressed, the people and agencies involved started gravitating towards one of these two camps. Swords were perpetually drawn on both sides with each camp opening so many inquiries and investigations against the other that it became impossible to identify who had the upper hand.

And whether they won or lost, each camp stood to suffer heavy collateral damage; it was inevitable. Both camps had made it clear that they were in it for the long haul, that they could play this game of one-upmanship better than the other and that they would stoop to any level to emerge victorious. Everyone was in danger and there was nothing or no one too dear, which is an ideal situation to reach a compromise.

The next morning the media personnel, who had been up and waiting for information all night, were overjoyed when the NIA informed them about Sathe's motive in the Kuberia case. The dominating headlines were: 'The final link has been resolved' and 'Only the motive was left, that has been disclosed'.

Yatin Sathe had moved to the Arthur Road Jail from the NIA lockup. He was satisfied with the arrangements made for him in his special cell. He had accepted that he would not get bail any time soon, so he had decided to make his life in jail as comfortable as possible. A mobile phone, an iPad, a water dispenser, food from home, clean bedding, a fellow prisoner to serve him and protection from the gangs in jail—all had been arranged unofficially for him.

Two days ago, former commissioner Mahavir Tomar and former encounter specialist Dilip Verma had been to the NIA office for questioning. After that, Sathe's cunning mind had got to work. He realized that the members of the two camps were playing him like a football. But in the present circumstances, no camp seemed to have the upper hand and neither could be sure of absolute victory. This was an ideal situation for Sathe to find opportunity in adversity. He grabbed the chance to become the referee instead. No matter who won or lost, the referee wasn't going to be affected.

The first delivery from Sathe in the form of motive of 'supercop' had taken place successfully. But he was yet to deliver the second instalment to the NIA.

The word 'supercop' was trending on social media. Ever since the NIA had told the media that Sathe's motive in the Kuberia incident was to become a supercop, the journalists had been busy exaggerating and dramatizing the news.

Accepting the NIA's statement as the truth, each and every news channel in the country broadcast the news that API Yatin Sathe of the Mumbai Police had executed the Kuberia incident so that he could later solve the case and emerge as a supercop. But his plan had gone awry, which led to the murder of the sole witness in the case, Hasmukh Jain. According to the NIA, Sathe had accepted this sequence of events.

A supercop is someone who goes above and beyond the regular demands of the post to create the image of an effective policeman. The fame of such a cop outshines that of film stars and cricketers; his very name makes the underworld and criminals tremble in fear; the most powerful of politicians call him directly; the media longs to interview him; he rules parallelly within the police department and remains untouched by the most senior of officers; he gets allotted the most number of high-profile cases and encounters; he is a person the corporate honchos desperately want to befriend. This was the glamour Sathe had seen seventeen years ago in his mentor Verma and rival Nitya Shetty. He wanted to make a bigger name for himself.

The media expounded on how Sathe wanted to compensate for the career setback he had faced by being away from the police force for seventeen years. In the last ten years, there had been no supercops in the state of Maharashtra. Sathe wanted to fill that vacuum. He wished that after a few years, when he retired, his name would be instated in the Mumbai Police's hall of fame. It was also communicated that Sathe wanted to launch a high-profile and modern security and detective agency. The tag of a supercop would have aided such a venture.

It seemed that everything had been set right in twenty-four hours; all's well that ends well. The way listeners await the end of a religious discourse, it seemed as if both camps were waiting eagerly in the same manner. But one pent-up outburst spoilt the entire show.

In the last eight years, the media had failed to remain neutral. Most channels and outlets were either devoted to the central government or to another party. Under these changed circumstances, social media maintained the sanctity of journalism. 'BhadaasForMedia.com', also called Bhadaas, was one outlet that published the inside scoop on major issues and scandals and was largely neutral.

A lot of media personnel went against the sycophant policies of their bosses. News that could not be reported in the channels and newspapers they worked for was published on social media anonymously. Such news pieces were also put out when the reporter was sure about something but had no evidence to back his/her claim. BhadaasForMedia.com had provisions in which the reporter could post an article without disclosing his/her name. It served the dual purpose of providing an outlet for pent-up frustration while ensuring that the job of a reporter remained secure.

Now, an article posted on Bhadaas dismissed the supercop theory in the Kuberia case. It connected the Kuberia case, the Hasmukh murder case and the extortion case, complete with a timeline of the sequence of events and how the parties involved had backpedalled several times.

The article propagated that by believing the supercop theory, the NIA was weakening its own case. It explained how Yatin Sathe would benefit under the various sections of law by using this theory.

The article had piqued the interest of all the people connected to these cases.

Here's what the article on Bhadaas read like:

The motive of wanting to emerge as a supercop is complete hogwash. With this theory, Yatin Sathe stands to benefit the most. Going forward, when the proceedings advance in court, Sathe's lawyers will present three arguments.

Firstly, under the law, it is required that motive has to be to cause an explosion, but Sathe's motive was not to cause an explosion. He did not want to harm anyone. Gelatin is not explosive by itself; it requires a detonator, which was not found by any investigating agency. Therefore, the allegation that Sathe's intention was to cause an explosion is false.

Secondly, it's easy to get your hands on gelatin. No special training or arrangement is needed to handle it. There is a detailed mention of how to handle explosive materials in the Explosives Act.

And thirdly, according to the law, a terrorist's motive would be to cause harm to the public or public property. But in this case, Sathe's target was two members of Kuber's family whose names were mentioned in the threat letter. It was the threat of possible action against a private individual, not a terrorist act against the public.

What will eventually happen is that Sathe will escape a stringent law like the UAPA and be booked under the IPC and Explosive Acts only. This will be similar to what happened in the case of actor Sanjay Dutt in the 1993 serial blast case, in which a strict law like TADA was not applied to him. Instead, he was punished under the Arms Act.

Sathe can meet a similar fate and then be in a less bad situation comparatively. He will get bail. The case will go on for years. First, the sessions court will announce its verdict, then the appeal against this verdict will be filed in the high court, and then the appeal against the high court's decision will be filed with the Supreme Court. A review petition against the decision of the Supreme Court will be filed and there will be another decision. Till the time this protracted legal battle ensues, Sathe will be out on bail. When he finally gets sentenced, he will have become a senior citizen and will try and use that in his favour.

In India, from killing a deer to killing people sleeping on the footpath by driving over them, the cases against the rich and famous have gone on for over two decades. Sathe's case might be the same.

The premise behind this act could be to make the agency accept Sathe's supercop theory as it is. If these doubts can arise in the mind of the author of this article, why have they not come to the experienced officers of the investigating agency and the legal department? Or is the investigating agency feigning ignorance despite being aware of each fact?

The writer has been covering this case since the first day, so please pay attention to these points:

Sathe always fought NIA custody and sought to be in jail. In turn, the NIA always contested Sathe being in jail and sought his custody for itself.

1. Then, former commissioner Mahavir Tomar accused former home minister Sardeshpande of extortion, and he mentioned Sathe. Sathe had not spoken about this case to anyone until then.
2. Sathe's mentors Verma and Tomar spent hours at the NIA office. The question is: Did they meet Sathe and plan with him, or were they being interrogated?
3. Sathe had a change of heart at the next court hearing. Unlike before, he requested to be in the NIA's custody, so that he could record his statement against the former home minister.
4. In the next court hearing, the NIA also had a change of heart and told the court that Sathe should be sent to judicial custody because he had disclosed the motive.

Sathe's biggest defence in court had been to question the absence of a motive, which the NIA had been unsuccessful in getting him to reveal. What happened suddenly after Tomar and Verma's visit? Was a deal struck, as part of which Sathe revealed the motive? What made Sathe surrender his biggest defence?

We must question whether Sathe, Tomar, Verma and the central agency have come to some agreement, based on which Sathe will reap long-term benefits and Tomar and Verma will be let off lightly? Despite Tomar and Verma's suspicious roles in the case, they have not been arrested and are being treated as witnesses.

There are two camps in this case: the first one has the state's ruling party, the state's home ministry, the state's ATS, the Mumbai Police, the ACB and the journalists supporting the state. The second camp has the Centre's ruling party, the NIA, the CBI, the ED, former commissioner Tomar and reporters supporting the central government.

So far, both the camps had been quarrelling, but now they seem to agree with this supercop theory. Didn't anyone think it was suspicious and absurd? Why this sudden consensus?

Had Yatin Sathe not agreed to declare a motive, there would not have been a consensus between the two camps. Sathe, knowing that he would not be acquitted quickly and honourably, decided to take maximum advantage of his limitation. A vicious person like him, with a devious mind, would not have done this without being given a safety net. He would have sought some assurance, monetary compensation for his family, a lesser sentence and provision of amenities in prison.

Sathe may think of himself as a smart alec, the new facilitator of this 'opportunity in adversity' deal, but he is nothing more than a joker and a pawn. Tomar and Verma's company is akin to riding on the back of a lion. Till the ride lasts, it's all good, but the moment you get off, the lion will devour you. Sathe needs to understand this MESSAGE. He is not half as smart as his guru, Verma.

Yours,
Unknown

Sathe had no doubt about who the author of this article was. In his cell inside the jail, reading the article on his iPad, and based on the language, sentences, style and furiousness expressed, he recognized the unknown author. Though the IP address could be used to trace the writer, it was not required in this case. No one knew this reporter better than Sathe because, seventeen years ago, Sathe had been at the receiving end of reporter Sanjay Trivedi's words.

But the last bit worried Sathe. He read it again: 'Sathe may think of himself as a smart alec, the new facilitator of this "opportunity in adversity" deal, but he is nothing more than a joker and a pawn. Tomar and Verma's company is akin to riding on the back of a lion. Till the ride lasts, it's all good, but the moment you get off, the lion will devour you. Sathe needs to understand this MESSAGE. *He is not half as smart as his guru, Verma.*'

The way the word 'message' had been highlighted did not escape Sathe's notice. Sathe felt as if Trivedi was trying to send him a message. He remembered what he had learned the night before his arrest, when he had left the ATS office after his interrogation.

A day before Sathe's arrest

Sathe had left the ATS office at night after a marathon session of questioning. Stopping his car on the way, the NIA officers had shoved into his hand the summons to appear for questioning the next day. Then his partner, Gajanan Jhende, had messaged and asked to meet. Sathe had arrived at the GPS location Jhende had sent. He had switched off the lights of his car and waited. After some time, Jhende arrived and got into the car.

Dilip Verma's special man, Jhende, who was out on parole, told Sathe about all the developments that had taken place in the case in the twelve hours that Sathe had spent at the ATS office. Finally, he gave Sathe Verma's message.

Actually, it had been a threat disguised as a message. Sathe was warned not to mention Verma in front of the investigators under any circumstances. In return, Varma would take care of Sathe's girlfriend, Nina Dias, in case anything unexpected happened.

Sathe knew that right from parking the Scorpio outside Kuberia to Hasmukh's murder, he might have led the team, but the people who had helped him were sourced by Verma. All of them were his henchmen. One indication from Verma, and they would have done to Sathe what they had done to Hasmukh.

One hidden meaning of Verma's message was that in case Sathe was arrested and incriminated Verma, Nina would be sent to the same place as Hasmukh. Now, Sathe was not as worried about Nina's life as he was about his black money, which Nina was to transfer to offshore accounts over the next two days.

Sathe's mind was in turmoil. On the one hand, he had led from the front in carrying out all the crimes. For twenty years, he had held all of Verma's dark exploits close to his heart. Like a faithful disciple, he had stood by Verma through thick and thin. But still, his guru had not only expressed distrust but also issued indirect threats.

Sathe, in a fit of rage, had turned on the ignition of his car. In a hurry, Jhende had disembarked just in time. What Sathe did not know was that the instant Jhende alighted from the car, the mobile in his pocket had vibrated. It had been the ATS team that had surrounded him and subsequently arrested him.

Driving at a high speed in anger, Sathe had thought of reporting for questioning the next day and fleeing with Nina at night. But unfortunately, Sathe was prematurely arrested by the NIA the next day.

Present

Sathe was in jail once again. The seventeen years, when he was out on bail, flashed before his eyes. He had left no stone unturned to stay afloat and remain relevant while out of the police force.

He had worked in the media as a consultant to crime shows, authored two books, created a messaging app and even joined a political party, but everywhere people had tried to take advantage of his notoriety rather than putting his skills to use. Despite the reinstatement, everyone wanted to cash in on his ignominiousness, just like the two camps were doing now.

Sathe had wanted to become a supercop, but he felt like a prostitute, someone who could be taken advantage of whenever, however and by whoever.

Verma, Sathe's idol, had laid the foundation to turn the CIU into 'criminals in uniform'. Now, he had broken Sathe's heart. Sathe started assessing the guru–chela (teacher–disciple) relationship, as suggested in Trivedi's article.

Then, he began to examine the truth from a different perspective. He had found the wanted criminals through mobile and internet surveillance, but Verma had hogged the credit for carrying out the encounter. But when a collective mistake was made in the line of duty, he had been made to bear the brunt of it alone.

Seventeen years ago, Sathe had not wanted to kill Nawaz. He had wanted to get a confession out of the alleged terrorist. Nawaz's death had been unintentional. Everyone had been involved in getting rid of the body, everyone had gone to jail, but despite being the CIU chief, Verma had been spared an arrest.

In the fake stamp scam of 2003, arrests were made from constables to a commissioner. But Verma had not been arrested. In the disproportionate assets case, Verma's junior Nitya Shetty and a lot of other policemen had been arrested, but Verma had evaded it once again despite having unaccountable money and assets. In the case of a fake encounter, Verma's subordinates went to jail, but he was acquitted.

In the last twenty years, Verma's contemporaries and rivals had been marginalized and punished for different reasons, but he alone had survived. He had survived each and every time by sacrificing his disciples.

Sathe's introspective thinking took him back to the Mahabharata, in which Guru Dronacharya had requested the thumb of his disciple Eklavya as guru dakshina (the tradition of offering payment or a gift to one's teacher or guru after the completion of training), only to ensure that his other disciple, Arjun, remained the best archer. Verma was the kind of guru who, for his own survival, would ask for the thumbs of both Arjun and Eklavya. He had done something similar with Yatin Sathe and Nitya Shetty.

The mist of blind devotion towards his guru began to dissipate from Sathe's eyes. He had understood that Verma had such a strong network with the criminals that he could get Sathe killed inside the jail within a day. Till the time Sathe was alive, Verma's freedom was at risk. But if Sathe was eliminated from the equation, then Verma's freedom stood confirmed. Sathe was no novice any more and had picked up a few illicit tricks from his guru. It was the only way to keep himself safe.

Wiping his eyes that were brimming with tears, and with a heavy heart, Sathe decided to give Verma a special guru dakshina, which would be the last gift Verma would receive from any of his disciples. Through his connections in the Arthur Road Jail, Sathe got an urgent message delivered to someone outside.

It was 6 a.m. In the hill station of Lonavala, situated a hundred kilometres away from Mumbai, the night was giving way to dawn. Valley City, which housed five-star hotels and super-luxurious private bungalows, dotted the skyline. Many people from Mumbai came here to get some respite from the fast-paced life of the city and to recuperate. Dilip Verma had also come here the night before to spend the weekend with his family. After the Kuberia and Hasmukh scandals, Verma desperately needed the break.

His family was still sleeping when Verma, as per habit, got up early for his morning walk. Twenty-five years ago, when the underworld's carnage was at its peak in Mumbai, some police officers had jointly launched a cleanliness campaign to restrain the underworld by conducting one encounter after the other without making any distinction between real and fake.

Amongst these encounter specialists, Dilip Verma held the record for the maximum number of killings with over hundred encounters to his credit. As a reward, the CIU was created and Verma was made the chief. Of course, he faced both the allegation and case of a fake encounter. The credit for the CIU becoming 'criminals in uniform' from the actual 'crime investigation unit' was Verma's alone. Sathe had only taken the CIU forward on the course it had been put on by Verma.

Verma's old crimes were forgotten when he entered Dawood Ibrahim's locality and nabbed his brother from among his henchmen and dragged him to a police station. This feat had been a planned one so that his previous transgressions could be overlooked, and to give his political ambitions post retirement a boost. Verma had contested elections after retiring, but he had lost. Despite his contacts in the ruling party, he saw no future for himself in politics, which was why he had decided to return to the world of crime.

Criminals trembled when they heard Verma's name. He had direct links with the underworld and he settled all types of disputes, ranging from property to criminal issues. That's why, for protection, he always carried a pistol.

That morning, too, he had his pistol stuffed inside his sports jacket. Barely a few steps into his walk, he felt that something was amiss. Two people were walking behind him and two others were coming towards him. On the side of the road, too, three strong and sturdy men were exercising. They all wore sports jackets that seemed to conceal something. Verma realized that it was an ambush, either to kill or to capture.

Verma knew that either Mahavir Tomar or Yatin Sathe were behind this. His hand instinctively reached for his pistol, but then he let go of the idea of resisting. The opposite party had more members, were younger than him and could come at him from three different directions. A lake lay on the fourth side, so there was no escape as such. There was hardly anyone else on the road.

A silent agreement took place between Verma and the men around him. Verma would not resist. The men approached him and took out their weapons. Two SUVs came from behind. Verma was shoved into one of them. The cars headed towards Mumbai.

At that very moment, in Mumbai, armed men broke into Verma's home.

14

It takes nine years

2009

Kuber's dream residence, Kuberia, was under construction. The family was living in their palatial ancestral bungalow until it was ready. Kuber's son, Dhruv, was in grade four. Despite his young age, he had been enrolled into a lot of classes and tuitions to keep him busy outside of school. He was being groomed as the prince of the family.

One day, when the tutor was teaching him math, Dhruv interrupted him with a very innocent question. 'Sir, can you tell me what your per minute income is?' Such a question from a nine-year-old child caused worry lines to form on the head of the tutor. Dhruv was too young to be concerned about these matters, and a middle-class teacher's income is not so much that it can be calculated on a minute-by-minute basis. Nonetheless, the tutor did some calculations and told Dhruv that his income per minute was one rupee.

Dhruv could not believe it. He wondered how anyone could earn so little. 'Sir, my father earns one lakh rupees per minute. Right now, I am nine years old. By the time I am twenty-one years old, based on the present growth rate, my father's income will grow to five lakh rupees per minute.'

The tutor was astonished and, to verify Dhruv's claim, took out his calculator. Dhruv responded playfully with, 'Sir, Papa's monthly income cannot fit on the screen of this calculator. I want to do even better than him.'

Nine-year-old Dhruv's way of thinking made the tutor realize how restricted he was in terms of ambition. But he also realized that kids born into wealthy families like Kuber's could be given wings to soar higher than anyone else.

Dhruv went on to tell his tutor that on his last birthday, his father had bought a new helicopter that took flight from the Mahalakshmi Racecourse helipad roughly thirty minutes away from their home because they did not have a helipad in their ancestral home.

Present day

The headlines all across flashed that the country's most known encounter specialist had been arrested. Dilip Verma was to be produced before a court shortly. Inside the court, a crowd of reporters and cameramen had begun to assemble. Sanjay Trivedi also reached the court and prayed hard for Verma to be produced before lunch so that he could get to Bawla Masjid in time, when the Friday namaz ended, for an exclusive report.

The moment the anchor's question reached his ears, the reporter, Trivedi, started spewing rivulets of information.

'Early this morning, hundred kilometres away from Mumbai, in Lonavala, an NIA team arrested encounter specialist Dilip Verma. At the same time, NIA's second team raided Verma's Mumbai home for evidence. Both these operations were carried out under secrecy and under the protection of over a hundred armed soldiers of the central police force. The Maharashtra police was not informed, which makes it clear that the central and state agencies don't trust each other completely. The NIA's sources revealed that some cash, printouts, documents and illegal weapons were recovered from Verma's house. As far as evidence is concerned, my experience tells me that a sharp retired police officer like Verma would not keep any incriminating evidence at home. Also, Verma was questioned before but not arrested. This means that a person close to Verma tipped off the NIA, forcing it to take such forceful action. The question that arises is: Who is this accomplice of Verma's who snitched?'

In a police van, live telecast of this news was playing on a constable's mobile phone. A couple of other constables sat close to him and looked at the screen. Sathe was gazing out of the netted window of the van, listening to the reporter speaking. He was being taken to the same court for a hearing where Verma was to be produced presently.

This was the first case to be heard before the court that day. The courtroom itself was packed with Verma, Sathe, NIA officers, members of the media and lawyers. Everyone awaited the arrival of the judge.

Interestingly, among the people present was ATS's Nitya Shetty. It was a little surprising because the case was no longer the ATS's. Dilip Verma, Yatin Sathe, Nitya Shetty and Sanjay Trivedi, however, remained unperturbed. They had been witnesses to the ups and downs in each other's lives for the last two decades.

As soon as the judge was seated, the court was informed that the NIA lawyer had tested positive for COVID19 and hence, was missing from the courtroom. Taking special permission, the NIA's IG Rohtagi, began speaking. 'You know that the Kuberia case and the Hasmukh murder case are connected and being investigated by the NIA. The agency got a tip last evening, based on which it arrested two suspects. They gave the agency some important information pertaining to the case. They are small-time criminals who, along with the "criminals in uniform", carried out the crime. It was while questioning them that Dilip Verma's name came to the fore.

'Early this morning, an NIA team reached Lonavala and arrested Verma. Another team searched his house in Andheri and confiscated anonymous SIM cards, a laptop, documents and electronic gadgets. All this while we believed that Yatin Sathe was the mastermind and facilitator. But the fact is that, right from the beginning, Verma and Sathe have been equal players. They were both masterminds and facilitators. While Sathe led the operation on the ground, Verma was like the control room. If we use the analogy of a game here, we can say that Sathe was the captain and Verma was the coach. The team of criminals around Sathe and the "criminals in uniform" had been assembled by Verma. He identified them, convinced them, decided their roles, explained it to them and then executed the operation by making them collaborate with Sathe. It would not be an exaggeration to say that Verma had made Sathe the captain of this team.

'Dilip Verma is a retired police officer. Considered a supercop, he holds the record for carrying out more than a hundred encounter killings. The underworld fears him and his knowledge of the criminal world is unprecedented. Around twenty years ago, when the CIU was formulated, Verma was its chief. As chief, Verma initiated a young Yatin Sathe into his squad. Ever since, their unholy alliance has been at work. Last year, when Sathe became the CIU chief, both of them jointly hatched this conspiracy. The gelatin sticks found in the Scorpio outside Kuberia were procured by Verma from a company in Nagpur. He had them sent to Sathe. Seeing the Kuberia case slip out of their hands, the duo was worried. When Sathe called Hasmukh Jain to his CIU office a day or two before he was murdered, Dilip Verma had been present there and had pressurized Hasmukh to take the blame for planting the explosives-filled car outside Kuberia. Hasmukh refused to comply and was murdered. The additional manpower that was required to execute the murder was also arranged by Verma. We have those people's statements pinning the blame on Verma. The car that was used in Hasmukh's murder was also arranged by Verma, and traces of Hasmukh's DNA have been found in this car.

'All the people whom Verma involved in this crime were also paid huge amounts of money. Verma orchestrated Hasmukh's murder. The SIM cards found with the rest of the accused had been used to keep in touch with Verma. We, the NIA, know this because of the call detail records. Incidentally, most calls between the accused and Verma were made using the Internet and were not normal calls. Evidence of Verma being in touch with the accused has also been found in the IPDR, the internet protocol detail record, in which the telephone company has records of each user who uses the company's network to log on to the internet. Through this, the IMEI number, or the device number of the mobile, the IP address of the origin and destination point, information about the website or communication app used and the user's location, time and date of use can also be found out.

'In addition to all of this, we have recovered an unlicensed weapon from Verma's home. Where Sathe's motive was to become a supercop, Verma's motive was to earn money. After retiring from the police, Verma contested the Vidhan Sabha elections. He lost the polls and crores of rupees. He then decided to use his supercop reputation and recover the lost money by extorting builders, businessmen and industrialists and from the income derived through settlements done in the underworld.

'In total, the NIA has statements of accomplices, technical evidence and motive against Verma. He is not a regular retired officer. He is an exceedingly dangerous man who can tamper with evidence if he remains outside. He may even threaten the families of the accomplices who have testified against him, or he may flee. He needs to be questioned in custody. The money trail and the amounts handed out to the accused need to be traced. His DNA sample needs to be matched with the sample found in the vehicle used in Hasmukh's murder. We may make more arrests based on the information Verma gives us during interrogation. This is why we request his custody.'

The judge looked at Dilip Verma's lawyer, who informed the judge that Verma would like to plead his own case. The judge granted permission.

Verma began to speak. 'Of the two so-called accused with whom the NIA is linking me, I am acquainted with only one. When I was in the police, he was my informer for twelve years. I do not know the other person. After retiring, I started running an NGO and, on account of being a social worker, many people come and meet me. It is possible that the second suspect met me through some social work programme. There have always been two camps in the police department, and my rival camp has always tried to implicate me. In this case, there is also the issue of a tussle between the Centre and the state. Since I am attached to the ruling party in the state, I am being targeted by the central government's agency.

'The recovery of the weapon that the NIA is talking about is a pistol that was gifted to me twenty-five years ago by an erstwhile police commissioner who was happy with my work. It is not an illegal weapon. On account of the Covid lockdown, I have been unable to get the licence renewed. I have put my life on the line for the country, I have killed more than a hundred criminals in encounters and freed Mumbai from the clutches of the underworld. Understandably, I am on the hit list of the underworld. In that case, what's wrong with keeping a weapon for self-defence? If the NIA thinks that I am a big player who knows how to twist the law around, why would I make the imprudent mistake of keeping incriminating evidence at home?

'To question a person based on their call detail records and IPDR, NIA does not need to keep me in custody as these records are documentary evidence. They cannot be considered main evidence because their value lies only in their capacity as corroborative evidence. Whenever the NIA calls me for questioning, I am ready. Previously, too, the NIA interrogated me for hours and found nothing. The remand application of the accused who were arrested earlier with Yatin Sathe does not mention my name or involvement. Then, all of a sudden, arresting me like a terrorist and producing me before a court in a dishonourable manner is akin to abusing my contribution towards the country and Mumbai. It seems the NIA has arrested me as an afterthought. As if part of a conspiracy, I am being pushed into this case. And if I am even half the mastermind and facilitator the NIA is making me out to be, then the remand application of the arrested suspects would have at least mentioned me. Is it possible that the mastermind, out of nowhere, falls into the lap of the NIA? I object to the NIA requesting my custody and seek bail.'

The judge then asked the NIA. 'After questioning the other accused in the case, the NIA must have uncovered the conspiracy. Why didn't you arrest Dilip Verma then?'

Rohtagi, in response, took out some documents which his junior placed before the judge. He said, 'This is the case diary in which the investigating officer recorded the daily activities undertaken and the progress made. Under a provision of Section 172 of the CrPC, the inquiry officer is required to maintain a record of the investigation on a daily basis so that it can be ensured that the officer has actually conducted a serious investigation and not acted on the basis of his whims. The case diary plays an important role as a record, but it cannot be used as evidence during a trial. Nevertheless, in 2005, in the case of *Siddhartha vs State of Bihar*, Supreme Court Justices K.G. Balakrishnan and B.N. Srikrishna reiterated that the investigating officer is required to maintain a case diary during the entire investigation, and if the court has any doubt as to the manner in which the case was investigated, or on the conduct of the inquiry officer, it has the right to refer to this case diary.'

Rohtagi saw the judge going through the case diary, so he paused. He spoke again when the judge lifted his head. 'The case diary gave us a hint about Verma's role. But that time he was a mere suspect. His name did not crop suddenly. During the investigation, a lot of secrecy needs to be maintained. Especially when the suspect is a former police officer like Dilip Verma, who knows how to trick the investigating agency. He is a tough man and it's very difficult to get him to open his mouth. Verma misled the NIA from the very beginning. He lied during his initial interrogation about not being in touch with Sathe recently. Our evidence and witnesses clearly disproved Verma's claim. His initial questioning did not take place in custody, but he lied then. We need to question him in our custody and get him to speak the truth. That's why the NIA wants Verma in its custody.'

The judge rejected Verma's bail application and granted the NIA ten days custody of Verma.

Watching the news on his TV, Mahavir Tomar was troubled. He was wondering how a clever man like Verma, who always managed to stay safe, had got entangled in this case. Tomar was sure that someone had sabotaged Verma. How were the two henchmen, who supposedly implicated Verma, arrested suddenly? Someone must have tipped off the NIA about them, leaving the agency with no choice but to arrest Verma. But arresting and then questioning them would have taken time. After all, it was not possible to arrest someone like Verma within twelve hours. This meant that someone first ratted Verma out to the NIA, post which the agency decided to nab Verma. The henchmen were caught after this and a story was fabricated, that Verma was arrested on the basis of their confessional statements.

It was also possible that the person who had leaked information to the writer of the unknown blog could have given the NIA information against Verma. In the face of such incriminating evidence, it would not have been possible for the NIA to stick to their original agreement. It would have led to slander, which the agency could not risk. It was meaningless to doubt Yatin Sathe as he himself was the focal point of this entire arrangement. Then Verma was also going to get Sathe's final setting done inside the jail after a few months. Tomar thought that he was probably overthinking the whole situation and that the NIA's story about getting information on Verma through the two henchmen might be genuine.

Tomar felt as if he was inching close to a safe zone. The reason for this was that he knew the true motive behind the Kuberia incident, and that was his armour. Verma and Sathe did not know anything about this motive. Had they known, they would not have been arrested. The other accused arrested in the case could not have even dreamt of what this motive might be. Verma and Sathe's arrest exhibited the seriousness of the NIA towards the case and diverted attention away from the actual motive.

It was in search of this motive that Sanjay Trivedi raced to Bawla Masjid as soon as the court hearing was over. He heaved a sigh of relief at making it in time and fixed his eyes on the main door. Within no time, after offering the Friday namaz, the worshippers started streaming out of the masjid.

Moments later, Aman Choudhury also emerged from the masjid. His well-exercised body was covered in a white Pathani suit and a matching white cap on his head. The Ma Amba locket was not visible around his neck. Leaning against his Range Rover, Choudhury found journalist Sanjay Trivedi looking at him with a wry smile. He paused for a second before slowly walking up to his car and opening the back door. Trivedi, meanwhile, opened the front door on the other side and got in.

On the back seat, strong and sturdy NIA men sat on either side of Dilip Verma. After the court hearing, he was being taken to the agency's office. Squashed in the middle, Verma wondered who had ratted him out. For the first time in his life, Verma felt cheated. He knew that the NIA's story of getting information from the two henchmen was made up. Sathe, Verma knew, had no reason to do this because he himself was in deep trouble. Also, he had been loyal to Verma for two decades.

Finally, Verma's needle of suspicion rested on Mahavir Tomar. He knew Tomar was an expert at switching sides. Tomar had incriminated the very home minister who had placed his hand on his head and made him commissioner in the first place. A few days ago, someone had informed Verma about a recent audio recording of Tomar's, in which he could be heard saying: 'Whoever is caught, right or wrong, doesn't matter. Let them get arrested, but save me and I will spend whatever money is required in return.'

Verma had thought of the recording as faff, but now doubt had ingrained itself in his mind. He was troubled and agitated and tried to shift his weight around, but he had no room to move between the two NIA men.

After changing his clothes in the backseat, Aman Choudhury sat in the driver's seat.

'You come here every Friday to offer prayers?' Sanjay Trivedi asked.

There was no response.

'Since when have you had your men following me?'

Again, Choudhury did not respond.

'You are Muslim. Your name, Aman Choudhury, is such that you can pass off as both Hindu and Muslim. You have taken advantage of this fact.'

Choudhury, who was driving now, was dressed like an executive in formal clothes. He took out the Ma Amba locket from the glove box and put it around his neck. Trivedi missed the pistol in the glove box because his eyes were locked on the shiny locket around Choudhury's neck.

'You are a Muslim but roam about with a Ma Amba locket around your neck. Any secret behind this?'

Choudhury did not say anything. He simply kept driving.

They stopped right outside Arthur Road Jail. While entering the jail, Sathe's gait reflected a strange confidence.

Sathe, who was settling into his special cell after returning from the court, was happy that his guru, Dilip Verma would become his cellmate soon. What brought him even more happiness was that Verma had no idea that Sathe was behind all this, that Sathe's trick of shifting the blame onto someone else had worked. Sathe had managed to sow a permanent seed of distrust between Tomar and Verma.

The NIA had used Verma's henchmen's statement as the official basis for arresting Verma. But it was Sathe who had handed over to the NIA details pertaining to Verma, his two accomplices, the communication between them and evidence implicating Verma. Sathe thought the game would become safer for him. After all, Verma would not be as powerful inside the jail as he was outside of it. Sathe felt that he had got an extension of a few years on his life. He had also managed to get his special guru dakshina delivered to Verma and had successfully delivered the second instalment of NIA's deal.

Sathe knew that no one would believe that he had struck an opportunistic alliance with his longtime foe, Sanjay Trivedi. After years of rivalry, Sathe had realized that Trivedi belonged to that clan of clingy yet sedulous reporters who were only interested in information. Whether that information came from a good or bad source was immaterial.

In order to find an opportunity in adversity, Sathe had sent inside information to Trivedi via his girlfriend, Nina Dias. Trivedi had lapped it up and used it in the unknown blog, thus making a mountain out of a molehill.

Next, Trivedi had to turn the mountain into Mount Everest. Though Sathe was behind bars, the effects of the fucked-up situation he had created were felt everywhere.

'Here, there, everywhere. In this case, you and this bullshit were all over the place.'

For a moment, there was complete silence, after which Trivedi said to Aman Choudhury, 'That night after the late court hearing, you drove off in front of me in this car. After a few hours, when Mahavir Tomar left the chief minister's house, you also came out from the house in the same vehicle. Your presence at two important places related to this developing matter within a span of a few hours led to alarm bells ringing in my mind. Then I remembered that I saw you for the first time the day you found the Scorpio outside Kuberia. I had noticed the gigantic locket around your neck and was informed that you were in charge of security at Kuberia. You were the first to notice the suspiciously parked Scorpio.

'One night, by chance, I saw this car of yours outside my house. You were talking to two bikers, and I think you had hired them to keep an eye on me. I was breaking one news after the other in this case, maybe that is why you wanted me under surveillance. I am sure that some other reporters are also being watched. Now, because the Range Rover is an expensive car, it gets noticed in my lower-middle-class residential area. The watchman informed me that your car had been spotted there three times in the past week.

'It's understandable for me to become suspicious under these circumstances, don't you think? So, using the registration number, I traced the name of its owner first and then his address. After that, I got to know of your glorious background. It was easy from there. I only had to pay attention to the places that were developing focal points in this matter.'

Here, Sanjay Trivedi took out his phone and started showing Choudhury one photo after another. 'When the high court handed over the investigation of the extortion case to the CBI, you were there. In this photo, your car can be seen outside the CBI office. There is even a photo of you talking to Sathe's lawyer outside the sessions court. Before the ED left to interrogate the home minister, your Range Rover was spotted outside the ED's office.'

Then Trivedi played a video. He spoke after it ended. 'Apart from photos, I have this video as well. Instead of sending Sathe to a lockup, he was sent to judicial custody in Arthur Road Jail, which is infamous for corruption. Then you went to that jail and ensured arrangements for Sathe's safety and comfort. For this, you engaged the biggest middleman there. Unfortunately for you, that middleman was known to me because of my years of crime reporting. During this sting operation, he arrogantly told me all about you.'

Then, pointing to the backseat of the car, Trivedi continued to speak: 'A khaki-coloured file was kept on the backseat of your car. It was labelled "Kuberia Helipad". You were seen in a lot of places with that file. I spoke to my sources in the agencies and departments associated with the helipad. All the dots connected after that and everything fell into place.'

'Why are you telling me all this?' Aman Choudhury finally spoke.

'For reaction. I am not one of those reporters who reports based on half-baked and unconfirmed information. I belong to the old school of journalism. If I did not think that balanced journalism was necessary, then by now your news would have gone viral. I'm sure you would have managed mainstream media, but how would you control social media? It is important to know your side of the story.'

'Why should I give you a reaction?'

'I knew you would respond like this, which was why I told you such a long story. You see, you don't have much of a choice. Weigh all your options and you will realize what I am saying. In any case, by hook or by crook, the reality will be revealed and you will be in trouble, my friend. Sooner or later, I will get to the bottom of the entire matter. Maybe in two days, I think. Then don't say that you should have been consulted, or why I didn't cross-verify this information with you. It's better if you explain now, before it's too late. I have an idea of the true story, I only want to hear your version of it.'

Choudhury looked at the reporter in anger, but Trivedi wasn't done. He said, 'And don't give me that supercop bullshit. We both know that it's hogwash, a cover-up, a rattle placed in the hands of the media and the public to amuse them. The whole theory about Sathe doing this to become a supercop was created to either benefit Sathe or to fool everybody else. Despite it being an open-and-shut case, things are being done for Sathe's benefit. Why? There is a reason. I think this story started much earlier, but the reality is yet to surface. Actually, in this case, all the people involved are busy saving themselves and, to save themselves, it was important that Sathe agrees to a settlement.'

Aman Choudhury appeared troubled. For a moment, there was silence. He parked the car outside a coffee shop and gestured that he was going to get some coffee.

Getting out from the other side of the car, Sanjay Trivedi said, 'If you want to give a reaction, do so. If not, that's fine, too. But understand this, you are not the only smart one in this situation. Sathe also made the same mistake.'

Choudhury returned with two disposable glasses of steaming coffee. Trivedi reached into his pocket, took out four pills and gulped them down with his first sip.

Before he knew it, Trivedi felt as if a bomb had exploded in his brain. Darkness engulfed him. He lay sprawled on the floor, his legs and hands not moving. Choudhury bent and held his finger in front of Trivedi's nose. He was still breathing.

15
That will be all

Ten days later

Chaos ensued in Sanjay Trivedi's room at the hospital. An attendant rushed to summon the nursing staff and a senior doctor was promptly called in.

Moments ago, Trivedi's fingers had moved and he had slowly opened his eyes. It was all hazy at first, but then his vision cleared up. A saline drip was attached to his wrist. Trivedi looked at the cardiac monitors, the mechanical ventilators and the other equipment around him. He did not remember how he had got here.

For the staff, he was the patient who had slipped into a coma during surgery and regained consciousness after many days. One by one, they began to stream into his room.

With a faltering step, Dilip Verma entered Arthur Road Jail. He had been here several times, but it was his first entry as an inmate. His ten-day remand with the NIA was over. Despite tough questioning and employing all possible methods, the NIA had been unable to get the country's number one encounter specialist to open his mouth. Now the court had sent him to judicial custody in Arthur Road Jail. After the procedural checking, he knew Yatin Sathe waited for him in his special cell. As soon as Verma entered, Sathe touched his feet in obeisance.

For the last ten days, there had been complete silence on the Kuberia and Hasmukh murder cases. The matter had disappeared from the news as well. The results of the Vidhan Sabha elections held in five states of the country were out. The credibility of the ruling party at the Centre, the Jan Bhakt Sangh, was at stake. The main opposition party in every state alleged that all the machinery and agencies that came under the central government had been assigned election duty at the cost of neglecting everything else.

The results were a shocker for the Jan Bhakt Sangh. In three big states—West Bengal, Tamil Nadu and Kerala—they had lost by huge margins. The toadies of the central government in the media were busy righting the wrong that had followed. Election news hogged all the limelight. Everything else was history.

The moment Aman Choudhury entered Trivedi's room, the attendant saluted him and left. Trivedi was better now.

'Welcome back. You are lucky. Not everyone comes out of a coma so quickly,' said Choudhury.

Trivedi, after regaining consciousness, had been informed by the doctors that he had been brought to the hospital in an unconscious state. He had undergone a complicated brain surgery that had mostly gone well, but some complications had led to Trivedi slipping into a coma. Even the nursing staff had reiterated to him that he had got a second lease on life.

Choudhury got up, turned on the TV and put on the news channel that Trivedi worked for on mute. He pointed at the TV and said, 'You no longer work there. The anonymous blog that you wrote? Well, your channel got to know about it. In any case, you had become a burden for the news channel; they did not want to spend money on your treatment. Your operation and post-recovery costs will be equal to the salaries of at least four reporters.'

Trivedi's face contorted in confusion when he heard this. He glanced around the hospital room equipped with hi-tech medical facilities. Aman Choudhury did not miss this.

'You are in Kuber Super Speciality hospital. Your medical expenses are being borne by the Kuber Foundation.'

'Why?'

'The answer to your question is hidden in that long story of yours. The one you narrated to me ten days ago, before you fainted. You had figured out a lot of things, but there were some links that you were not able to connect because you missed some vital facts. I completed your story over the past ten days. Thanks to your move, thanks to my experience with the R&AW, thanks to the policeman on our pay and thanks to Sathe, we now have information that we did not have before. In this story, Aman Choudhury, Sanjay Trivedi, Sathe, Verma and Tomar are mere characters.'

'The story begins with the central character, Yatin Sathe. Everyone thought that Sathe had been reinstated, but that was not completely true. Sathe had been reinstated on the condition that he complete a job.

First, Sathe's mentor, Dilip Verma, met him. Because of their teacher–disciple relationship, Verma was aware of Sathe's tight financial situation, which he took advantage of to get Sathe to agree. Sathe was told that he could be reinstated, but that he would have to do some 'special' work in return. Sathe was shown a rosy picture about being given high-profile cases to solve, and an important posting through which he could make good on his tainted image and stand to gain financially. Verma narrated a plan to Sathe, as per which a car laden with explosives was to be parked outside a rich industrialist's house. The investigation was to be handed to Sathe. Then, after a few days, two so-called terrorists were to be shot in a fake encounter. This was to garner applause from the media and give Sathe the tag of a supercop.

Citing his old connection with Mahavir Tomar, Verma told Sathe that he would enjoy the former commissioner's full support. Sathe did not really have any other choice, which was why he agreed. Then, Verma told him how he would re-enter the police force. Everything went according to plan thereafter. On account of COVID19, Commissioner Tomar reinstated suspended police officers, including Sathe, to make up for the shortage in the force. The way Verma had recruited Sathe was how Verma himself had been recruited a few days ago. Sathe had a reason to risk it all. So did Verma.

Retired encounter specialist Dilip Verma, who had ruined his financial standing after losing the elections, was given a conditional offer by his mentor, Tomar, to find a way out of his financial crisis. Commissioner Tomar came up with a dangerous plan. First, the commissioner tried to coax some other capable officers into it. But they were all either settled or did not want to take such a big risk. For the execution of the plan, Tomar needed a daring and needy officer, and his search ended with Yatin Sathe. Tomar had done his complete homework with regard to Sathe. In order to recruit him, Tomar knew he needed Verma. He offered Verma a deal worth crores and paid him an advance. Verma had to first recruit Sathe and then, for Sathe's support, he had to assemble a 'criminals in uniform' team to execute the special plan.

Both Sathe and Verma were greedy for money and eager to get out of their hopeless situations. As per Commissioner Tomar's plan, Sathe was reinstated. Normally, reinstated officers are given a side posting, but ignoring all rules, Tomar made Sathe the head of the important and high-profile CIU. After becoming the head of the CIU, Sathe was under probation in a way. Tomar first gauged whether Sathe could handle big cases or not. The five most high-profile cases that took place in Mumbai post Sathe's joining were handed over to him for investigation. Tomar also got Sathe to extort crores of rupees on a monthly basis. He allowed Sathe to bypass senior officers, be they ACPs or joint commissioners, and take orders directly from him. Overall, Tomar tested Sathe as a criminal in uniform, which Sathe passed with flying colours. It was only after this that Tomar launched him into the big game.

So, Tomar recruited Verma and Verma recruited Sathe. Unaware of the 'true motive', they were essentially pawns. If something went wrong, their arrest was guaranteed. Tomar, however, knew that if something went wrong, there would be no evidence of his direct involvement in the case. His dangerous plan was ready to be executed. Sathe was ready to carry it out and Verma had assembled the support team.

Sathe and Verma only knew that they had to park the car loaded with explosives and then, on the pretext of a fake encounter, show that the case had been solved. But despite such meticulous planning, an unexpected blunder came to pass.

According to the plan, Sathe parked the Scorpio outside Kuberia. The fake number on the car belonged to an escort car in Kuber's fleet. This was done so that the car would be easily spotted by the Kuberia security staff and they would inform the police. The moment the local police station was called, the CIU's Yatin Sathe was to reach the spot.

The police found gelatin sticks, a threat letter, the Jai Bharti team's jersey and a bag in the car. Based on what was decided, Commissioner Tomar exerted all his power to ensure that the CIU, headed by Sathe, was given the investigation of the case.

Then came the turning point, which was not part of the plan. A so-called terrorist organization, the Jaish-ul-Hind, claimed responsibility for this incident. The person who claimed responsibility on social media was not a member of the Jaish-ul-Hind, but a terrorist from Indian Mujahideen, serving a sentence in Tihar Jail. He had procured a mobile phone in jail and posted a false message. Even though he or his organization had not done this, and when no one was taking responsibility, he saw an opportunity to enhance his terrorist profile. Later, even though Jaish-ul-Hind distanced itself from the Kuberia scandal, the flawless plan had been disturbed. All major investigating agencies in the country went on high alert. After the Delhi Police submitted its report on the matter, the NIA's interest in the matter was piqued.

A terrorist sitting in Tihar Jail had unknowingly unravelled the plot.

Maharashtra's home minister, Sardeshpande, and the Mumbai ATS were unaware of Commissioner Tomar's scheming. The ATS managed to trace Hasmukh, the owner of the Scorpio, despite the missing chassis and engine numbers. Since it was predetermined that the case would be handed to the CIU, Sathe did not exercise as much caution as he usually would have. The NIA, too, found out the truth through CCTV footage. Meanwhile, DIG Palande and Nitya Shetty of the ATS continued to leak information to opposition leader Jitendra Nagpure via IPS Naren Arya, to ensure the matter would not get swept under the carpet. The case took a political turn. Direct allegations were levelled against Sathe and he was removed from the investigation.

Sathe's friend Hasmukh was the sole link through which the others could be nabbed. Commissioner Tomar wanted to leave no clue behind, so he ordered Hasmukh's murder. Sathe, with his accomplices, killed Hasmukh, but the ATS managed to solve the case. This goof-up led to the 'true motive' taking another beating.

In the interim, the NIA arrested Sathe. Now, had the NIA not arrested him that day, the ATS would have done so, or he would have fled or been killed. After Sathe's arrest, Sardeshpande suspected Tomar's involvement in the case. He had Tomar disgracefully removed from the post of commissioner. To save himself from arrest by the NIA, Tomar switched sides. To prove his loyalty to his new political bosses, he incriminated Sardeshpande in the multicrore extortion case. The moment the high court ordered a CBI inquiry into the case, Sardeshpande resigned. In response, the state government triggered several inquiries against Tomar.

All this while, the NIA had been unable to get Sathe to divulge the motive behind the Kuberia incident. To build pressure, they even applied the UAPA to his case. A strict law like the UAPA meant that Sathe would not get bail. This was when Tomar and Verma met Sathe at the NIA office. Tomar convinced Sathe to give a statement against Sardeshpande in the extortion case. The stage had been set. All the possibilities of the matter hurtling ahead were clearly visible now.

At this point, however, the real danger lay in the disclosure of the true motive and the story behind it. If the motive came to the fore, a catastrophe would ensue. The state government would run into trouble and players from both camps would be exposed. The supercop theory came into being at this point. Convenient for all, it was Tomar's idea.

After Sathe's motive of wanting to be a supercop was accepted, the NIA declared its investigation successful. It established that Sathe worked alone, thus significantly diminishing the possibility of Verma and Tomar's arrest. The opposition leader, Nagpure, who had been very vocal until now, adopted a startling silence. This pointed to an agreement between the ruling party and the opposition.

The NIA got Sathe sent to custody in jail as per his wish, making everyone think Sathe was happy. The person who gained the most in all of this was Mahavir Tomar, who, despite being the mastermind, remained safe.

But Tomar and Verma made a mistake that would cost them. They took Sathe to be weak. They thought that Sathe had accepted his fate and would spend the rest of his life in jail or trying to get bail.

Sathe had realized that he was just a pawn. Verma and Tomar were using his shoulder to fire at others. The entire plan was devised in a way that if something was to go wrong, only Sathe and the people below him would get caught. He had considered Tomar and his guru, Verma, to be his well-wishers. He had trusted them, as a result of which he was in jail and Tomar and Verma were free. Sathe had also understood that

Verma and Tomar had plans to kill him, which they would carry out eventually. He decided to become the wazir instead of a pawn. Everyone thought he had been taken care of. Sathe knew he had to teach the people who had used him a lesson. He knew that Tomar was the bigger player and, to nab him, Verma would need to be caught first. Just as Tomar had once planned to recruit Verma in order to get Sathe onboard, now Sathe plotted to get Verma involved and bait Tomar in as well.

Sathe used his mortal enemy, reporter Sanjay Trivedi, to his advantage.

Through his girlfriend, Nina Dias, Sathe surreptitiously sent information on the real boss of the 'criminals in uniform' to Trivedi, who was already doubting the supercop theory and the way the case had gone cold.

Based on the information received from Sathe's girlfriend, Trivedi started investigating the matter further. Because the tip had come from Sathe, Trivedi was suspicious initially. But Sathe's questions were valid, prompting Trivedi to dig deeper.

After his independent investigation, Trivedi realized that the supercop theory was nonsensical. He wrote the truth in an anonymous blog post, which mentioned how this theory was a pre-planned move to weaken the case against Sathe in the future as well.

Trivedi also got to know that Verma and Tomar could easily get rid of Sathe in jail. Through his blog, Trivedi left a message for Sathe. When Sathe's girlfriend met Trivedi, she told him that Sathe had an iPad inside the jail and would be able to read his blog post. Sathe understood the message and the danger to his life. He knew that to stay alive he had to break Verma and Tomar's partnership by sowing the seeds of mutual doubt in their minds. He planned a special guru-dakshina for Verma.

Based on information received from Sathe, the NIA first arrested two of Verma's henchmen and then Verma himself.

Sathe, with the help of the NIA, plotted things in a way that everyone would think that the henchmen had ratted Verma out. Through this move, Sathe broke Verma and Tomar's partnership and created a situation where they began to mistrust each other. He emerged as a confidant and true friend of Verma's, who was still smarting from Tomar's supposed betrayal. Also, Sathe now had Trivedi in his court. The danger of being killed in jail by Tomar was equal for both Sathe and Verma. And, sitting in jail, Verma considered Sathe to be his most trusted friend and began planning to settle scores with Tomar.

Trivedi, meanwhile, working on the basis of Sathe's information, was close to identifying the true motive. In search of evidence corroborating this motive, he had filed three RTI applications in different government departments. Kuber's well-wishers in those departments had informed his son, Dhruv.

Moving ahead in his investigation, Trivedi was on the lookout for that one moment when he could expose everything. At this point, if he had exposed the true motive and the story behind it corroborated with evidence, then all arrangements done by agencies, government, Kuber and others, to keep the true motive under wraps would have been exposed, causing discomfort to all.

Not only did Kuber have money in abundance, but also luck. Just before the big reveal, Trivedi met Aman Choudhury. It was while he was with Choudhury that Trivedi suffered a brain stroke and slipped into a coma.

Another significant development took place. Kuber was impressed with Trivedi and his ability to get to the bottom of this complicated issue. No one else had got as close to identifying the true motive which was 'Operation Kuberia helipad'.

Kuber owned a lot of helicopters, but to use them he had to go to Mahalakshmi Racecourse, which was thirty minutes away from Kuberia. If he could save this time, he would save five hundred and fifty crores a year.

There were two helipads on the rooftop of Kuberia, but they were useless because residential areas in Mumbai do not have permission for helicopters to take off or land. Also, since Peddar Road was home to several millionaires and billionaires, these powerful neighbours were bound to raise objections. Several NGOs would also jump in citing noise pollution caused due to the landing and take-off of helicopters. If anyone filed a PIL (public interest litigation), the matter would go to court.

Clearance would also be needed from the state police, the environment ministry and the civil aviation ministry. A valid reason was also needed to overrule so many possible objections so that on the basis of the 'reason', necessary clearances could be sought from the government.

Therefore, in 2013 itself, Mumbai's then police commissioner came forward to 'help'. This was similar to the 'help' they were now getting. One day, the Indian Mujahedeen sent a letter threatening to kill Kuber. In addition, the Mumbai Police received a so-called intelligence input. Now, no one suspects such letters and inputs. If you are resourceful, you can easily plant them.

The commissioner of Mumbai in 2013, who was a 'criminal in uniform' himself, wrote to all the departments and ministries concerned just a day before his retirement, stating that Kuber's life was in danger, and that he should be allowed to fly directly in and out of his home as an exception. Such a strong recommendation from the commissioner eased out the path to getting the permissions needed. In the next two months, the file was passed quickly from one table to the next. When money is not a problem and there is a valid reason to seek clearance, the bureaucracy does not hesitate.

But before the last clearance could come through, the state and central governments changed. The Jan Bhakt Sangh came to power. Jitendra Nagpure became the chief minister for the first time. The new government knew about Kuber's cordial relations with the previous government. Therefore, as retaliation, permission for the helipad on Kuberia was not granted. The 'criminals in uniform' in Nagpure's government presented a new intelligence report, which said that Kuber's life was not in danger. Intelligence inputs were once again managed. With this, the matter got stuck for five years.

After five years, when elections were held again, Nagpure's party was removed from power. A new coalition government came to power in Maharashtra.

At this point, senior IPS officer Mahavir Tomar made a grand entry. Tomar's service record was impressive but controversial; his ambition was to become Mumbai's commissioner, but there was a problem. In the race for the post of commissioner were a lot of officers senior than Tomar. They could only be bypassed if a hefty bribe was paid to the ruling political party. Tomar took advantage of being Kuber's family friend. He contacted Kuber's young and enthusiastic son, Dhruv, and told him that he was aware of Kuber's helipad project, which had been lying unfinished since 2013. Now that the state government had changed, an operational helipad at Kuberia could become a reality. Tomar also told Dhruv that if he became the police commissioner of Mumbai, he would ensure the helipads became functional. Twenty-one-year-old Dhruv trusted Tomar. And not being able to stand up to his son's insistence, Kuber agreed to accept Tomar's help.

Tomar took a hundred crores from Kuber and bribed the ruling political party. He became the police commissioner of

Mumbai, bypassing his seniors. When Dhruv asked Tomar how he planned to get the helipad operational, Tomar told the boy 'leave it to me'. Kuber, knowing that Dhruv was yet to be more acquainted with the ways of the world, appointed Aman Choudhury to coordinate with Tomar. A retired R&AW officer, Choudhury knew how to deal with officers like Tomar.

But Tomar also kept Choudhury in the dark about his plan. Understandably, Kuber, too, was totally unaware of Tomar's dangerous scheme until it failed and was exposed. Choudhury knew that Tomar could go to any extent, but he did not know what that extent was. He was under the misconception that he was Tomar's handler, but even he ended up becoming a pawn.

Tomar's plan was in action. Kuber had only helped a little. The criminal in uniform residing inside Tomar thought that not only would he be able to pay off Kuber's loan, but also earn hundreds of crores.

As stated earlier, Tomar's plan was predetermined: an explosives-laden vehicle would be found outside Kuberia, followed by an encounter of two so-called terrorists a few days later, and then the use of the helipad would be approved in the name of security. But this plan had crumbled in a phase-wise manner.

Neither Kuber, nor his son Dhruv, nor Aman Choudhury had the slightest idea about the conspiracy Mahavir Tomar had hatched in his mind. In the garb of getting the helipad sanctioned, he had crossed all boundaries. Kuber, once aware of the entire situation, was livid. After talking to both the camps, he made one thing clear—whatever Tomar had done had been of his own free will and the Kuber Group had nothing to do with it. Kuber cut off all his ties with Mahavir Tomar and dropped the helipad project for the time being.

All the planning, the drama, the twisting of the rules, Hasmukh's murder, arrests and ruined careers seemed to have been for nothing. It all seemed to be to pay the price of fulfilling someone's ambition of becoming a police commissioner, for an IPS officer to be able to repay the loan he had taken to pay his political masters for the post of commissioner. So that a commissioner-level officer could turn the CIU into 'criminals in uniform'. So that the richest man in the country could have an operational rooftop helipad at home, something no other businessman in the country could boast about. So that the owner of billions of rupees could save an additional five hundred and fifty crores each year. So that a rich and stubborn boy like Dhruv could be indulged.

So many people had paid the price for one man's ambition to become a commissioner—Hasmukh with his life, the home minister with his chair and the likes of Verma and Sathe with their freedom.

Yatin Sathe, Dilip Verma, Aman Choudhury, Sardeshpande, Sanjay Trivedi and Hasmukh Jain had been reduced to mere puppets. Mahavir Tomar, despite orchestrating so many crimes, was free, while Sathe and Verma were in jail. Tomar had used the political bosses, entrepreneurs, the system and the criminals in uniform to his own advantage. There was doubt, conjecture and theory against him, but no evidence based on which he could be arrested.'

Mahavir Tomar circulated an audio file to the media, policemen, acquaintances and relatives. The idea was to control the recent damage done to his image and question all the inquiries initiated by the state government against him.

The audio clip went viral. In the clip, Tomar could be heard conversing with senior officer Ajay Dubey who had taken over as DGP in Maharashtra. As per the state government's instructions, Dubey was investigating the complaints raised against his own batchmate, Tomar. Both of them had talked on the phone about this. In the clip, first Tomar could be heard requesting his DGP friend to drop all the complaints against him. In response, Dubey told Tomar that the investigation against him could be stopped if he took back the allegations he had levied against former home minister Sardeshpande.

Tomar had recorded this conversation without Dubey's knowledge. Tomar wanted to use this to seek relief from the court by claiming that the ongoing investigation against him was prejudiced. The immediate effect would be that DGP Ajay Dubey would be penalized and Tomar would benefit. By doing so, Tomar had not only broken the trust of his well-wisher, friend and batchmate Ajay Dubey, but also sacrificed Dubey's career for his own benefit.

When it came to fulfilling his own goals, Tomar never hesitated to sacrifice colleagues, well-wishers, juniors, financiers or political bosses. This was how he had survived and grown in the police force.

'This is whom we call a smart player. Compared to him, people will call us immature. He has changed the entire game with just one audio clip. It is believed that the mind of an IPS officer runs at optimum capacity, but the brains of officers who start their careers as sub-inspectors, after clearing the tough Maharashtra Public Service Commission exam, are no match for Tomar's brain. After masterminding this entire fiasco, Tomar Sir is outside and people like us, who were his pawns, are languishing in jail,' Sathe said to Verma.

Sathe was targeting Verma's ego. The audio clip had reached them in jail after being downloaded on an illegally procured mobile phone. Both of them had heard it many times. They understood that Tomar had broken his friend's trust and sacrificed his career for his own personal gain and to improve his image.

Sathe was trying to use Tomar's latest trick for his own benefit. The way Sachin Tendulkar would read the mind of a bowler, similarly, Sathe was trying to read Verma's mind. Sathe had knocked down Verma's wicket, but he would emerge as a player only after taking down Tomar. He would also ensure that he had exacted revenge on all those who had used him.

Sathe had full faith in Verma's chicanery. He hoped that a devious bastard like Verma would have some back-up plan through which Sathe could reach Tomar. With the objective of instigating Verma further, Sathe continued speaking,

'*Verma Sir, please understand the chronology.*

Whose plan was it? Tomar's.

You procured the explosives on whose demand? Tomar's.

Who provided the police vehicle to bring the explosives from Nagpur to Mumbai by road? Tomar.

Who was dealing with Kuber? Tomar.

Who got the money from Kuber? Tomar.

Who was dealing with the former home minister? Tomar.

Who recruited you? Tomar.

Who allotted everyone their tasks and decided their roles? Tomar.

Who gave the money that was distributed to small-time criminals involved in the conspiracy? Tomar.

With a heavy heart, I had to kill my friend Hasmukh. Who gave the order to kill him? Tomar.

Who implicated former home minister Sardeshpande to save himself? Tomar.

Who is creating trouble for the state at the behest of the Centre by changing sides? Tomar.

Who implicated his well-wisher and friend, IPS Ajay Dubey, for his own benefit? Tomar.

Who went to jail? Verma and Sathe and others. Who did not go to jail? Tomar.

In his career, who created and eliminated numerous Vermas and Sathes? Tomar.

After a few months, when Verma and Sathe are murdered in jail, who will benefit the most? Tomar.'

Hearing Sathe's diatribe, a shiver ran down Verma's spine. He knew that not only was Tomar capable of getting someone killed in jail, but had also done so earlier. It was not just a matter of fake encounters. In the last thirty years, Verma himself, at Tomar's behest, had carried out several unofficial killings only because the victims had stood in Tomar's way. At Tomar's bidding, Verma himself had registered fake cases against many businessmen, bookies, hotel owners and builders, extorting crores under the pretext of reaching a settlement.

Tomar even carried out contract killings in the guise of encounters by taking money from the underworld to eliminate opposing gang members. Through this, he not only made crores but also made a name for himself. From setting weekly extortion targets for his subordinates to assigning important postings, Verma had seen Tomar do it all. Tomar was the capitalist of the police force, who would earn money by wrong means and then buy a premium posting for himself by paying off the political bosses. In his thirty-year-old association with Tomar, Verma had seen Tomar use devious means to move ahead in his career and prosper financially. Tomar, meanwhile, knew as much about Verma as a snake knows about the venom it carries in its fangs.

Terror was evident on Verma's face. If the man who had carried out a hundred encounters was fearful of Tomar, you can guess how cruel Tomar could be.

Sathe could see his plan working. He said, 'The CIU now notoriously stands for "criminals in uniform", but who is the biggest criminal in uniform? If Yatin Sathe is the captain of the team and Dilip Verma is the coach, then Tomar is the president of the cricket board. There is evidence implicating us and the others, but Tomar never left any clue behind that could implicate him. He is beyond harm.'

Dilip Verma smiled at the mention of the words 'evidence' and 'clue'.

'To cut your long story short, it can be concluded that Tomar executed his devious plan without keeping Kuber in the loop.'

'Now you are conveniently pushing Tomar aside by saying that he did whatever he did at his own level. What did he stand to gain?'

In response to Sanjay Trivedi's question, Aman Choudhury said, 'He had taken an off-book loan from Kuber to become the commissioner. It must have been Tomar's plan to pay off the loan by getting the helipad clearance as well as asking for some money in return once the work was completed. Anyway, Kuber's idea of "some money" is much more than "a lot of money" for most people.'

Sanjay Trivedi, lying on the hospital bed, erupted in laughter at the way Choudhury compared Kuber's 'some money' with 'a lot of money' for others.

Choudhury responded to Trivedi's laugh by saying, 'If our intentions were wrong, why would we have borne all your medical expenses, which run into lakhs of rupees? Wouldn't we have left you to die? If you had not collapsed in front of me that day, you might have exposed everything by now and declared us criminals. People would have believed you. As it is, it is the tendency of people to consider billionaire businessmen and successful politicians iniquitous. The armed forces, encounter specialists and people within the judicial system are equally bad, but they are considered holy cows. This is why a person like Mahavir Tomar roams free with the tag of being a brave officer. He eliminates whoever comes in his way to save himself. No one managed to reach as far as you in unravelling this matter. Kuber knows the difference between competent and incompetent people.'

'And why did you narrate the story to me with so much extra insight, intelligence and judgements?'

'Because Tomar did not spare me either. Kuber had made me in-charge of the helipad project, but without my knowledge, Tomar hatched a conspiracy under the pretext of completing that very same project. Kuber was angry with me as a result. Thankfully, he did not fire me, but I have been transferred to a side posting outside of India as punishment. This may be our last meeting. Tonight, I leave India. I thought of talking to you before that. We investigated on the basis of your lead and then the whole story came to light. That's why we felt it right to tell you this. Even if we would not have told you, you would have found out sooner or later. Kuber has been informed in advance about this meeting of ours.'

'Does Kuber know that, despite being a Muslim, Aman Choudhury dons the garb of a Hindu?'

Before answering Trivedi's question, Choudhury straightened the locket hanging around his neck and said, 'Kuber has always known, but his family and the rest of the security team are unaware. Kuber knows his family very well, hence he did not want everybody to know. For Kuber, money is god, but for the rest of the family, especially Dhruv ...' Choudhury left his sentence hanging.

Dilip Verma told Sathe that he had recorded one conversation with Tomar without his knowledge. Generally, Tomar was always extremely careful, but because this conversation had taken place during the initial stages of planning, Tomar had his guard down. Now, Verma was apprehensive about using this clip against Tomar because it also implicated him.

Sathe reminded Verma that they were already behind bars, while Tomar was free. If Tomar got rid of them in jail, this piece of evidence would become useless. 'By holding on to this evidence against Tomar, you will not get a Param Vir Chakra for bravery. People's fate lines are etched on their hands, but Tomar's seem to be on his butt. Don't hit him on the palm, if you have to, hit ...'

Verma told Sathe about the person from whom the audio clip could be collected. Sathe called his girlfriend, Nina Dias.

The moment Aman Choudhury left; Sanjay Trivedi received a WhatsApp audio clip from Nina Dias. He immediately identified the people talking in the clip, but he wanted to be sure.

Trivedi called Nina Dias, who in turn dialled Sathe and got everybody on a conference call. Sathe and Verma confirmed their presence. Verma declared that he had recorded this audio during a conversation with Mahavir Tomar. In the clip, Tomar could be heard saying to Verma: 'You get the car parked outside Kuberia, I will take care of the rest.' The rest of the conversation in the three-and-a-half-minute audio clip elaborated on Tomar's role in the entire fiasco.

The moment the conference call ended, Nina Dias got rid of the anonymous phone and left for an undisclosed location. Based on Sathe's advice, she was to go underground for a few days. Even Sathe and Verma destroyed their phone and iPad and dumped them in the garbage bin of the prison's kitchen. Both of them knew that in the next two or three days, the NIA would raid their jail cell to search for the electronics.

Sanjay Trivedi, meanwhile, had recorded the conference call without the knowledge of Varma, Sathe and Nina so no one could go back on their words. Lying on his bed in the hospital, Trivedi wrote a long report, which he intended to publish as a blog, on his mobile phone. It was his most sensational and dangerous report as a journalist. Before posting it online, Sanjay Trivedi glanced at the heading again: Mahavir Tomar: Chief of the 'Criminals in Uniform'.

'This is the breaking news of the hour ... the biggest arrest in the Kuberia explosives case and the Hasmukh murder case. Mahavir Tomar has emerged as the chief of the "criminals in uniform". Tomar was the mastermind behind the conspiracy.'

The news anchor was almost hollering. 'The NIA has matched the voices of Tomar and Verma in the audio clip that has gone viral. Sathe and Verma have also confessed to Tomar being the mastermind. It is clear that Mahavir Tomar carried out the crime while he was in office. The NIA has also made it clear that Tomar executed this crime while he was the Mumbai

Police commissioner. The NIA sources say more evidence will come to light soon. It is worth noting that the entire scam was exposed through an unknown blog.'

Utter chaos ensued inside and outside all newsrooms across the country as they relayed the breaking news of the hour. Panicked individuals ran back and forth between desks, as if the country itself was under threat. Screams and shouts, interspersed with expletives, added to the bedlam.

Images and videos of siren-blaring police vehicles, Kuber's photographs at Kuberia, file photographs of Hasmukh Jain and live footage of the arrested Mahavir Tomar being taken to court dominated TV screens across the country.

About the Authors

Sanjay Singh and **Rakesh Trivedi** have over two decades of experience in investigative journalism. Their stellar career graph features prominent news channels such as Zee News, Times Now, NDTV, News18 and ABP News. They have blown the whistle on numerous scams and conspiracies, including the Telgi stamp paper scam.